Dear Reader,

There are some books I remember reading, and others—a very special few—that I remember living: books where I'm pulled in so quickly and so deeply that I lose myself in the setting, the story, and the characters and their dilemmas. *The House in the Orchard* by Elizabeth Brooks is exactly this kind of book, and exactly the kind of escape reading—of the smartest and most sophisticated order—that we are all looking for right now.

I was hooked from the first chapter when Maude, a thirteen-year-old girl living in the late 1800s, finds herself, after the unexpected deaths of her parents, living with Miss Greenaway (a woman she's never met) out in the Cambridgeshire countryside. I've always loved Elizabeth Brooks' ability to make settings come alive—from Maude's uptight London house to her train ride through the countryside to the Orchard House itself, every space in this story absolutely transported me. I love, too, that we have the ability to discover Orchard House with Maude, and take in its wonder and mystery through her eyes.

The cast of characters also comes to life under Maude's careful, watchful gaze—accounted for in her spirited diary entries that range from whimsical to voyeuristic to dangerous, and serve as a window into important moments in British history and big, noteworthy themes: education and other rights for women, class differences, loss and grief, da[illegible]ghterhood, and loyalty between siblings. And though *The House in the* [illegible] takes place a century and a half ago, the emotional dynamics between [illegible] rs are so recognizable that anyone who has ever fo[illegible] a loved one, uncovered a family secret, or struggle[illegible] society places on them will find themselves in these [illegible]

The House in the [illegible] absolute master class in perspective—and in how to craft an unreliable narrator—with such delicately laced themes of sacrifice, the urge to belong, and, ultimately, revenge, that I remain mesmerized by it, even long after first reading. I hope you will be too.

Best,

Masie Cochran, *Editorial Director*

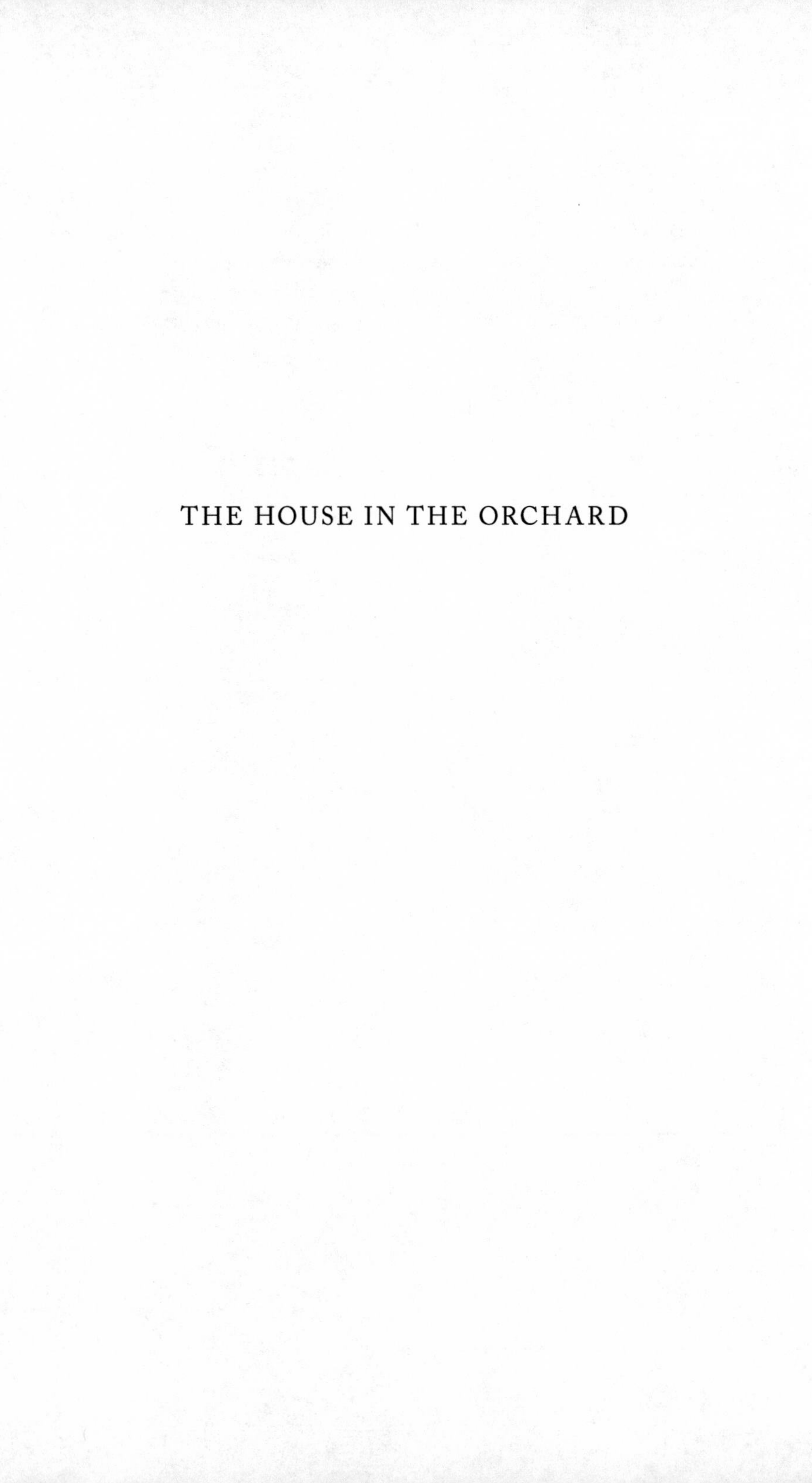

THE HOUSE IN THE ORCHARD

Published by Tin House, Portland, Oregon

Distributed by W. W. Norton & Company

Library of Congress Cataloging-in-Publication Data TK

Printed in the USA
Interior design by Diane Chonette

www.tinhouse.com

THE HOUSE IN THE ORCHARD

ELIZABETH BROOKS

 TIN HOUSE / Portland, Oregon

Orchard House
Sawyer's Fen
Cambridgeshire
13 May, 1941

For much of my life I have been suspicious of formal documents. Pious declarations in the name of "I, the undersigned" make me squirm: they have a solid and trustworthy appearance, but they are not solid, and not to be trusted. How can they be?

Nevertheless, I need a will, so I am sitting up in bed "on this thirteenth day of May, 1941," to write one, and I have engaged the vicar and his wife to call by this afternoon and witness me sign.

I am not—as far as I know—mortally ill, but I am feeling old, and I care what becomes of Orchard House. I want my brother Frank's son—my nephew, Jonathan—to have it, in the event that he survives this wicked war. Yesterday, courtesy of the "announcements" column in the Times, I learned that Jonathan and his wife have a baby son, and it pleases me to picture a child, or children, growing up here.

It goes without saying that Frank will dislike the arrangement and suspect mischief on my part, but I will not be discouraged on his account.

My nephew will be surprised to learn of his inheritance, since he was four years old when we last met, and he surely remembers little, or nothing, of me. I remember him, however, and it is in memory of those weeks we spent together in the winter of 1912 that I am resolved to make him my sole heir. I wish him and his family joy of the place.

Signed: Maude Louise Gower
(Maude Louise Gower)

In the presence of

S. H. Yates
(Rev. S. H. Yates)

Lucille Yates
(Mrs. L. J. Yates)

PEGGY

September 1945

"Frank, if you would only listen. I'm not saying I want to leave you and move in here. I'm not even saying I'm tempted . . ."

When there's no reply, Peggy turns from the window, but her father-in-law is gone. She hears him descend the stairs, and the latch clicks on the front door, and when she peers down from the window he's there, on the paved terrace, looking out across the garden.

Peggy pivots hands on hips, taking in the overflowing bookcase, and the hairy cat basket, and the four-poster bed with red curtains. Aunt Maude's bed. The mattress is as high as a pony's back—how ever did the old lady manage getting in and out?

Laurie would love it if they moved here. Not just the Gothic bed but everything: the wild garden, the expanse of rooms, the freedom. She tries to imagine it bare and uncluttered, her four-year-old son zooming up and down the stairs, wings outstretched and guns ablaze, laying claim to all the emptied space. He'd bring the place to life, if anyone could.

Peggy lifts the heavy sash, throwing the window open. Laurie is pottering in the garden, picking up leaves and windfall apples, chatting to himself. The evening is full of peaceful smells: rain, cows, grass. There's not much in the way of a view, because of the mist. Across the meadow she can just make out another house, but its walls have crumbled, and the roof has fallen in.

"Frank? Are you all right down there?"

Peggy rests her folded arms on the sill and leans out. Down below, she can see the drizzle settling on her father-in-law's hat and soaking through his light coat. It's not like him to stand and suffer. She wonders what he's thinking, but there's no way of telling with Frank. Never is, never was.

There's no doubt he's heard her question—Frank is sharp at ninety-one—but he doesn't reply. She leans out even farther and tries again.

"Are you all right?"

"Not really, no."

Peggy goggles her eyes theatrically, although she wouldn't dare if he could see her. In all the years she's known him, it's the first time Frank has answered such a question with anything other than, "Perfectly." When the telegram came to say his only son had died—shot down over Le Havre in the summer of '44—he made no complaint but withdrew to the sitting room with his newspaper. When he found Peggy in the kitchen, weeping with no shame over the washing-up bowl, he'd said, "Now then, my dear, Jonathan wouldn't have wanted a fuss."

Peggy rests her chin on her arms and looks out at the flat, misty meadows, half in love with the tranquillity, half missing London. Before she can think of a suitable reply, Frank declares, "It's no place for a child, Margaret." Never Peggy, with him. Always Margaret. "It's no place for anyone. We can employ people to clear it out, and evaluate it, and so on . . . There's no need for you to be involved, at all. It was a mistake to come."

Peggy is wary of being bullied.

"But Frank, the thing is . . . your sister left Orchard House to Jonathan . . . and maybe he'd have wanted me and Laurie to keep it? You know how Jonathan hated London. Remember how he used to talk about moving away and buying a cottage with a bit of land, keeping a few chickens . . . ?"

"Not here."

"Maybe not, but—"

"Jonathan is dead. We must think what's best for you and Laurence."

Does Peggy need to enumerate the ways in which this place might be preferable to a slim, terraced house in Hendon, where they live cheek by jowl with Frank's daughter and son-in-law, not to mention a lodger and maid-of-all-work? She begins but gives up. It's off-putting when Frank simply stands there like a post, narrow and erect, with nothing but the crown of his hat and his rain-soaked shoulders visible.

"I'll come down," she calls, shutting the window.

As Peggy returns to the room, the house seems to close around her, and the outdoor smells are smothered by a strange, mingled sweetness—rotting fruits, dead flowers, and violet soap. Perhaps her father-in-law is right. There is something about this house, something off-kilter, and she's not sure she likes it. Slowly she circles the room and stops in front of the fireplace. There's a mirror over the mantel, and a middle-aged woman looks out: a tired face, with no flesh to spare, beneath an ugly felt hat.

"Are you afraid?" Peggy asks her reflection. "What frightens you most?"

She asked the same questions of her husband, once upon a time. Six years ago. September 1939. They were in bed, curled together, loose-limbed and drowsing, and she meant it—of course she meant it—in the context of the war that had been declared that day. She meant, *Are you more afraid of killing, or being killed?* But Jonathan was too close to sleep to understand, and he answered out of a dream of childhood, with a puff of laughter, half-ashamed, "What frightens me most? I'd have to say my father."

Peggy and the mirror-woman glide away from one another as she inspects the objects in the room—the disordered clothes, the books and papers, the souvenirs from foreign parts. The woodworms have been busy with a portable desk, and it sheds dust as she lifts the lid with the tip of one finger. There's a silver bracelet inside, and a leather-bound notebook with a creaky spine.

The first page in the notebook reads:

The Private Diary of Maude Louise Gower
January 1876

Peggy takes a moment to admire the grace of the handwriting, and its dizzying old age. The 1870s? She thinks vaguely of dresses with bustles, and penny-farthing bicycles, and people living innocent lives, dreaming gentle dreams. Aunt Maude would have been a child.

Softly, she replaces the book inside the desk and lowers the lid.

Trailing down the stairs at Orchard House, Peggy surprises a tortoiseshell cat in the shadowy hallway. It's hiding between a pair of wellington boots and a pile of wooden crates, and she feels its gaze before she sees it. The cat dashes out of hiding and bolts past her, up the stairs. She stands back to watch it go, before carrying on to the bottom.

There is a scattering of apples in one of the crates, and Peggy's mouth is dry. It's been hours since she had anything to eat or drink. She reaches for one, but her fingers close on clammy skin and the fruit caves in. On closer inspection it's obvious that every single one of the apples is rotten, whether they're brown and speckled with mould, or green gold and riddled with holes. She roots in her pocket for a handkerchief and wipes the pulp from her hand.

There's a study, to her left, with shelves and shelves of books; practically a library. Peggy doesn't read much—not as much as Jonathan did—but she likes being surrounded by books. They are a friendly presence. Her eyes skim the shelves, and she sees Euripides, Mrs. Beeton, and John Buchan side by side on one shelf.

There's a large table in the middle of the study, and a smaller desk in the corner, with a telephone. Peggy puts the receiver to her ear and is surprised to hear a thrum; for some reason she expected it to be disconnected. She sets it down quickly, before the operator has a chance to speak.

She can't help but indulge the thought of keeping the house. It would be a sin—wouldn't it?—to turn it down and return to London, where all her life's horrors unfolded. Peggy remembers, with a shudder, the last time she saw Jonathan, at King's Cross, and the dishonest brightness she'd insisted upon, in the name of courage. ("Off you go, now! Good luck!") She remembers the cloud of dust where her mum and dad's house once stood, and the strip of floral dressing gown—mum's dressing gown—spiked on the railings. She remembers the night her own house was hit—Laurie had been staying with Frank in Hendon, thank God—and the way her feet left the ground before she made it to the shelter at the bottom of the garden.

She will miss her fellow typists at the Ministry of Information, but it's not as if she's got a job there anymore. Most of the girls have scattered, made a fresh start for themselves. It's time she did the same.

This place, though? Orchard House?

Peggy wishes there were someone she could have sent in advance, to clear the place out and give it a thorough clean. If she'd arrived to find it empty and bare, it might not have felt so uncanny, and Frank might have been more complaisant. They could have called it a blank slate and started from scratch.

She glances over the shelves and pockets *Smallwood's Guide to the English Counties: Cambridgeshire*, for later.

Frank is standing in the same spot, swigging from his hip flask. He drinks like a fish—he even managed to drink his way through the war, when alcohol wasn't to be had for love nor money, but he never seems drunk. He's a tall, straight old man, severely handsome, long widowed. Before he retired, nearly thirty years ago, he was an obstetrician. Peggy often wonders, uncomfortably, about that; Frank has the steady nerves of a good doctor, but none of the manners. Doubtless he's saved lives in his time but even so, she would not wish to give birth under those cool grey eyes.

Frank hesitates before offering the hip flask, but she ignores his scruples and enjoys a sip. He flicks one of his looks at her: a rapid up and down that she's not supposed to notice. She's wearing slacks today, and Frank doesn't approve of women who wear slacks, or drive cars, or drink.

Peggy pulls her cardigan tight. It's a chilly evening; feels like autumn. Cambridgeshire is said to be a bleak county, isn't it? She thinks of it as windy and exposed, with a shortage of hills and trees. She shivers and waves at her son, who is making a heap of twigs and leaves at the far end of the orchard. He seems to contemplate her for a while before waving back. Some people—that awful kindergarten teacher at the school in Hendon—think Laurie is backward, but he's not. Laurie may keep his thoughts to himself, but he has plenty of them.

Frank gestures at one of the paving slabs.

"Maude bricked it up," he says. "Blocked it off."

"What?" Peggy's thoughts are still with Laurie.

Frank takes another gulp from his flask, and points again.

"There used to be a trapdoor, right there, opening onto the cellar steps."

"Oh?"

"Yes. There's a vast cellar underneath this house, with only one entrance, and the very first thing my sister did, when the house fell into her hands, was to brick it up."

"But why would she do that?"

"It's an eerie thought, isn't it?"

Sometimes Frank's aversion to direct questions seems to verge on the obsessive.

He carries on: "Don't you agree that it's an eerie thought? A whole set of dark, musty, underground rooms, which you would live above day by day, but never set foot in, or see, if you moved in.

Alternatively, you could sell the place and buy a nice new-build in Hendon."

Peggy smiles drily, but he is far away with his own thoughts and doesn't notice. Laurie is wading through the long grass, peeling bark from a twig.

"Aunt Maude can't have been all bad if she willed her house to Jonathan," she observes.

"Oh, she'll have had her reasons."

"*Bad* reasons?"

Frank takes another swig, as if that will do in place of an answer.

"You know Jonathan stayed here once, as a child?" he says.

"I only know because Maude mentioned it in her will."

Peggy presses her lips together, silently urging her father-in-law to say more. She's learned, over the years, that her best bet lies in silence. Questions and expectant glances only annoy him.

"He was very small," Frank says. "Four or five years old. His mother and I went down with the flu, and there was nobody else to look after him. I was really very unwell—too ill to be consulted, so my wife arranged for him to stay here, at Orchard House. I would never have allowed it."

Peggy stretches the silence for as long as she can bear, but in the end she has to ask, "Why not?"

Frank is sinking down inside himself. Peggy wills him to break the fall and lift his eyes to the world, where the sky is dove grey and the leaves are turning to gold, and she is pleading for knowledge.

"Jonathan came back in one piece, didn't he?" she suggests. "Aunt Maude looked after him all right?"

Frank is staring across the garden at Laurie, who is rattling twigs against the tree trunks, and talking urgently to himself.

"Jonathan was like that, when he came back from Orchard House," says Frank. "Living for the stories inside his head, unwilling to talk to me, no longer trusting me entirely. I never discovered what lies he'd been told. My sister was obsessed with hurting me, for the best part of seventy years, and although she rarely succeeded, that was one occasion upon which she did. There was an imaginary game he kept playing, but refused to explain, called 'the lady on the stairs.'"

Frank shudders as if he feels a sudden pain, but when Peggy reaches out to steady him, he shakes her off and drains the last of the brandy, like a parched man gulping water. Usually it's hard to believe he's an old man—his shoulders are so correct, and he speaks with such fluency—but it shows on occasion. Peggy looks at him now and notices how skeletal his face has become since Jonathan died, shedding such plumpness and colour as it ever had.

Frank says, "I've decided we shan't stay here tonight, after all."

Peggy drags her gaze away from the paving slab, where he claims the trapdoor used to be. It is noticeably squarer than the others that surround it and, beneath the moss and lichen, a darker shade of grey.

"We shan't?"

"No. We'll head up to Cambridge and take rooms in my old college. Or rather—they won't want you and Laurence at St. John's—we'll find a hotel."

Peggy frowns. "That place where we bought the milk—Willowtree Farm—they were advertising bed and breakfast," she says. "Perhaps if you don't wish to stay in the house—"

"Willowbrook Farm," he corrects her. "If it's all the same to you, I'd rather we left the village altogether and headed for town."

Peggy thinks fleetingly of Cambridge hotels (a hot bath, a stiff drink, a good meal, with any luck . . .) but shakes her head.

"You go, if you must. I don't mind running you down to the station, but Laurie and I will stay, as planned."

"Peggy—"

She raises her palms. "I'm sure you're right about Orchard House, and I'll end up selling it, but just let me see. Give me time to think."

Her father-in-law never shouts. When he's angry, he turns his head away.

"Oh Frank. I can't believe that you, a man of science, believe in ghosts?"

She laughs as she says it, meaning to provoke him, but he will not be provoked. He makes no sign of having heard her.

The rain comes on heavily, soon after Frank has left. Peggy calls her son inside and settles him in the kitchen with his colouring pencils and exercise book. She watches for a while, and listens while he tells her about his newest drawings, but once he's fully absorbed she leaves him for another exploration of the house. She's not sure whether she's searching for reasons to stay or reasons to go.

It's hard not to dwell on the inaccessible cellar beneath her feet, but she pauses by the study window to watch the rain bludgeon the garden. It's a wilderness out there, with roses growing up the apple trees, and grass up to your knees, and masses of ivy. But this tells her nothing categorical about Aunt Maude. Perhaps the old lady never noticed her garden. Or else she was too frail to tend it herself, and too shy to have anyone in. Or maybe she liked it jungly.

"Who were you?" she asks out loud, tensing for an answer that doesn't come, and berating herself for being absurd.

Peggy can't find a linen cupboard, and the only bed that's made up with sheets and blankets is Aunt Maude's. It's a perfect monstrosity, with its great posts reaching to the ceiling and its crimson curtains. She tries not to consider the probability that the old woman died there.

"What an exciting bed," she tells Laurie. "You won't mind sharing with me, will you?"

Laurie doesn't mind. He's full of bread and milk and fresh air; too droopy-eyed for a story. He snuggles under the quilt and they begin their usual Our Father, but they haven't got as far as "Thy will be done" before he's away. She kisses him softly on the forehead and leaves the unfinished prayer hanging in the air.

There's a scuttle of coal and a pile of kindling next to the hearth, and she manages to get a fire going. With the curtains drawn over the window and the bedside lamp switched on, the room is cosier. Peggy changes into her pyjamas as discreetly as if she were being watched and climbs under the covers. Supper is a cigarette, a cup of tea, and the packet of cheese sandwiches she made this morning, before they left Hendon. She takes a bite and opens *Smallwood.*

The historic county of Cambridgeshire lies in the east of England, and is bordered by the counties of Lincolnshire to the north, Norfolk to the

Someone is climbing the stairs. Peggy stops chewing and swallows. The floorboards creak as the intruder walks the length of the landing and stops outside her bedroom door. She slides out of bed and reaches for the poker. Laurie hasn't woken. She pulls the covers up and drops them over his face, but she can't conceal his little, humped shape.

Another creak. Peggy raises the poker like a sword and flings open the door. The tortoiseshell cat trots in, pausing to sniff at her bare feet.

Peggy's shoulders slump as the cat leaps onto the bed. She swears under her breath and gives the fire a rough stir. It occurs to her that singing might help, and she hums a few lines of "Boogie Woogie Bugle Boy," but the silence is deeper and darker when she stops.

Laurie doesn't move as the cat picks its way across his body, to the empty half of the bed. It stops to knead the quilt, making tiny pricking sounds as it catches the threads with its claws.

Peggy moves the portable desk from the end of the bed, where it's in the way of her feet, and places it on the chest of drawers, opening the lid for another quick look at the diary. The child's writing is elegant but clear, and the first entry begins in January 1876 with an address: not *Orchard House, Sawyer's Fen, Cambridgeshire* but *17 Erskine Place, Bloomsbury, London.*

Peggy shuts the desk and goes back to bed, where she tries again with *Smallwood's Guide.*

The city of Cambridge is situated on the River Cam, on the southern side of the county, approximately fifty-five miles from London. Renowned for its university, whose foundation dates back to the early years of the thirteenth

She yawns and tosses the book aside, and the cat makes no objection when she rubs it between the ears. Her eyes rest absently on the little desk, while she sips her tea and eats her sandwich. When she's finished she gets up, dusts the crumbs from her hands, and brings the diary back to bed.

The cat waits until she's settled before it walks up her body, to the pillow, and peers under the covers. She lifts them up and it slinks inside, its tail brushing her face as it makes its way down to her feet.

Peggy opens the notebook and begins to read.

The Private Diary of Maude Louise Gower
January 1876

17 Erskine Place
Bloomsbury
London
Monday, 10 January, 1876

It is cold without Ebenezer curled up on my lap; I wish Miss Wilson hadn't frightened him away. There's no fire in my bedroom and no colour: I sit on a dark patterned rug, in front of a dark empty hearth, surrounded by dark wooden furniture. Ruth has draped all the mirrors in the house with black cloths, including the one on my dressing table, in case Pa's spirit gets trapped in the glass. Servants are such foolish and superstitious creatures, as Mamma is fond of observing. All the same, now that the light is fading, I am glad I can't see into my mirror. Things that were quite normal last week have become dark and twisted this week. For example, I used to like hearing the trains go in and out of Euston station, but the noise they make has changed since Pa died: they used to squeal with excitement and now they wail.

17 Erskine Place has always been a forlorn and unsettled house, but never to this degree. Our lodgers are unhappy on account of the "Untoward Circumstances of Mr. Gower's Demise," although nobody will tell me what that means. I only know that Pa was away on business when he died and that his body was brought back to London with some difficulty and delay. One of our first-floor tenants, fussy old Mr. Paley, maintains that our address has become an "abode of rumour and death" and that his nerves will not stand it, although Cook says he is only trying to reduce his rent. Whatever else you may say about 17 Erskine Place, it <u>is</u> one of the most respectable boarding houses in Bloomsbury. "Genteel board and residence close to Euston station," as the advertisement says in the <u>Times</u>. "Pleasant, airy rooms; superior table d'hôte; select society."

Mamma wrote the advertisement, and I think she puts it beautifully. She makes it sound like a house in a book, or a dream.

I won't be able to write for much longer because I can't find a candle and I need to go and have my supper.

I wish Frank would come home. My brother is the most important person in the world now, excepting Ebenezer the cat,* and the only person I can talk to about Pa. Why doesn't he come? If he knew, really <u>knew</u>, how much I need him, he would come at once. In three years' time, when I am sixteen and my brother Frank is a qualified doctor, I will go and keep house for him. This is my only comfort, now that Pa is gone.

There are pleasant places in which to be grief-stricken, and not-so-pleasant places: my brother's college rooms in Cambridge belong in the former category; 17 Erskine Place, Bloomsbury, in the latter. Doubtless Frank's college rooms will be as warm as toast, whereas my bedroom has been freezing ever since the awful news came, as if a small fire in my grate might cause offence to my deceased pa, or our mourning household, or our neighbours in Erskine Place, or, quite possibly, God himself. Nobody seems to realise, perhaps they don't care, that it's rather difficult to write a diary when you're all bundled up in shawls and mittens, and the joints won't bend in your fingers.

Miss Wilson said, "There is a fire in the parlour should you choose to be sociable."

But I don't choose to be sociable! I want to write my diary and think about Pa. Besides, it's all very well for Miss Wilson; she spends half her time below stairs, toasting her dainty feet on the hearth and gobbling sweets.** Apparently the dead have no objection to kitchen ranges being lit.

* And Mamma, of course.

** My dear governess had four beaux at the last count, and they all gave her sweets at Christmas. Two of her beaux are clerks and one works for the post office, but the butcher's boy is also smitten and he brings her toffees and peppermints incessantly. Imagine being loved by a butcher's boy! He's not even handsome and he smells like blood.

Tuesday, 11 January, 1876

Miss Wilson came in this morning as I was trying to arrange my hair. She dawdled about, pretending to tidy my bookshelf whilst casting critical glances at the back of my head. (I have lifted the cloth from my mirror, Miss Wilson! I can see you!) I expect she was disappointed not to find Ebenezer doing dreadful things to my clothes with his claws, as that is her usual excuse for clapping in his face and shooing him away, but Ebenezer was long gone; he made his way down to the kitchen while I was still half-asleep. Cook is nice and she understands cats.

It was ten times harder to make a proper job of my hair under the critical eye of Miss Wilson. Naturally she didn't offer to help! It's extremely difficult to tie ribbons when you are unused to doing it by yourself, and I am not allowed to ask Ruth or Nettie because they are run off their feet this week. Our house has been filling with relatives in advance of Pa's funeral, hordes of aunts and uncles and goodness-knows-whats, and there are rooms to be aired, beds to be made, carpets to be beaten, and so on and so forth. Dozens of ways, in fact, for a redundant governess to make herself useful. (I hardly need mention that my lessons stopped with the news of Pa's death. Mamma has ruled that I must continue with my needlework, but I am not expected to apply my mind to the more taxing subjects.)

Miss Wilson picked up an arithmetic book and walked with it to the window, leafing slowly through the pages. I was surprised, because ordinarily Miss Wilson is no great enthusiast for arithmetic, but then she said, "What time is your brother expected?" and I realised she was only pretending to be absorbed by the book. She glanced at her own reflection in the grimy window while she waited for my answer, and smoothed her neatly coiled braids. I yanked my ribbon into a hopeless knot and gave up on hairstyling; Ruth or Nettie will simply have to come and help, no matter how busy they are.

Frank's train is due at noon, but I couldn't see what business it was of Miss Wilson's. I replied by asking, "How is Mr. Briggs?" (Mr. Briggs being the butcher's boy, more commonly known as Jack), which managed to be a perfectly polite question and an elegant snub, all in one. I am writing this up several hours later, and it still gives me a glow of satisfaction.

Nettie did my hair creditably for a kitchen maid. I would have preferred Ruth to do it, but she was busy with Mamma's breakfast tray.

When Nettie had tied the last ribbon, she turned me round so that we were face to face, and planted her hands on my shoulders. I expected her to say it was pretty (it would have been the natural and normal thing to say), but she screwed her mouth into an odd smile and said, "Poor ducky."

Nettie often calls me ducky and I don't like it, but I suppose it is her way of being kind.

It feels as though there are dozens and dozens of relatives settling like pigeons over our house, but in fact there are only five. I know this because Miss Wilson and I had to join them in the dining room for breakfast. (Ebenezer is lucky; I wish I could have a saucer of cream in the kitchen.) I don't understand how any of The Relatives relate to me, because nobody has seen fit to explain, and I do not recall seeing any of them before in my life. However, over the course of breakfast I succeeded in putting names to faces, as follows:

> *Uncle Talbot: Large. Greasy waistcoat. Gobbles.*
> *Aunt Judith: Uncle T.'s wife. Grey hair and skin. Pince-nez on chain.*
> *Aunt Janet: Irritable. Complained about noise, smell of gas jets, flavour of porridge.*
> *Cousin John: Silent. No distinguishing features.*
> *Cousin Amelia: Very old indeed. Deaf. Possibly Cousin J.'s mother?*

Everyone was seated when I came in, and Aunt Janet muttered some precept about tardiness, which may or may not have been a quotation from the Bible. The lodgers (those who don't pay to have their breakfast in their rooms) had already been and gone. Aunt Judith said, "How very like her dear mother she is—in appearance, at least," which might have been a kindly thing to say, if it hadn't been done in such a dour tone of voice while she cleaned her pince-nez. Nobody mentioned Pa. Nobody called me "poor ducky" or anything like it. At least the fire was lit in the dining room, but it smoked and gave off scant heat, and the porridge was tepid. There were fried kidneys and bacon on the sideboard, but only Uncle Talbot ate them.

Breakfast passed slowly. I think The Relatives may be collectively mad, because I couldn't understand half the things they said to one another. At times they appeared to be speaking in code: for example, more than one mention was made of The Feline, as in, "I presume The Feline will not be showing its face at the funeral?" which elicited a flurry of tutting, and blushing and glances in my direction. I thought about this for a long time before daring to say,

"Ebenezer?"

"Who is Ebenezer?" said Aunt Janet.

"My cat."

They all looked at one another. Uncle Talbot leered and said, "Oh, we're not talking about *Ebenezer*!"

Whenever they weren't talking, an awful silence arose, and the clock ticked too loudly. A train thundered out of the station as I was scraping out my porridge bowl, making the windows rattle in their frames. I don't usually notice that, but Aunt Janet closed her eyes to show how much it pained her.

I must say, it is a great comfort to be likened to Mamma, even by Aunt Judith. Mamma looks like an actual angel, with her golden hair and her melancholy eyes. I studied my reflection in the silver teapot and allowed myself a tiny smile, despite the fact its bulbous sides had compressed my forehead and distended my chin. The truth is that I *do* resemble Mamma, and I *am* pretty, although I would never be so vulgar as to acknowledge it out loud. I have never been allowed to wear black before and it suits me well; it makes me look older, paler, and more distinguished.

"I gather she's bookish," said Aunt Janet at one point, with a nod in my direction.

"Oh yes!" said Uncle Talbot, as if he knew anything about it. "Quite the bluestocking, I hear."

Well! Other than the Feline/Ebenezer conversation (if that can be called a conversation) I hadn't uttered a single word since entering the dining room, but at the charge of bluestocking I gave an involuntary squeak and slopped tea in my saucer. A hideous, staring silence ensued. I drew three long, slow breaths, which is Cook's advice for keeping tempers in check, and said, "If you please, I am nothing of the sort."

Well, I am not. Admittedly I like to read, but only in the sense that all ladies like to read; I shall never be an intellectual female, like awful Ann in Frank's poem. (Frank wrote a very funny poem about the female "students" at Cambridge, which was published to great acclaim in his college newspaper last spring. I have it in my desk drawer; I will find it and copy it here. It really is very funny.)*

The aunts tightened their lips when I spoke, and for some reason Uncle Talbot winked at Miss Wilson, which makes me like him least of all The Relatives. After that, everyone left me alone. They talked amongst themselves about how horrible London is, and how they never get such foggy weather in St. Albans.

**A Lesson for the Ladies, by Mr. Frank Gower*

Sally wished to have a home
And make that home a heaven.
Scornful Ann had loftier dreams,
Like "X plus Y makes 7."

Sally got a husband
And a cottage by the sea.

Annie said, "I'd rather get
A varsity degree."

Sally filled her little house
With songs and fresh-baked pies
While Annie got a frown line
And a squint in both her eyes.

Sally was her husband's joy,
Her gifts were sweet and homely.
Annie's head was full of facts
But Annie ended lonely.

After breakfast, Mamma summoned me to her room. I must have hesitated outside her room for a full minute, my fingers playing on the handle of the door.

What was I was afraid of? As strange as it sounds, I wasn't frightened of the fact that Mamma is dying. I suppose she's been doing it for so long, ever since I was born, that I've grown used to it. Mamma keeps on dying the way other people keep on living. Besides, now that Pa is gone, Mamma cannot die before Frank is ready to leave university and be a doctor. If she did, I would belong nowhere and to no one, which is inconceivable.

No. The answer came to me as I twisted the doorknob and entered her room. What I'm afraid of is whatever it is she's feeling, regarding Pa. She doesn't seem grief-stricken in the ordinary way.

The night after the news about Pa being dead came, I got up (or dreamed I got up) and heard (or dreamed I heard) Mamma pacing her bedroom floor. Also, the noise of something smashing, and Mamma shouting raw, crude words. I lurked on the stairs with my hands over my ears, and definitely felt awake, but I could still hear the shouting, and my father's name mixed up in it.

Mamma was just as composed as ever when I saw her the next day, and she was equally composed when I stood beside her bed this morning, which makes me suspect that I am the one with the disordered mind. Surely Mamma would never raise her voice, or pace about, or smash things on purpose, or use words like the ones I heard? She radiates calm and light, like a figure in a stained-glass window. Her cheeks are as white as her nightgown, and they have a sheen that makes me want to stroke them, although, of course, I wouldn't dare. I doubt anyone has ever dared touch Mamma.

The china shepherdess is missing from her mantelpiece, the one with the pink dress and the wide-brimmed hat, but that doesn't prove anything. More than likely it has been moved, or perhaps Ruth broke it when she was dusting.

Back to the events of this morning: Mamma told me to take the breakfast tray from her lap, so I put it out on the landing, although she'd hardly eaten a thing. Cook had done her a soft-boiled egg, and the sight of the orange yolk oozing over the rim of the shell made my mouth water, which is a shameful admission to make, even in a secret diary. How can I be hungry when Pa is dead? Especially as I'd only just finished my bowl of porridge.

"Shall I read to you, Mamma?"

I like reading aloud to Mamma; it means I can talk without saying stupid or insensitive things. Poetry is her favourite and

Tennyson is her idol, but she prefers being read to, rather than reading herself, because her eyes tire quickly. Pa's favourites were *Punch* magazine, the *Times* newspaper, and novels, and his favourite writers were Charles Dickens and William Makepeace Thackeray.

"Tennyson?" I murmured, but I was thinking of those old copies of *Punch*, which Frank keeps in a box under his bed, and I felt madly inspired to suggest reading something funny. I don't know what got into me this morning.

"No, thank you, Maude." Mamma closed her eyes and lay back on her pillows, her forehead puckered in a frown. I think she was in pain. "I don't want you to stay. I only wish to tell you that Frank has telegraphed; he shan't be able to come until tomorrow."

I should have folded my hands, nodded sedately, and said, "Very well, Mamma." I wish that's what I'd done; it seems so easy now that I come to write about it. As it was, I'm afraid I lost my mind in a rather literal way: I scrabbled to find it, but it wasn't there.

"Oh no!" I cried. "No, no, I was counting on Frank to come *today*!"

Her frown deepened and I burst into tears, and suddenly I wasn't crying about Frank, I was crying about Pa, and I kept sobbing out his name, over and over again. Mamma's face hardened and she said "That father of yours!" with such ferocity I didn't know what to think, and I found myself weeping all the more loudly and ran to my room.

*

If Frank doesn't come soon, I shall die. No, that is a sad inaccuracy. I shall almost certainly *not* die. The danger is, rather, that I shall lose my composure again. I wish I could weep like Mamma, bowed and silent behind a spotless handkerchief, instead of shaking and hiccoughing and exuding too much liquid from my eyes and my nose. Also, I hate the way crying makes my face turn red. I don't cry often, but when I do, I disgust myself. I think I disgust Mamma too, although she is too gracious to say so.

On account of my misbehaviour I've been locked in my room with no luncheon and no tea, and only the prospect of bread and milk for supper. Ebenezer is with me, but he is restless and would rather walk along the curtain rail, mewing at the ceiling, than sit on my lap. This diary is my best comfort. I wish I could say I have no appetite but the later it gets, the more my thoughts turn to soft-boiled eggs and toast.

Wednesday, 12 January, 1876

I spent the morning loitering on the stairs, listening for Frank. It's a pity all our front bedrooms are occupied at present, otherwise I'd have waited by one of the windows. It wasn't possible to watch from the parlour, because that's where Pa's coffin has been kept ever since Saturday, when the undertakers came. They propped the lid open to begin with, so we could pay Pa our respects, but they nailed it down this morning. Imagine standing at the parlour window, with <u>that</u> at one's back! I couldn't have done it for the world.

Truly, I began to think Frank would never come. A dozen times or more I jumped, hearing a carriage turn into Erskine Place, but although some of them slowed, none clattered to a stop.

Miss Wilson happened to be passing through the hall when Frank rapped on the front door, so it was she who admitted him. I was surprised: my beloved governess has been known to refuse to answer the door, on the grounds that it is "menial work." I wanted to call over the banisters and remind her of that, but I didn't, for fear of having my ears boxed later on. (Incidentally, Miss Wilson looks well enough in mourning, although with her brown hair and flushed complexion I don't believe she looks as well as I do. Her crape dress is second-hand, and the black is turning rusty.)

Frank bounded in with his hat in his hand and his hair on end. "Morning, Miss Wilson! Or is it afternoon already? How do you do, Nettie?"

He sounded rattled and out of breath, rather than sorrowful. I said, "Frank?" and he ran to meet me on the landing. When he flung his arms around me and lifted me up, I confess I almost smiled.

"Miss Mouse!" he cried, whirling me round and round until I was afraid we would both topple down the stairs. "How is my little Miss Mouse?"

"Frank?" I said, once he'd stopped. "Don't you think you ought to bear yourself more gravely?"

He put me down and kissed the top of my head.

"I'm sorry," he said. "I will bear myself more gravely for your sake."

"For <u>Pa's</u> sake, you mean."

Frank didn't acknowledge the correction; he just tousled my nicely combed hair. I extricated my face from his waistcoat and pushed him away, the better to search his face, but he wouldn't meet my eye. It was very strange. Pa used to say, "Frank by name and Frank by nature," and I had always found it to be true. Today, my brother's mouth was oddly rigid, as if he were angry; his manner was boisterous, as if he were happy; his gaze kept sliding to one side, as if he were guilty; and the rims of his eyelids were pink, as if he were sad. What was I, what am I, to make of that?

"You're quite right to observe the proprieties," he said. "I approve. And now I must see Mamma."

He planted another kiss on my head and elbowed me aside.

Miss Wilson and Nettie were still in the hall, looking up at us, so I tried not to let my astonishment show.

I don't understand anything anymore. When did Frank stop loving Pa? And how? And why? I suppose it's one good reason for writing a diary. If I put all these conversations and happenings into words, and order them on a page, they might begin to make some sense.

By the time I caught up with him, Frank was standing in front of the landing mirror with his gloves between his teeth, flattening his ruffled hair. The black drape that Ruth had hung over the glass, for the sake of Pa's wandering soul, lay on the floor in a twisted heap. I picked it up as Frank muttered through his gloves, "What a place to hang a mirror! I can't see a thing!" and then, spitting them out, "Do I look a tiny bit respectable now, Mouse?"

I was meant to say, "Dear Frank, you could never look respectable," but I found it impossible to joke with my head full of dark-coloured questions. Perhaps it was just as well he didn't wait for my reply before tapping on Mamma's door and entering when she called.

"Frank!" Our mother raised her head from the pillow and stretched out her arms. "Darling boy!"

"Hello, Mamma."

My brother is always soft and quiet in her presence, and he is never like that with anyone else (except once, with me, when I had scarlet fever and everyone thought I was going to die). Nevertheless, Mamma always seems extra-specially fragile in Frank's presence, and Pa had the same effect on her. I suppose it's because she's pretty much bed-bound, whereas both of them are, or were, so ruddy-cheeked and boyish, with the scent of the outdoors always on their clothes. I watched Frank bending over the bed in his dark coat, and her arms winding round his neck like silken cords to pull him down. Mamma has not worn mourning since Pa died, but then she is always in her nightgown, and who ever heard of a black nightgown?

"I nearly stayed away," said Frank.

Mamma stroked his hair out of his eyes. "It's as well you've come. People would have talked."

I wanted to stand there and listen, and I wanted to go away and <u>not</u> listen, so I compromised by parting the curtains and looking out of the window. I like the way the glass is kept clean in Mamma's bedroom; mine is always spotted with soot, and I can never see as much of the railway line as I would like. I blew a circle of mist and wrote my initials (M. L. G.) and Pa's (G. P. G.), before rubbing them away with my sleeve. The fog was thick and cold today. Soon, Frank would have to follow the hearse to the cemetery at Tower

Hamlets and stand among the bare trees and stone angels, watching Pa's coffin being lowered into the earth. I felt sorry that Frank would have no better company than Uncle Talbot and Cousin John (and, I suppose, Pa's old friends, and men from the publishing house), but I was also thankful that ladies do not attend funerals.

It was quiet in Erskine Place. There was only the postman, delivering letters to the other side of the garden square; a three-legged dog sniffing at the foot of a lamp post; and a tall, cloaked woman, pacing up and down the pavement like a lost soul. Perhaps she was waiting for someone, or killing time before an appointment. I remembered the heroines in Pa's stories (he used to make them up for me if there was nothing juicy in the newspapers) and tried to make a romantic figure of her, but there wasn't much to go on, since I couldn't see her face. In one of Pa's stories, her hooded cloak would have been made of black velvet or satin, whereas in fact it was green wool, much mended, with mud at the hem.

Up and down the woman walked, her head bowed, her arms wrapped tightly about her person. I kept changing my mind as to whether she was in bodily pain, or mental anguish, or deep thought, or whether she was merely cold. When a carriage turned into Erskine Place she ducked into the square and watched, from behind the railings, as it passed.

"Maude?" It was Mamma. "Come away from the window."

Frank was sitting on the edge of her bed, holding her hand, and their faces were wet with tears. Frank smiled broadly at me, as if that might convince me all was well.

Ruth and I braved the January air to stand on the front step and watch the cortège depart. The aunts watched from the parlour, as did Nettie, Miss Wilson, and Cook, and a couple of the lodgers. Mamma was too ill to leave her bed.

I was cold (I wasn't wearing my outdoor things) but Ruth had a shawl, which she wrapped around us both. I suppose it was rather undignified, to stand like that with one's parlourmaid, but I felt so sad that I couldn't bring myself to mind. The black horses snorted and stamped a great deal as the coffin was loaded into the hearse, and when they tossed their plumed heads I thought of the circus we went to, Frank and I, with Pa, and the acrobat lady who stood on the horse's back as it galloped round the ring. Except, of course, that the circus horse had been piebald, and its plumes had been red and green and gold.

Frank climbed into the second carriage and sat down opposite Uncle Talbot, and I thought how young and lean my brother looked beneath his top hat. Uncle Talbot was having a private smile about something; Cousin John was fidgeting with his collar; the undertakers looked positively bored. I closed my eyes. It was all so mean and drab. There ought to have been ten times as many horses, and they ought to have been sleek and polished, and all the church bells in North London ought to have been tolling, and the streets ought to have been thronged with crowds. I shivered and opened my eyes as the horses strained against their harnesses and the wheels rumbled into motion.

Ebenezer chased a dead leaf down the steps and I stooped to pick him up, but he didn't want to be held.

The cortège turned the corner into Euston Road, and the unknown woman—her hood bowed, her arms still tightly wrapped around her body—followed a few paces behind. Ruth and I stayed on the doorstep after they'd gone, staring down the street as if we were waiting for something else to happen, but nothing did.

Friday, 14 January, 1876

Pa is buried and The Relatives are gone at last. Cousins John and Amelia went home yesterday afternoon; Aunts Janet and Judith and Uncle Talbot left this morning. I was summoned to the parlour to make my farewells, while Frank went to find them a cab.

I can't think why they wanted to see me; none of them had anything of interest to say. I kissed the ladies' powdery cheeks and tried to get away with shaking Uncle Talbot's hand, but he said couldn't he have a kiss as well? so I gave him one very, very quickly, making sure to hold my breath, because of his stale smell. Miss Wilson was with me, and Uncle Talbot kept trying to wink at her. She was lucky; she didn't have to say anything, or kiss anyone; she had only to keep her eyes on the rug.

I sat on the horsehair sofa next to Miss Wilson, and The Relatives proceeded to bombard me with snippets of advice. "Be sure to behave yourself" was the long and short of it, as if I were still a baby in the nursery, whereas in fact I shall be fourteen in April. "A little less reading, Miss Bluestocking!" was Uncle Talbot's contribution, and if he intended to make everyone smile, I'm pleased to say he failed signally.

Pa's coffin is gone, but the area it leaves behind, formerly an innocent, rectangular table where we played games and took tea, is irremediably coffin-shaped. I looked across at Aunt Janet and thought, "That space, between your eyes and mine, was filled by my father's dead body until two days ago."

Last night, and the night before, I dreamed that I was buried in the cemetery at Tower Hamlets. Pa was calling to me, but I couldn't answer him on account of a stone angel, which was pressing its hand across my face and stuffing my mouth with wet earth. I could never tell this dream to anyone, except for you, dear diary, because what if it proves that I'm mad or wicked? What then? I suspect that normal people (normal females, anyway) would never entertain such ugly ideas, even in their sleep. Nettie sometimes tells me her dreams, but they are always funny, like the one where she mistook a pudding for her hat.

"I can't help wondering what's to become of the child when her poor mother . . . ?"

This was Aunt Janet. Rather than say the word "dies," she allowed the question to trail away, which struck me as a surprising delicacy. We all know that Mamma is dying (do we not?), and Aunt Janet has dealt bluntly with every other topic during her stay, from the inferiority of our wallpapers, to the stunting effects of Bloomsbury air, to Almighty God's disdain for Peevishness in Girls.

"Goodness me, *I* don't know!" Aunt Judith replied, and she laughed a trilling little laugh, which didn't suit her at all.

"There is no need to flare up, Judith; nobody is asking you to adopt the child."

If they had been cats, they would have arched their backs and hissed.

Sunday, 16 January, 1876

Last week, grief was a knife in my heart; this week, it feels oddly like boredom.

Frank ought to be back in Cambridge, he says so himself, and yet he stays: draping himself over sofas, flicking through medical textbooks, smoking Pa's cigars. He manages to be full of jokes and laughter (I cannot get him to talk seriously about anything) without being the least bit happy. I know, although they make no comment, that the servants consider him a nuisance.

This evening, my brother and I sat in front of the parlour fire, playing backgammon. I was cross-legged on the rug; he was lounging in an armchair; the inevitable Miss Wilson was perched on a stool in the corner, doing her embroidery. I rolled a double six and moved another checker off the board. It occurred to me that Frank is now the master of 17 Erskine Place, and that nobody has authority to scold him. If he wishes to drink Pa's brandy, or put his feet on Pa's chairs, or bend the pages in Pa's books, he may do so with impunity. I suppose Mamma might reprimand him if she wished, but she never would.

"When you are a proper doctor, with your own practice, I shall no longer be 'Miss Mouse,'" I said. "I'll be your housekeeper, and you will have to do as I say in the matter of smoking and drinking and mistreating chairs."

I was half-serious, but only half. It's true, I did want him to sit up properly and put Pa's brandy away and be the old Frank whom I could thoroughly understand and talk to, but I also wanted to make him smile.

Frank refilled his glass and pushed the backgammon board aside with his foot. He did smile, although not—it must be said—in my direction.

"No doubt you're aware of your pupil's high ambitions, Miss Wilson? The future she has mapped out for herself?"

Miss Wilson returned his smile, furtively, and looked down again at her sewing.

"The acme of Miss Mouse's desire is to keep house for her brother," Frank went on, pushing the backgammon pieces around at random. Clearly, the game was aborted, which was all the more annoying because I'd been about to win. I was not afraid of Frank (what an idea!), but I was afraid of the mood he was generating tonight. It excluded me by including Miss Wilson; it had him laughing at me and soliciting her smiles. If I said anything, anything at all, I knew they would both find it droll.

I got on my hands and knees to retrieve the backgammon pieces that Frank had scattered. The set had been Pa's, and I was loath to lose any part of it. I couldn't see their faces, down there at floor level, only their feet. Miss Wilson crossed and uncrossed her ankles in their dainty button boots, while Frank drew invisible patterns on the rug with his outstretched toe.

When I got back to my room, I practised writing things in Miss Wilson's hand. (I find people's handwriting interesting, although I keep this a secret in case it isn't quite ladylike. Miss Wilson's hand is especially easy to copy as she writes like a dunce.)

I wrote, "I am no bird; and no net ensnares me," which is a quote from Pa's favourite scene in Jane Eyre. I also wrote, "My name is Miss Wilson and I am in love with the butcher's boy." Finally I did her clodhopping signature—*Ellen Wilson*—half a dozen times at the bottom of the page.

Monday, 17 January, 1876

I woke from my usual nightmare a few hours ago, only to doubt that I was really awake. I got out of bed and stumbled round the room, and for a while it seemed my door had gone from its usual place, but I found it in the end and let myself out. I felt my way downstairs and along the landing to Frank's room and beat softly on the door with my palms. I do not like wandering the house at night: What if I were to meet one of the lodgers? What if ghostly old Mr. Paley were to emerge from his room, all dressed for bed? Or the German professor, Herr Schulz, with his bristling beard? I beat a little harder and whispered, "Frank!" My face was wet and my breaths came strangely, and all my insides were drumming and thrumming, but I still remembered to be quiet so as not to disturb Mamma. (I'm pleased about that, now I'm sane and awake; it's proof of <u>some</u> degree of self-possession.)

It was funny, seeing Frank barefoot in his nightshirt, with a lighted candle in his hand. His face was bleary and bemused, and his hair was a haystack.

"Maude?" He rubbed his eyes. "Whatever is the matter?"

"Nothing. Nothing really. I had a nightmare."

I thought he would send me back to bed, but my appearance must have been more compelling than my words because he looked me up and down with a sigh and said, "Poor little Mousey." He had me come inside and sit on the bed, and while I shivered and cried he swaddled me in his dressing gown and poured an inch of brandy into a glass.

"Sip this," he said, pressing it into my hands, and I said "Thank you" without passing comment on the fact that Pa's liquor bottles had taken up residence in my brother's bedroom. (There was also a bottle of Madeira on the washstand.) I didn't taste the brandy, but it was pleasant to sniff at its evil, gunpowder scent.

Frank put his arm round me and patted my shoulder. Apart from the height and bulk of him, and his hairy legs, it was as if we were children again.

"You can tell me your bad dream," he yawned, "if it helps."

I remembered the flavour of the dream, but not enough detail to make a coherent description.

"Frank?" I asked, instead. "Who is The Feline?"

He stopped rubbing my arm, but his voice remained light. "The Feline?"

"Uncle Talbot kept talking about The Feline. Not to me, but . . . I heard him. A couple of evenings ago he was laughing, after dinner, and he told Cousin John that he could think of worse ways to die than curled up in a cosy little basket with The Feline. And then one day, when we were all at breakfast, he said, 'I don't suppose The Feline will show its face at the funeral?' And there were other times as well."

Frank let go of my shoulder and laid his hands on his lap.

"What did everybody else say?"

"Very little. Aunt Judith gave him a mean look when he mentioned it at the breakfast table; I don't think she approved."

My brother stood up and walked to the mantelpiece. There were various oddments on the shelf—a clock, a handbell, a watch, a nutcracker doll, a box of matches, a candlestick—and he picked them up, one by one, only to put them down again.

"Frank?"

"Hmm?"

I paused, unsure how to express myself. "Frank . . . was Pa somehow killed by a cat?"

He put the matches down with a laugh and looked at me fondly. "Oh Mousey," he said, which would have been nice—quite the old Frank—if it had been accompanied by a straight answer.

"It's all very well for you to laugh—"

"No, our father did not die at the hands—paws—of a cat."

"Then—"

"I will tell you all—or rather, I will tell you something about it tomorrow, but only if you go to bed this minute, and fall asleep, and dream about nice things."

"Such as . . . ?"

He combed his fingers through his hair. "Whatever you like. Sugar and spice and all things nice. Understood?"

Frank gave me his candle, and I gave him the untasted brandy before making my way back to bed. I am writing this entry in pencil, so as not to spill ink on the blanket.

Tomorrow (today, in fact!) I may at least have one answer, to one question.

The daylight, such as it was, began to fade around four o'clock this evening. I went to my brother's bedroom and found Ruth packing a valise with the few clothes and books Frank had brought with him.

"Oh Ruth! Is Frank going back to Cambridge immediately?"

"Not immediately, Miss Maude." She glanced up. "He says he'll be leaving in the morning; he asked me to arrange his bags."

"Where is he now? I haven't set eyes on him all day."

"I left him in the parlour, miss. He came in from his walk half an hour ago, looking ever so cold and out of sorts, so I lit the fire and sat him down, and Nettie took him some tea."

I scuttled downstairs. If only I'd known, I'd have gone to him straightaway; it's not as if I was doing anything important. Miss Wilson had instructed me to sort through my mending, but I couldn't get on because Ebenezer wanted to sit on top of the sewing basket, and I didn't like to object.

Ebenezer *knows* things. Sometimes I think he is laughing at us, all of us, the entire human race.

When I entered the parlour, I found Frank sitting on a low stool in his greatcoat and boots, with only the fire for light. He was gazing into the flames as if there was a sad story there and he was reading it to himself. I knelt down and laid a hand upon his knee.

"Hello, Maude." He stroked my hand.

There was a cup on the hearth, cold to the touch, full of strong, brown tea. I almost said, "I wouldn't have turned my nose up at that when it was hot; nobody thinks to bring *me* a cup of tea!" but Frank looked so far away that I didn't have the heart.

"Are you thinking about Pa?" I said.

"In a way."

I followed his eyes to the fire, to see if I could read what he was reading, but however hard I tried they were just coals and flames to me.

"You're cold," he said, gathering my small hands inside his large ones and blowing on them, as if to kindle fire from a spark. Once upon a time it would have made me laugh and wriggle, but today I felt closer to crying.

"Will you tell me things now?" I said. "Last night you promised you would."

Frank squeezed my hands, and I took that for a "yes."

"Will you tell me why you're angry with Pa?"

"Because he let us down."

"Oh no, I'm sure he didn't!" I cried. "Or if he did, he didn't mean to."

"He did mean to."

My lips wobbled. "But we love him, don't we, Frank? Remember that time he took us to the circus? We love Pa, don't we?" Sometimes, when I speak, I sound more like a silly child than I really am inside.

Frank breathed over my cold hands again. "Pa hurt Mamma, which is the same as hurting you and me. Do you see, Maude? He shamed and humiliated our own mamma."

Nobody could humiliate our mother, even if they wanted to; you might as well try to humiliate the moon and stars. I wanted to argue with Frank and explain how he was wrong, but it was difficult to grapple with words like "hurt" and "shame" and "humiliate." I couldn't get hold of them, somehow.

"You'll need to be more particular, if you expect me to believe you," I said, "because Pa never would have struck Mamma, or shouted at her, or said cruel things."

"No," Frank conceded. "No, it wasn't that kind of hurt."

"What then? And what does 'The Feline' have to do with it?"

A light hand tapped on the door and pushed it ajar. I glanced across the room at Miss Wilson, but she was nearly invisible in the twilight: the slight shape of a dark dress in the doorway; the gleam of an eye.

"Forgive me. I have been looking all over the house for my pupil . . ."

"Frank!" I seized his hands as he let go of mine. "Please tell me about The Feline."

"Come in, Miss Wilson." Frank got to his feet. "No need to apologise."

I got up as well, in a bid to keep my brother's attention.

"Frank! Please, won't you finish . . ."

He extracted his hands from mine and patted my cheek.

"Oh Maude, don't you know?" he said. "Surely you know already? The Feline is a vicious, predatory beast who lures foolish men to their doom."

"You're not talking about an actual cat though, are you?"

"Oh yes, Miss Mouse, I am. The Feline is very actual, very real. She is a mighty, insatiable, flesh-eating cat with sharp white teeth and glossy fur."

I suppose I should have been grateful that he was talking at all, but I couldn't help wishing he'd talk to <u>me</u>. Whom was he addressing? Himself? I'd say he was sharing a joke with Miss Wilson, if it weren't for the fact that he'd turned away to poke at the fire.

"The Feline beckons men into her lair, and when they come, she plays with them awhile before eating them alive."

I was, am, wholeheartedly confused. We were obviously discussing a metaphorical, rather than a zoological, cat, but that was no help at all. Symbolical cats are only useful if you know what they symbolise.

"Miss Maude?" said Miss Wilson from the doorway. Her voice had gone lower and quieter, in keeping with Frank's. "Go upstairs, if you please, and fetch your mending."

I did as I was told. When I came back, Frank had gone and Miss Wilson was alone by the hearth with a little smile on her face, knotting and unknotting her fingers.

Me: "Miss Wilson, did you understand what my brother was talking about just now?"

Miss Wilson (after a long pause, which rendered me hopeful of an intelligent reply): "I'm not . . . or rather . . . yes and no."

Good heavens. One of these days someone will give me a straight answer to a straight question, and I swear I shall faint from the shock.

Tuesday, 18 January, 1876

I have promised to tell my diary everything and therefore I will make this entry, although I don't like to. Quite apart from anything else, it is difficult to describe an event I only half heard, half saw, and less than half understood. When I recall it, I want to throw china objects at the wall, as Mamma may have done the other week. Or else I want to weep and shout. Or else I want to wash. I want to sit up to my neck in the bathtub, scrubbing and scrubbing and scrubbing, until I'm pure and sweet-smelling, in body, mind, and spirit.

I woke from my usual nightmare—stone angels, and rain, and figures hunched over spades, shovelling soil—and lay still while my heartbeat righted itself. I thought about my bad dream.

Throwing my shawl around my shoulders, I felt my way to the door. You may be sure, dear diary, that I was quiet—even quieter than I'd been the previous night.

The corridor outside my room was <u>not</u> entirely quiet, but then it never is. Even at the dead of night, Euston station is alive—I suppose the whole of London is alive—and its hectic pulse reverberates through the house. There are inside noises as well: creaking joists, rattling windows, the snores and whimpers that people make when they are asleep.

I tiptoed along the landing, pausing every few seconds to listen. It seemed to me, although I couldn't be sure, that there were other, less explicable sounds as well: creaks and rustles, whispers and failed attempts at whispers, a muffled noise that might have been a laugh. "Ghosts!" was my first thought, and I was just weighing up the competing terrors that presented themselves (return to the solitary darkness of my room, or make my way down the haunted stairs to find my brother?) when a door opened softly, farther down the corridor, and Frank himself emerged.

He was coming out of Miss Wilson's room, and Miss Wilson was there too, holding a candle. The two of them stood in her open doorway in their nightgowns—without shawls, or robes, or anything that might make them half-decent. They did not notice me: I was wearing a long, dark shawl over my nightdress, and I managed to make no sound at all.

I will never understand how, or why, they should wish to stand so close to one another in their <u>night things</u>. It makes my skin crawl. Miss Wilson's hair—of which she is usually so vain—was hanging over her face and sticking up at the sides. Her right hand was flat against my brother's chest and I heard her whisper—amongst other, less audible whispers—"Do you promise me solemnly, Frank?" to which he answered, "Dear, sweet girl!"

Nobody should press his or her face against another person's face (and neck!) the way she proceeded to do. A couple of times I've felt Dr. Nesbit's hot breath on my face as he peered inside my swollen throat and under my eyelids, which was horrible enough, and not nearly so intrusive. At one point they looked as though they were trying to eat each other from the head down. Occasionally Miss Wilson broke off to say, "Shh!"

I would have fled, but I didn't dare move until they'd parted, at long last, with much lingering and touching of hands. Frank crept downstairs and Miss Wilson withdrew to her room, shutting the door behind her.

I spent the rest of the night shivering between my sheets and thinking.

Miss Wilson is a servant, but she is a very different proposition from, say, Nettie and Ruth. They are, and always have been, merely Nettie and Ruth, neither pretty nor plain, old nor young, nice nor not-nice, as necessary and uninteresting to our household as the coal scuttle, or the dining table, or the curtains over the windows. Miss Wilson is more like Mamma, in the sense that they both have Defining Qualities. (Of course, I do not mean that Miss Wilson is <u>like</u> Mamma in any other sense!) Mamma's Defining Qualities are gentleness, purity, and beauty, but I find it much harder to name Miss Wilson's. Is there any word that means "attractive" and "odious," both at the same time, or is that what's meant by a paradox?

It's all very well to think, and to write long diary entries, but I need to decide on a course of action.

Friday, 21 January, 1876

It has been impossible to write until now, on account of the upset on Tuesday (of which more presently) and then because I was ill, actually ill in bed, as a result of Miss Wilson's cruelty. She even induced Mamma to commit an injustice, which is perhaps the worst part of the whole business, although I am confident Mamma herself has done nothing wrong by being misled, and that it is my governess's soul, and hers alone, that finds itself in *dire jeopardy*.

I was tired on Tuesday morning, after my wakeful night, and depressed, and quite at a loss. I came downstairs to breakfast, only to find that Frank had left for Cambridge on an early train without saying goodbye. ("He said goodbye to your mother last night, on his way to bed," said Ruth, when I complained to her, and that was that. I am forbidden to say, "Yes, but what about *me*?" in any context whatsoever; Mamma calls it a coarse and childish species of question.)

On the upside, Miss Wilson was miserable too. We ate our porridge in silence, except for the odd sigh and stifled yawn. Mrs. Bristow (lodges on the third floor in the small room at the back) came in, looking for her spectacles, but they weren't to be found and she decided they must be on her washstand after all. The coal-delivery men made their way, with lots of bangs and rumbles, round Erskine Place. The only things Miss Wilson said, unprompted, were: "Did *you* know your brother was intending to leave so early?" and "Were there any letters or notes on the hall table when you came down?" to which I was able to reply, truthfully, "No" and "No."

I took some bacon from the sideboard and wondered how it would be when Miss Wilson was Mrs. Gower, and the mistress of

Frank's house. The very idea of it, of Miss Wilson wearing my keys at her belt, and totting up my household accounts, and sitting next to my brother on the settee at night, made me choke on my first mouthful. I had to spit half a rasher onto my plate in order to cough, and of course she took notice of that. She gave me a weary look and rubbed her eyes.

"You're excused from lessons this morning, Maude. You may amuse yourself until lunchtime."

"How so, Miss Wilson?"

"I feel somewhat tired and unwell; I shall be quite recovered by the afternoon."

"Why are you tired, Miss Wilson? Did you have a restless night?"

I suppose I must have sounded sly, more sly than I intended, because her whole face sharpened and she gave me a look that said, "I've got the measure of you." I sipped my tea demurely and speculated on how best to proceed.

What Miss Wilson doesn't seem to realise, and the thing that strikes me as most unfair, is that it was only a joke. In fact, it was the merest idea for a joke; I hadn't gone further than experimenting on a rough piece of paper.

"Dear Mr. Briggs," I wrote, but that was much too chilly. "Dearest Mr. Briggs, Darling Mr. Briggs, My Darling Jack . . ."

I did not hesitate because I found it difficult to mimic Miss Wilson's hand, but because I wasn't sure how a love letter ought to go.

"My Dearest, Darling Jack." (I settled on that in the end. She ought to come across as forward, which was scarcely a deceit given what I'd witnessed the previous night.)

> *My heart is no longer mine. You have won me over with your gentlemanly overtures and your gifts of peppermint creams, and I cannot pretend anymore to a coolness I do not feel. Let us be married quickly, just as soon as the banns are read. As your wife, the wife of the handsomest butcher's boy in London, I know I shall be happier than a queen. Perhaps, with enough ambition, we may be the proprietors of our very own butcher's shop one day, and we shall bring up our many children to make the finest blood puddings and pork pies. How many children shall we have, dear*

That was as much as I wrote, and you must admit it has the potential to be funny. It made <u>me</u> laugh. Anyway, I wasn't necessarily going to deliver it to Jack Briggs the butcher's boy; I might have sent it to Frank instead, since he enjoys a good joke. Or I might have simply finished it off for my own amusement and destroyed it. We will never know. Just as I was getting into my stride, Miss Wilson walked in with her perpetual suspicions and her, "What are you up to, Miss Maude?"

It's possible I blushed, because when I said "Nothing!" she folded her arms and raised her eyebrows.

I'd been sitting by the cold fireplace with my writing on my lap, but as she approached I leapt to my feet, nearly knocking the ink bottle onto the hearthrug. Things might have turned out better if I <u>had</u> spilled the ink and caused a distraction. As it was, Miss Wilson lunged for the paper I was hiding behind my back and secured it before I had time to gather my wits. She is taller than me, so she was able to hold it at arm's length, above her head, and study it at leisure. I leapt and snatched and pleaded, but she twisted away from me and carried on reading.

I gave up; there was nothing else for it. Miss Wilson went red in the face and I felt sure she was going to burst into tears, but to my astonishment she neither cried, nor spoke, nor laid a finger on me. Instead, she stood very still when she'd finished reading, chewing the inside of her cheek. After a while she folded the paper and left the room.

I ought to have been disturbed by her uncharacteristic restraint. Miss Wilson is not unwilling to use the slipper on my hands or legs, and in the past I've been beaten for such run-of-the-mill sins as laziness and "stupidity" (so-called, much she knows about that!) and having dirt under my nails. On Tuesday morning, I was foolish enough to think I'd got away with it, that she would have a good cry in her room, burn the letter in the grate, and never raise the matter again.

I was wrong. In a few minutes she returned, looking less like a woman who'd been weeping tears of humiliation and more like the cat that got the cream. I swear she was extra tall, extra calm, extra poised as she opened the door and announced, "Your mother wishes to see you right away, Miss Maude."

It was as much as to say, "Checkmate."

I didn't plead, unless you count the way I looked at her, and neither did she relent. Smilingly, she shook her head and held out her hand.

My governess escorted me to my mother's bedroom door, and waited politely while I summoned the courage to knock. Truth be told, I had rather she'd dragged me along by my hair and hurled me through the door.

Mamma was lying with her eyes closed and the offending letter in her hand. I must have stood at the head of her bed for a full minute, waiting for some acknowledgement. I knew she was awake because she'd said "Come!" when I knocked.

At last she opened her eyes, took a long look at me, and closed them again. My mother was especially beautiful that morning, with her hair spreading like pale fire over the pillow. If I were standing at the gates of heaven, and St. Peter gave me such a look before shooing me away, I don't think I could have felt much worse.

Mamma's slim fingers lifted the paper.

"You wrote this?"

I thought of replying, "It was only a joke!" or "Wouldn't you like to know what Miss Wilson did last night, with Frank?" but in the end I whispered, simply, "Yes."

Mamma: "What do you wish me to do, Miss Wilson?"

Miss W.: "Whatever you see fit, ma'am."

M. (long, weary pause): "What is the time?"

Miss W.: "Half past ten."

M. (even longer, wearier pause): "Very well. Put Miss Maude in the coal cellar, where she may ponder her behaviour until half past ten tonight; twelve hours will be enough, I suppose."

Mamma closed her lips and folded her hands over her breast. Miss Wilson looked like someone with a head full of questions, which she couldn't bring herself to ask. I had a head full of objections, rather violent ones, which I didn't dare voice. We both stood staring until my governess murmured, "Ma'am," bobbed a little curtsey, and steered me away. As we reached the door, I glanced over my shoulder, but Mamma kept her eyes closed, like a sculpted queen on the lid of a tomb in Westminster Abbey.

Even in daylight hours, the coal cellar bears an uncanny resemblance to my nightmare. The darkness is complete in there, without so much as a rim of light around the door, or the pavement hatch through which the delivery man pours the coal. The silence, too, is so utter that it buzzes inside your ears, except when the occasional pedestrian stomps across the hatch with a brief "bang-bang" of his or her boots. As for the January cold: if I were a better philosopher than I am, I might say I was grateful for it on that terrible Tuesday, because it distracted me from my other woes.

Cook came at some point (without permission, judging by her furtive manner) bearing a blanket, a hunk of bread, and a mug of hot broth. The tin mug is usually reserved for tradespeople; for example, after the chimneys have been swept, the sweep will be taken to the kitchen and given beer in the tin mug. Therefore, as glad as I was of the broth, there was a horrible ignominy involved in drinking it. Likewise, the blanket was a blessing against the cold, but it was scratchy and it smelled of "scullery" and "backyard" in the worst possible senses (heaven knows what it's normally used for), and I was ashamed to pull it round my shoulders. Cook was in too much of a rush and a worry to say much, but she kissed me on the cheek and whispered, "Take heart!"

I would have laughed, if I could still laugh, when I thought how Miss Wilson scolded me, last week, for letting Ebenezer shed hairs on my new dress. "Look at me now, Miss Wilson," I thought. "Perched on a hill of coal, in clouds of dust, wrapped in a foul-smelling blanket, and all because of *you*!"

My fingers were so stiff with cold that I dropped the bread, halfway through eating it, but I was hungry enough to fish for it in the dark and polish it off nonetheless. It tasted of soot, and my back teeth crunched on a shard of coal.

Miss Wilson's parting shot, before bolting the cellar door, was an admonition "to spend this time wisely and thoughtfully, and to regard the experience as a gift, rather than a punishment," meaning, presumably, that I should dwell on my sins for twelve hours, and repent of them. In fact, I *did* spend some time thinking about my own badness (although I did it of my own accord, and *not* in deference to Miss Wilson), but the exercise only depressed me further and made me cry. Pa would not have been amused by my "Mr. Briggs" prank, because he was always kind to the servants, and only ever laughed at them in private. I tried to comfort myself with the thought that Frank would find it funny, before recalling that he is in love with, perhaps even engaged to, Miss Wilson, so would be obliged to find it offensive.

After that, my thoughts went on a very gloomy wander indeed. As if Pa being dead were not bad enough, now Frank was apparently intending to marry Miss Wilson, and all my hopes and plans for the future were scattered to the four winds. Equally bad was the look on Mamma's face before she pronounced my sentence. I couldn't seem to expel it from my mind. It wasn't anger I'd seen in her eyes, or even disappointment, but the utter, utter weariness of disgust.

I lay down on my side, because I didn't care anymore about being dirty. The cold was like a hundred sets of tiny teeth, biting through the holes in the blanket. I hoped I might fall asleep, but I didn't, I just lay there thinking and thinking and thinking. At one point I said, out loud, "Dear God, I wish I was dead," which is probably a mortal sin, but I only said it because it was true.

My arm is aching with so much writing. Not only have I finished this diary entry in one go, sitting up in bed, but I have also written an account of what happened in a letter to Frank (omitting the scene I witnessed outside Miss Wilson's room on Monday night, since I don't have the words for what they were doing, and the memory of it makes me squirm).

God did not answer my prayer in the coal cellar—that is to say, I emerged alive—but I was extremely ill. My teeth were chattering so hard by half past ten, when Miss Wilson and Cook came to release me, that Miss Wilson said I must be acting up, which I swear I was not. I fainted on the way upstairs, and Cook insisted on carrying me, despite remonstrations from You-Know-Who. That night, and the whole of the following day (Wednesday), I kept to my bed with a sore throat and a fever. I heard Ruth saying Dr. Nesbit ought to be called and Miss Wilson insisting it was nothing but a cold, "and no less than she deserves," to which dear Ruth responded darkly, "Be it on your head, Miss Wilson!"

I confess I prayed harder than ever that evening that I might die—or very, very, very nearly die—if only to spite my governess.

Monday, 24 January, 1876

I've been ill all Saturday and all Sunday. Miss Wilson has never wavered from her belief that I'm merely suffering from a cold—in which case I hope she catches it, and we will see how she likes it.

Ruth has been bringing me breakfast in bed, and she brought it again this morning. Tea, sugared porridge, buttered toast, and a soft-boiled egg!

I gave Ruth a guilty look as she propped my pillows behind my back. "Miss Wilson says that Mamma says I've been wallowing in luxury too long. I'm to get up today, and resume my usual routine."

"What a good idea," said Ruth. "But you can have your breakfast first."

Whenever Ruth is undermining Mamma (which she does, very subtly, every now and then), her voice goes brisk and firm, and she won't meet my eye. I didn't argue. With any luck, Mamma will never know about the soft-boiled egg.

There was a letter from Frank on the tray, and I waited till Ruth had gone before opening it.

St. John's College
Cambridge
22 January, 1876

Dear Miss Wilson,

I referred back to the envelope, but the addressee was, unmistakably, me. "Miss Maude Gower." It wouldn't be the first time in his life that my brother had made such a blunder; he has a tendency to carelessness. I suppose I ought not to have read on, since it wasn't my letter, but I'm afraid I did. I can only give an approximate transcript, as I no longer have the original to hand:

Dear Miss Wilson,

Ever since leaving London I have been pondering you, and my association with you, in a spirit of self-censure. My conscience—not to mention a timely letter from my sister—suggests that my recent behaviour has fallen short of the gentlemanlike standard to which I aspire.

I shall always regard you with the very deepest respect but there is, categorically, no question of a more intimate bond ever existing between us. If I have given rise to contrary expectations my own poor conduct is to blame, and I apologise accordingly.

Yours sincerely,
Frank Gower

Miss Wilson came in as I was starting on my egg. She was carrying a piece of paper, and I recognised my brother's sloping scrawl across the page.

"A letter for you, Miss Maude." Her voice sounded strange, and it crossed my mind that she really had caught my cold. "The envelope was accidentally addressed to me, which is how I came to read it."

"Ditto," said I, and we swapped. As we did so, I noted that

a) although Miss Wilson had admitted to perusing my letter, she had not apologised for doing so, and

b) the whites of her eyes were pink.

We both began reading immediately, but her letter was shorter than mine, and she finished first. She screwed it into her fist and left my room without saying a word, only shutting the door very sharply behind her.

St. John's College
Cambridge
22 January, 1876

Dearest Maude,

I scarcely know whether to laugh or cry! Throughout the long and illustrious history of rodents, was ever there a sillier or more endearing little mouse than my own sister? I read your letter to my cronies yesterday evening, when we met for a smoke in Hartwell's rooms, and it went down a treat, you may be sure! Henry Simpson says you are a comic genius and one of the other fellows—MacLeod, I think it was—thinks I ought to put you on the stage. What do you make of that idea?

In all seriousness I should like to know what, in heaven's name, gave you the idea that I—Francis George Henry Gower, your most respectable brother and chief scion of the Gower clan—might be matrimonially inclined towards Miss Wilson, of all people? Really, Maude! Your governess is a bonny enough lassie (as MacLeod would put it) but she is no Helen of Troy, and you know I could never settle for anything less. Besides, I had thought that you were to keep house for me (in the absence of said Helen) once you have completed your metamorphosis from Incompetent Child to Domestic Angel, and I have completed mine from Student to Medical Man? Is this not our long-cherished plan? It seems a shame to drag Miss Wilson into the scheme. She's got such a dreadfully martyred way of talking, and she doesn't know how to play whist, and she sends me to sleep when she reads aloud. (You can't have forgotten her "Marley's ghost" already? It was barely a month ago!)

There, now. Does this satisfy you, you ridiculous child?

Be of good cheer, Mousey. I know life is hard at present, and it's worse for you than it is for me, since you are stuck at home with little to do. I will come and visit you soon, or perhaps you will come and visit me? The chaps would be more than honoured to make your acquaintance.

Your affectionate brother,
Frank

Tuesday, 25 January, 1876

~~Hurrah, hurrah, hur~~

Miss Wilson has upped and gone! This very morning she set off for Brighton (where her parents and sisters live) without apparent concern for references, or pay, or serving periods of notice, or anything!

I have been dreaming of this day ever since she came, two years ago, but now it is come I don't know what to do. I was going to fill an entire page with "Hurrahs!" and, as you can see, I did make a start—but I don't have the heart for it somehow. Perhaps, since Pa died, I've become too old and grave for hurrahs.

It was Nettie who brought me the news. She came into my room while I was dressing, full to bursting with it:

"Oh miss, you'll never believe it!" she said. "I've just come from your mamma's room—she rang for fresh coals—and while I was there, Miss Wilson knocked and entered, as brisk and cool as you like, and announced that she's off, without so much as a by-your-leave!"

I froze in the middle of pulling my stocking over my right knee.

"What did Mamma say?"

"Why, nothing at all! Your poor mother hardly had time to blink, Miss Maude, let alone speak. As soon as that governess of yours had said her piece she swept off like a queen, and she's in her room now, packing up her things."

I went to Miss Wilson's room after breakfast. I don't know why. Curiosity, I suppose.

The door was ajar, and I saw her without being seen. She must have finished her packing, because the bedroom looked neat and bare, and there was a carpetbag on the floor with its clasps buckled up. Miss Wilson herself was sitting on the edge of the bed, cloaked, bonneted, and booted, with Ebenezer on her lap! He was kneading her cloak and shedding hairs everywhere, that is to say, he was doing all the things Miss Wilson hates most in a cat, but she simply sat with her head bowed, stroking him from the crown of his head to the middle of his shoulder blades. When I tapped on the door she looked up, but I couldn't make out her expression because the daylight was behind her. Miss Wilson's grimy window has the same outlook as mine: the train sheds, the gasworks, the higgledy-piggledy rooftops of Somers Town.

Ebenezer jumped down and rubbed against my ankles. I didn't know what to say, so I bent to caress him.

"What do you want, Maude?"

"The confusion over the envelopes," I said. "It was a genuine mistake on Frank's part, I'm sure. There was no malice in it."

"I didn't think there was."

"There is no malice in my brother."

"No, none at all. Only carelessness."

I might have defended him, if I hadn't already had the same thought and recorded it in this notebook, two or three pages back.

Wednesday, 26 January, 1876

Ebenezer always makes his way to the kitchen around eight o'clock at night for his supper; failing that he always, <u>always</u> appears in the morning for his saucer of cream. He didn't come last night, though, and he didn't come this morning. I have been round and round Erskine Place, tapping on a saucer with a fork and calling his name, and I would be there now if Mamma hadn't heard me from her bed and ordered Ruth to haul me indoors.

I know what's happened to Ebenezer. It came to me with such a start this afternoon, as I was embroidering the last of Frank's initials onto a handkerchief, that I stabbed my thumb and smeared the cambric with blood. <u>Miss Wilson is the culprit</u>. She has kidnapped Ebenezer and taken him away to Brighton, not because she loves him but because she hates me.

I rushed onto the landing when I heard Nettie going past, and told her my conjecture. I thought she would shriek and drop her dustpan (at the very least!), but all she said was, "I don't think that's likely, ducky. I saw Miss Wilson off at the door myself, and she only had the one bag for her clothes and whatnot. She'd have had a job fitting a big, fat, wriggling cat in there too."

Which only confirms my alternative and much more horrible suspicion: that Miss Wilson has done away with Ebenezer. That she has murdered him, and dumped his poor body who knows where? Under the ragged bushes in Erskine Place; in the depths of the coal cellar; in the sewers. I didn't bother sharing my idea with Nettie, given her unreceptive mood, but I mentioned it to Cook this evening. We were standing together on the basement steps, whispering, "Ebenezer!" into the darkness, and listening (in vain) for an answering "Miaow."

Up until tonight, I credited Cook with a sensitivity and intelligence beyond her station. Well. Up until tonight, I was wrong. She actually snorted (snorted!) at my theory and said, "Miss Wilson? Murder the cat? Don't be so silly, Miss Maude."

What is the matter with everyone? Why is the world so stupid and hateful? It was never like this when Pa was alive.

Sunday, 30 January, 1876

I have nothing interesting to tell you. Ebenezer is still missing. If I were a man I would go to Brighton and discover the truth, but I am not a man. I am merely a girl or, as Frank would have it, a mouse.

Friday, 4 February, 1876

Mamma summoned me to her bedside this afternoon. It is seventeen days since we saw one another last.

Mamma is very thin. Her skin has become yellow white, rather than snow white, and for the first time in all my life I felt no secret impulse to touch her. When I asked how she was, she made no answer. She has the air of someone trying hard to hear a distant voice.

I thought she wasn't going to speak at all, but suddenly she asked, "How have you been occupying your days, child?" By way of reply I spouted, rather desperately, a list of ladylike pursuits: from sewing (true), to pressing flowers (not quite so true),* to making an album of inspirational maxims (not true at all). I didn't lay claim to piano practice, since the piano is audible throughout the house, and she would have known I was lying.

I read aloud two stanzas from "The Lady of Shalott" before Mamma told me to stop. She said she was too sad for Tennyson.

* I picked some snowdrops in Erskine Place on Monday and promptly forgot all about them. I found them yesterday, quite by accident, crushed inside my coat pocket.

Sunday, 20 February, 1876

Improving one's deportment is a ladylike activity, of course, though it had slipped my mind until today.

This morning I walked around my room, balancing the <u>Tales of Ancient Rome</u> on my head. Each circuit was approximately thirty feet, and I performed it two hundred times, which means that I walked over a mile today without leaving my bedroom. The book fell off my head thirteen times.

I wish something interesting would happen.

Tuesday, 29 February, 1876

Something <u>has</u> happened; a terrible thing. I believe I have wished it into being, though I never meant to. What shall I DO? I don't know. I can't write.

Wednesday, 1 March, 1876

All the same, I can't <u>not</u> tell you, and I feel better able to write today.

There must have been a great commotion in the early hours of Tuesday morning, but I slept through everything and only woke when Cook came into my room. The darkness was starting to thin, and even with my curtains closed I could make out the shape of her face and the white of her apron. I shut my eyes and tried not to shiver, because Cook never, ever comes to my room; Cook belongs in the kitchen.

"Miss Maude?" she said.

Her rough hand caressed my hair and she shook my shoulder. I opened my eyes and we peered at one another through the dimness. I said, "Is it Mamma?" and the world seemed to hang on a thread while I waited for her nod.

How singular: not having to knock before entering Mamma's room; not having to think of something sensible to say. Nettie was in there, tidying round the bed. The little laudanum bottles, which always stood so neatly on the dressing table, were strewn over the floor and she was gathering them up.

"Please don't!" I protested when she made to embrace me, and to do her justice, she didn't. She bobbed a curtsey instead and said, "I'm so terribly sorry, Miss Maude," before hurrying from the room, the small, empty bottles chinking in her apron pocket with each step. I regretted my "don't!" at once. I hadn't meant for her to leave.

I only looked towards the bed, in the end, because not looking was worse.

In some ways, nothing had changed: the sight of Mamma's dead face still made the blood thunder in my ears. At any moment those heavy eyelids were going to lift, and the lips were going to part, and she was going to say something gentle yet terrible, the way angels do.

I waited at her side for a long time, wiping my damp palms over my dress, while the grey snow fell past the window. There was nobody to say, "What are you afraid of?" or "Go to your room now," or even "Mind your lovely new dress!"

In fact, my mourning dress is no longer lovely or new. The cuffs are frayed, and the black is fading to brown in patches.

It snowed all day. It was still snowing at dusk when I went into the square with Ebenezer's saucer and fork and began to call for him.

Weeks have passed since I'd last tried to find my cat, but I had a sentimental idea that God, in his pity, might choose today to perform a miracle. It was dark enough that I could stick out my tongue and taste the falling snow, without being seen from the other houses in Erskine Place. The flakes felt gritty against my teeth, and their flavour was soot. While I was standing in the middle of the square, I saw Frank arriving from the station, and Nettie letting him in.

Nettie was still standing in the open doorway when I got back. She'd done her best to resurrect the yew wreath, originally bought for Pa, by winding new lengths of black ribbon round the greenery. To my eye, it looked scruffy and second-hand, and however much she tried, it still refused to sit securely on its nail.

I made for the stairs, resisting a perverse temptation to glance inside the parlour. The coffin was there, with Mamma inside it, her eyes lightly closed and her hands crossed over her breast. That's how she used to lie when she was sleeping. I have tried to do the same, but I always wake up on my side with my knees bent and my hands balled under my chin.

I poked my head inside Frank's room, but he wasn't there, so I tapped on Mamma's bedroom door.

"Frank?"

My voice was quiet, but not so quiet he'd have failed to hear me. I could hear him: the creaking of the floorboards where he knelt, and the sobs he was smothering in the bare mattress.

"Frank?"

I sat down with my back against the door. It was a cold, dark place to sit, though no colder or darker than my bedroom. The sound of his distress was a terrible thing, but it didn't loosen my own tears in the way I'd hoped. I rested my chin on my knees and stared into the darkness with my eyes wide, trying not to blink. Suddenly I thought: "Pa in January. Mamma and Ebenezer in February. Whose turn will it be in March?"

"Frank!" This time I hammered with both fists, so that he would have to answer, but he only shouted, "Go to bed, Maude!"

I considered sliding a note under the door, but it was dark in our mother's room, so he was unlikely to see it, let alone read it. Besides, what would I write?

Don't shut me out, Frank.

Don't ever, ever leave me.

Thursday, 2 March, 1876

Frank was more like his old self today. This evening, he and I ate a picnic supper in his bedroom, since the dining room felt too grand for the two of us and he wouldn't countenance eating with the servants in the kitchen. Nettie was prevailed upon to light a fire and Cook brought a tray with cold mutton sandwiches, leftover suet pudding, apples, and cocoa. I sat cross-legged at the foot of the bed; Frank sat facing me, with his back against the headboard. I won't say it was a delightful occasion, because that would be vulgar, not to say immoral, in the circumstances; nonetheless it had a precious quality, and I shall keep it safe in my memory.

"We're like adventurers!" I remarked. "We've got a campfire to ward off wolves, and no chairs and no cutlery except for your pocketknife."

"I'm afraid we <u>are</u> adventurers," Frank sighed. "Real ones."

"What do you mean?"

"I mean because we're orphans."

My brother bit into a sandwich. I was silent while I considered our new status, and the more I thought, the more wistful I grew for a covered wagon and a wolf-infested wilderness.

"What will we do?" I said. "Or rather, what will *I* do? You will continue at the university, of course."

I hoped he'd reply, "What a silly question, Miss Mouse! Why, naturally you will come to live with me!" but he shrugged and said, "I suppose you'll have to live with one of The Relatives until I qualify."

His tone softened when he noticed my expression.

"Poor little Mouse. It won't be much longer than three years."

Three years! Three years may be no time at all in Cambridge, but as far as I'm concerned, it is eternity. I remembered the aching slowness of that first breakfast with The Relatives: how the clock ticked; how Cousin Amelia's jaw creaked as she chewed; how Aunt Janet complained about the porridge, and the gas lights, and the fog.

"Cheer up, Miss Mouse! You'll come through, and I'll visit so often you'll be sick of the sight of me . . . Oh now, don't *cry*!"

"But they are so old and disagreeable! They never smile—except for Uncle Talbot, and frankly I'd rather he didn't—and they talk to me as if I were some bothersome infant. I *hate* them. I want to live with you."

"And so you shall, as soon as I'm done with university."

"Frank, we will be together after the three years, won't we?"

"We will."

"Forever? You promise?"

"I promise."

He wasn't exactly laughing now, but neither were his words properly weighted. His eyes kept roving over the supper tray, and he picked up an apple and began to peel it.

"You won't . . ." I hesitated. "You won't go marrying someone and setting up house with her instead?"

"If you mean Miss Wilson—"

"I mean anybody."

Frank smiled as the red-gold peel spiralled from the blade of his knife.

"I hereby swear never to fall in love with anybody, never to contemplate marriage with anybody, and never to allow any person to keep house for me, excepting only my one true sister, Miss Mouse, otherwise known as Maude Louise Gower. So help me God."

He never looked up, he was too busy with his apple, but I watched his face carefully in the firelight.

"If I wrote that, or something like it, in an actual document, would you sign it?"

Frank threw his head back and laughed.

"Would you, though?"

"Oh Mousey." He wiped his eyes on his dressing gown sleeves. "I would, if it would keep you quiet."

I went to his desk and began to write. Frank bit noisily into his apple.

I, Francis George Henry Gower, hereby swear that nothing shall ever divide me from my sister, Maude Louise Gower. She shall always be first in my thoughts, as I am always first in hers.

Signed—

"There." I couldn't find any blotting paper, so I blew across the sheet until the ink was dry. "Read that, but if you can't sign it with the utmost seriousness, don't sign it at all. It has to be your free and solemn choice."

I stood at his side, pen and ink at the ready, while he read my words out loud.

"Well?" I said.

"Pass me the pen."

Frank held the apple between his teeth and pressed the knife blade into his hand. I didn't understand what he'd done until I saw the blood ripening, like a berry, on the pad of his thumb. He grinned at me.

"I can't sign your solemn, sacred thingummy in mere ink, now, can I?" he said. "A more grandiose gesture is called for."

Frank filled the nib from his wound and signed with a flourish. His blood mingled with the ink I'd been using, so his name came out blackish red.

There is something inarguably serious about a name written in blood. For all his light-hearted manner, I cannot look at it without believing, without knowing, that my brother is to be trusted.

Wednesday, 8 March, 1876

The Relatives arrived on Saturday, and today Mamma was buried in the cemetery at Tower Hamlets, alongside Pa. Frank says he will take me to see their grave before he returns to Cambridge, and of course I will go if he thinks it proper, although I would rather not. He says there is a beautiful stone angel with curly hair above their inscriptions, and I know he says it to comfort me, but it makes me remember my nightmare.

Naturally I eye The Relatives with a greater interest now that I know I must live with one (or more) of them. Aunt Janet's opening words, as she stooped to kiss my cheek, were, "First your father and now your mother!" as if my own carelessness were somehow to blame. Aunt Judith remarked, "I'd forgotten what a puny child she is," to which Uncle Talbot said, "Ah ha! Now, that's what comes of too much reading!"

Cousins John and Amelia said nothing at all.

Thursday, 9 March, 1876

I don't need an interpreter to tell me what inspired last night's dream. 17 Erskine Place was falling apart all around me: staircases were collapsing, windows shattering, pictures sliding off walls, furniture crumbling. Plaster dust drifted down like snow, muting the debris to a ghostly grey.

In real life everything—everything—is changing:

a) One of our lodgers, Mrs. Bristow, has disappeared without saying goodbye or paying her last month's rent.

b) Another one—Herr Schulz—is moving out tomorrow, having found new lodgings in Chalton Street.

c) Nettie and Ruth are going to be lady's maids for the Newby-Jones family on Walpole Square, which is a step up for both of them, but especially for Nettie. They try not to mention it in front of me, but their gladness is palpable.

d) Cook is leaving London in a week's time and returning to a former employer in York. I wasn't aware that Cook had any former employers; I thought she had always been here, serving us.

e) An estate agent came this morning and looked around our house. Apparently 17 Erskine Place must be sold if Frank is to afford to finish his studies.

I still don't know what's to become of me, but Uncle Talbot has proposed a meeting tomorrow morning, to discuss what he calls "the problem of Maude."

Friday, 10 March, 1876

The meeting took place, as planned. Everyone was in place when Frank and I entered the parlour. Aunts Judith and Janet sat beside one another on the horsehair sofa, staring over the heads of Cousins Amelia and John, who occupied the facing sofa. Uncle Talbot stood near the fire, leaning his elbow on the mantelpiece with a lord-of-the-manor air, although I couldn't help thinking that the mantelpiece ought to have been a couple of inches lower in order for his posture to appear perfectly blasé. (My thoughts tend towards the irrelevant at moments of high crisis; I have noticed it before.)

I stopped in the middle of the room and frowned at the Greek key pattern that runs round the edge of the hearthrug. Frank stood at my side. Nobody invited us to sit.

"If you take my advice, you'll put the child into service," said Cousin Amelia, without preamble. I lost my place in the hearthrug pattern, thunderstruck by a vision of myself in blackened rags, crawling up chimneys, coughing up soot—but was reassured by the horrified murmurs from the rest of the room and the touch of Frank's hand on my shoulder.

"Well? She has no money to speak of, and none of us wants her!"

I'm sure Cousin Amelia has never employed so many words in all her time at 17 Erskine Place. Cousin John nodded his agreement, but remained true to himself by saying nothing.

"There's no shame in hard work!" Cousin Amelia declaimed, before subsiding into the sofa and her usual state of acute deafness. She took no further part in the meeting, and did not react when Aunt Judith remarked, "That rather depends on what sort of work you mean!" and Aunt Janet added, "Miss Maude may be an encumbrance and a worry, but she is also a <u>Gower</u>!"

I almost warmed to the aunts at that juncture. (Almost.)

Meanwhile, Uncle Talbot posed by the fireplace, smiling to himself and stroking his whiskers. At one point he pulled an envelope from his breast pocket and began tapping it against his leg. In the outraged silence that followed Cousin Amelia's intervention he made a little "ahem," and when he was sure of everyone's attention he stared round the room, relishing the limelight. It was a shame that Aunt Judith spoiled the effect by snapping, "Oh really, Talbot, what <u>is</u> it? Spit it out!" just when he thought he had us in the palm of his hand.

I resumed my study of the hearthrug and resolved to look unimpressed, come what may. If Uncle Talbot were to announce he'd received notice from Buckingham Palace, that Maude Louise Gower was rightful heir to the throne, I would not turn a hair.

"I have here," he said, "two letters."

I looked up, despite myself, as Uncle Talbot drew two folded papers from the envelope. The room was silent, except for the ticking of the clock.

"The first letter is addressed to me, in my capacity as executor, by our late lamented friend Mr. George Percival Gower." (By which he meant Pa.) "This first letter was to be opened, by me, only in the event that both Mr. and Mrs. George Gower were deceased, before their daughter Maude had come of age. An eventuality which has, of course, most unfortunately, come to pass."

Aunts Judith and Janet exchanged glances.

"The second letter . . ."

A dramatic pause, to which everyone reacted correctly—except me. Aunt Judith leaned forwards in her seat, Aunt Janet's mouth went slack, Frank's hand tightened on my shoulder, even the cousins wore a listening look. I sniffed and sighed and made sure to discover an itch behind my ear.

"The second letter is from a Miss K. Greenaway, of Sawyer's Fen in Cambridgeshire."

He said it slowly, and with many a meaningful pause and emphasis.

I'd been bracing myself for a shock, but there was no need: neither the name nor the address meant anything to me (except that I always prick up my ears at mention of Cambridgeshire, because it is Frank's county for as long as he remains a student).

The general reaction, however, was much to Uncle Talbot's taste. There were gasps all round and one of the aunts emitted a strangled shriek. Frank's grip on my shoulder tightened to such an extent that I was obliged to protest and wriggle free. Cousin John shot to his feet, stared around the room, and sat down again.

Frank was the first to speak sensibly.

"I thought this meeting was intended to decide my sister's future?"

"Indeed it is," said Uncle Talbot.

"Then I fail to see what relevance Miss K. Gree—"

"STOP!" bellowed Aunt Janet. "Stop speaking at once."

Frank stopped. Aunt Janet folded her mittened hands on her lap, lifted her chin, and breathed deeply, in and out, several times.

"If it is absolutely necessary to bring this second letter into consideration," she said, "then the very least we can do, as civilised human beings, is to send the child from the room."

Everyone turned to look at me.

"Oh, but really, Aunt!" I exclaimed. This was too much! Dear diary, *you* see the absurdity of it, don't you? There we were, gathered together for the sole purpose of discussing *my* fate, and *I* was the one to be banished!

"Quite right, Janet." Uncle Talbot winked at me in an attempt (unsuccessful) to make me smile. "Quite right. Off you trot, Miss Maude."

I turned to my brother and seized his hands, but although he was kinder than the others, he was equally implacable.

"Go to the kitchen, Mouse," he said. "Perhaps you can persuade Nettie to play cards. I'll come and find you as soon as we're done."

"Frank!" I didn't so much drop his hands as throw them away, but he picked mine up, and held them tight, and kissed them.

"It's for the best," he whispered in my ear. "Trust me; I'll be your champion against all these old dragons; I'll make sure nothing bad comes to you."

I walked down the hall, hitting my heels hard against the tiles so that they would hear me going, and counted to ten before tiptoeing back. It is difficult to be stealthy in petticoats because they rustle so; undoubtedly it must be easier to be a gentleman spy. I'd hardly put my eye to the keyhole before Frank stuck his head out of the door and hissed, "Maude! Kitchen!"

I don't say he was angry, exactly. Frank is never angry with me, but he wasn't laughing either.

Downstairs, in the kitchen, Cook was reading the newspaper; Nettie was stirring sugar into her cup of tea; Ruth was sitting with her feet up on a chair. They did not pretend to be busy, even when they saw me, and don't forget it was gone ten o'clock in the morning. There was a heap of muddy potatoes on the table and I nearly said, "Those potatoes won't scrub themselves, you know," since it seemed the proper, mistress-like thing to say. However, I knew they would laugh, so I refrained. Such are the drawbacks of childhood, and a penniless, orphaned childhood at that. If Mr. Dickens were still alive, he might have put me in one of his books.

"What about a game of noughts and crosses, Miss Maude?"

This was Nettie, who had taken a piece of chalk from her apron pocket and started drawing a grid on the kitchen table. I expected Cook to remonstrate, but she merely turned another page of her Illustrated London News.

"No thank you."

"Come and join us anyway, miss." Ruth moved her feet off the chair and gestured for me to sit. "Tea's still hot."

"No thank you."

I wandered to the other end of the kitchen and studied my reflection in the hanging copper pots, listening, all the while, for any sounds from upstairs.

There was nothing for five minutes or so, and then there was shouting, upon which Cook removed her spectacles and said,

"Good heavens, that's never Master Frank?" and Ruth replied, "I think it is." Nobody stopped me when I ran upstairs.

Frank was roaring loud enough to rattle all the windows in the house: "I can scarcely believe that you, even you in your selfishness, would inflict such a fate on an innocent girl! A child. Your niece, for God's sake. My sister."

"Now Francis, control yourself. You are quite frenzied," Aunt Judith replied. (I had my ear to the door by now.) "I have already explained that if Talbot and I were in a position to take your sister, we would, but it isn't—"

"The same goes for me," said Aunt Janet. "If circumstances were different, then naturally . . ."

"Nonsense! What circumstances? You simply cannot bear to be inconvenienced."

"Enough." Uncle Talbot broke in. "Young man, there would appear to be two alternatives before us. Either we do as Cousin Amelia proposes, and put the child out to work . . . or this."

"But this . . ." Frank seemed lost for words, which was most unlike him, and most inconvenient for me. "My mother will be turning in her grave."

"Shall we keep our voices down?" Uncle Talbot snapped. "Walls have ears."

To my annoyance, Frank did begin to talk more quietly, and although I could still hear his teary, spitting passion, I could no longer catch what he said.

They talked inaudibly, on and on, so I went upstairs and peered through the smutty bedroom window at my old, familiar view. I tried pretending Ebenezer was with me, draped over my shoulder, but my imagination was too weak and I ended up more desolate than ever. I thought about running away, but couldn't think of anywhere to go. If I were a boy, I would join the navy and go to sea.

"There you are!" Frank spoke from the doorway. "I've been calling you." He was trying to sound cheerful, but he was trying too hard and it didn't fool me one bit.

I turned away from the window.

"What a face!" he said. "For heaven's sake, don't look like that, as if the sky is about to fall in!"

It's not as if I was unwilling to be reassured. If only Frank had been able to fix his eyes on mine, but apparently that was impossible.

He smiled with his mouth only and held out his hand.

"Ah ha!" Uncle Talbot grinned as we entered. "Well now, Miss Maude. Before you left the room, I think you heard me mention a letter, written by your late father, concerning his provisions—or perhaps rather his wishes—for you, in the event of your being left parentless?"

I managed an uncertain nod.

"It seems," he went on, with a sharp glance at Frank, "that your father has a cousin . . ."

"A cousin," echoed Aunt Judith sternly.

"A cousin by the name of Miss Greenaway. If ever you were to be left fatherless and motherless, it is—was—your pa's firm wish that Miss Greenaway should be your guardian."

I nodded even more slightly than before.

"I myself have written to the lady in question and apprised her of your father's letter, and she has replied, agreeing to take you on. In short, your brother will accompany you to King's Cross railway station in a week's time and travel with you as far as Cambridge, at which point you will go your separate ways: he to his college, you to your new home, a few miles away, in the village of Sawyer's Fen." Uncle Talbot let out a sigh of relief and rocked back on his heels.

"Miss Greenaway . . .?"

I thought if I said the name out loud I might find a memory, a shape, a colour, a timbre of voice, to attach to the unfamiliar name.

"And you say she is Pa's cousin . . . ?"

"Yes!" Aunt Judith snapped. "His cousin! I think your uncle has made that perfectly plain."

What interested me most was the unease that Miss Greenaway's name inspired, but I knew better than to say so out loud and expect a civil response.

"May I ask one question?"

The aunts shuffled and twitched. Frank thrust his hands in his pockets and glared at the fire irons.

"What is it?"

"This cousin of Pa's. Miss Greenaway. Is she . . . ?" (How to say it?) "Is she . . . quite respectable?"

Nobody seemed willing to reply, but glances were exchanged and the aunts pursed their lips. Frank snorted. My uncle chortled.

"She is Miss K. Greenaway of Orchard House, Sawyer's Fen, Cambridgeshire," said Uncle Talbot. "Really and truly, my dear, that is all any of us knows."

Orchard House
Sawyer's Fen
Cambridgeshire
Monday, 20 March, 1876

I spent hours writing that last entry, but I've had neither the time nor the will to write anything since. I seem to have done nothing for an entire week but run endless errands for one or another of the aunts, put my books and little treasures into a trunk, and take interminable lessons from Aunt Janet on the correct method for packing clothes. I suppose I should confess that I've also spent much time sitting at Pa's desk, staring into space. I stole his old tobacco pouch from a drawer, and have brought it with me as a memento. It has a sorrowful and lovely smell.

Now, here I am on the evening of Monday, 20 March, and 17 Erskine Place, Bloomsbury, is as flimsy and fragmented as a long-lost dream. I wonder whether I will ever see it again. Even if I do, both it and I will be changed, and someone else will have learnt to call it "home."

I did not expect a fanfare, but even so, the manner of our departure was terribly disappointing. When the moment came, Frank hurried downstairs shouting, "Hurry up, Maude, or we'll miss our train!" and Nettie cried, "Oh, but Ruth has popped out to the post office; she will be sorry not to see you off," to which Frank replied, "Can't be helped! Oh, drat these boots." Cook trotted up from the kitchen, wiping her floury hands on her apron, and kissed me on the cheek. Nettie shed a tear (which was something, I suppose) and said, "Good luck, ducky." The Relatives crowded the hallway, offering unoriginal pieces of advice about being good and remembering I was a Gower. Uncle Talbot made a joke, which nobody paid attention to, about how I must avoid wearing blue stockings at all cost, and the last thing I heard, as the door swung shut, was the sound of him laughing at his own wit.

It was all very paltry.

I have travelled on the train to Cambridge before, but last time I was with Pa (we were going to visit Frank at the university) and the hours flew by because we ate pear drops and chattered all the way.

This afternoon's journey could not have been more different. My brother was not in a talkative frame of mind. As soon as we'd taken our seats, he removed a large textbook from his valise, laid it across his lap, and told me to be quiet while he caught up on his studies. I wouldn't have minded, but he proceeded to frown fixedly at the frontispiece (a black-and-white engraving of Hippocrates) and neglected to turn a single page.

The only other passengers in our carriage were an elderly clergyman with a book and a man in a bowler hat, both of whom alighted at a suburban station north of London. Nobody else got in. As the train heaved forwards again I tapped Frank on the knee and said, "You're not angry with me, are you?"

"Why in heaven's name should I be angry?"

"I don't know. Because I'm going to live somewhere you disapprove of, with a person you despise."

"Well, that's scarcely your fault, is it?"

"No, it's not my fault at all."

We were agreed on that, apparently, so why did Frank's frown deepen? Could my new address really tarnish me in my brother's eyes?

"Frank? Why do you hate Miss Greenaway?"

"I have never met her."

"But you hate her all the same."

He squeezed his eyes shut and growled with frustration.

"Listen, Miss Mouse. What if I were to give you a puzzle, to keep you busy while I read?"

"Oh no—"

I thought he was trying to change the subject, but he held up his hand for silence and went on, "What is Miss Greenaway's Christian name? Do you know?"

"It begins with a 'K.' Katherine, perhaps?"

"It's Kitty," said Frank. "Presumably she was christened Katherine or Kathleen, if she was christened at all, but she goes by the name Kitty."

"Well? What of it?"

"What of it, indeed. That's the puzzle. Think it over while I try to read."

Frank retreated to his book and leafed through a couple of pages. I turned to the window and touched the cold glass with the tip of my nose. The suburbs had ended, and the view was dull indeed: hedges, fields, cows, barns. Frank was usually so good at making up guessing games, but I couldn't think where to start with "Kitty."

"Will you tell me the answer, if I can't guess?"

Frank smiled slightly, at the corner of his mouth, and turned a page.

Cook had supplied us with bread and cheese for the journey, but I'd lost my appetite (even I, who am always hungry!), so Frank had double portions. We rolled into Cambridge railway station as evening fell, and I opened the window in order to observe the crowded platform. Every woman between the ages of eighteen and eighty was Miss Kitty Greenaway for a few seconds, until I realised she couldn't be—whether because she was greeting someone else, or because she was loaded down with her own luggage, or because she was hurrying away without waiting.

"Mr. Francis Gower?" A man approached us with a guarded smile and an outstretched hand as we stepped down from the train. There was a tall, freckled girl hovering beside him, but she could scarcely be Miss Greenaway since she wasn't much older than me.

"You must be Mr. Stirling." Frank took the man's hand, with the cold manner that had become habitual to him ever since Friday morning, when The Relatives had decided my fate.

"This is my sister, Maude," Frank went on. "Maude, this is Mr. Stirling." I replied with my best "How d'you do?" upon which Mr. Stirling introduced us both to his daughter Emily—but nobody thought to enlighten me as to who in the name of goodness these Stirlings were, or why they'd come to meet our train, or what business they had with us at all. Perhaps I should have asked outright, or expressed my confusion with a glance at Frank, but I was afraid of seeming indelicate.

"You don't mind, do you?" said Mr. Stirling. "Coming along with us?"

Several seconds passed before I understood he was addressing me. I had no idea what to think, or say, or do in response, so I looked up at Frank.

"Mr. and Miss Stirling will be your neighbours at Sawyer's Fen," Frank said hastily. "They generously agreed to meet our train, and accompany you to your new . . . to Miss Greenaway's house."

"We were coming into town anyway," said Emily, "so you haven't put us out." It was the first thing she'd said and I couldn't help noticing that her voice was louder and rougher than mine.

Mr. Stirling fished for his pocket watch.

"We'd better get going." He held his broad hand out again, for Frank to shake. "Our train leaves in five minutes, and I'd like to make sure your sister's trunk is properly stowed."

"You're most kind," replied the new, chilly facsimile of my brother. He bowed ever so slightly at the girl and said, "Miss Stirling," by way of farewell. When he turned to me, I was half-afraid he might say, "Miss Gower," in the same unsmiling way, so I seized his elbow and took him aside.

"Frank?" I moved so close that my face brushed the lapels of his coat. I wanted to tell him I was scared, but apparently I was incapable of saying anything except his name.

My brother took me in his arms and hugged the breath from my lungs.

"You can come and see me as often as you please," he whispered into my hair. "We'll have great larks in Cambridge, you and I. We'll take a rowing boat along the river to Grantchester."

I could have stood like that forever while the people swarmed about us, but I was conscious of being watched, and I only resisted for a moment when Frank pulled away. Without another word, he picked up his valise and disappeared through the ticket hall.

I liked Mr. Stirling well enough, despite the roughness of his hands, and the windblown redness of his face, and the fact that his clothes, whilst neither ill-made nor dirty, were too coarse to be nice. Rather than wait for a porter, he lifted my trunk into the luggage van as if it weighed nothing at all, and when he let slip that he was a farmer, I can't say I was surprised. I said, "How lovely; I've never met a farmer before," which made him laugh. Emily didn't laugh; she went red in the face (she is as high-coloured as her father, which suits a girl so much less than a man) and muttered something rude under her breath. It baffles me that my slight remark, which was a mere statement of fact, should have provoked amusement in him, and irritation in her. I swear there was nothing ungracious in my manner.

The train, a small, local train with dozens of rural stops, left Cambridge on time. There were two other passengers in our carriage, and we didn't talk much. Mr. Stirling tried his hand at weather-related observations, but it had been a grey, flat sort of day, neither cold nor warm, and there was little to be said. Naturally, there was only one subject engrossing my mind, but I couldn't think of a Miss Greenaway–related question that would be both interesting and polite.

"Will she send you to school?" said Emily, all of a sudden. "Miss Greenaway, I mean. Or is she proposing to teach you herself?"

"Really, I have no idea." The question intrigued me, of course, but I could hardly engage with it while our fellow passengers, both of them middle-aged men, were peering at us over the tops of their newspapers. I wished we were alone, or that Emily had a softer voice. Mr. Stirling appeared to have nodded off.

"I'm learning Greek and Latin," Emily went on. "I'm going to try for the university in a couple of years."

Well! That made the newspapers rustle! The man on the left gave Emily such a glare that I blushed on her behalf. I was reminded of Frank's poem, "A Lesson for the Ladies," and half-inclined to quote a verse or two, but I could remember only the last couplet ("Annie's head was full of facts / But Annie ended lonely"), which risked falling flat on its own.

Emily was waiting for my response, so I said, "Indeed?" in a manner that Mamma would certainly have approved, as an economical way of expressing politeness and utter boredom at one and the same time. The conversation duly died.

My seat was next to the window, so I was able to turn my face away without appearing odd. I lolled about with the movement of the train and grew drowsy, but couldn't sleep. The darkening Cambridgeshire skies were too vast to be friendly, and the land was like an ocean that went on and on, as far as the eye could see, with tall-spired villages popping up here and there in its midst, like islands. It made me feel tiny and exposed, and sick with longing for London.

My dear diary, you're wondering why I've squandered so many pages on the prelude to my arrival, leaving myself short of time and energy to describe the event itself. Well, here is the truth: even though I have reached my destination, I have yet to meet Miss Greenaway herself! Neither can I tell you much about her house, since the night was pitchy-black when I arrived, and what little I've seen so far was by the light of a single candle.

It was gone eight o'clock when the train stopped at Sawyer's Fen. (Emily insists on calling it "the station," but I scarcely think it merits the name, given that it consists of an unlit sign and a bench. It is, at best, a "halt.") There was a wheeled contraption waiting for us: I suppose it was a cart from Willowbrook Farm (which is the name of Mr. Stirling's establishment) because there were bits of straw sticking to the seats, and a horrible mixed-up smell of milk, chicken feathers, horses, mud, and I-don't-know-what. It was impossible not to grimace, and I was thankful for the darkness because it hid my scrunched-up expression from the Stirlings. All anybody could see, by the driver's lantern light, were patches of uneven road and the jogging ears of the horse.

"That's Orchard House, up ahead," said Emily. I looked and saw a yellow dot, which grew larger and squarer by the minute, and eventually turned into a lighted window.

The woman who answered the door, candle in hand, was old, plump, and wheezy, and I did not warm to her. Mr. Stirling greeted her as "Mrs. P.," which was a relief because

a) it meant she wasn't Miss Greenaway, and
b) it implied servant status. (A gentleman would never address a lady as "Mrs. P.," would he? I'm uncertain on the point,

> but I think not. Only imagine Mamma's face if one of Pa's friends had said, "Evening, Mrs. G.!")

I am glad Miss Greenaway keeps a servant. I was afraid she'd only agreed to take me on because she needed a maid-of-all-work. This could still be the case, I suppose, but the existence of Mrs. P. makes it seem less likely.

Mr. Stirling carried my trunk upstairs, even though it was dark and he hadn't a spare hand for a light.

"Left at the top of the stairs," Mrs. P. called after him. "Keep going till you get to a door."

"Right-oh!" After a bit of thumping about and muttered cursing he returned, dusting himself down. "Where's Kitty?"

"Asleep. She's been as pale as whitewash all day long, and barely ate a thing for supper, so I packed her off to bed. She didn't like me for it—"

"Oh, I can imagine!"

"—but I wouldn't take no for an answer."

"You were quite right, Mrs. P.," said Mr. Stirling. "Quite right. Where would we be without you, eh?"

Mrs. P. didn't answer, which struck me as charmless. Most people would have made some little, trite response—"Oh, go on with you!" or "How kind!"—and although I might not have noticed if she had, I couldn't help noticing that she hadn't.

When her eye fell on me, she said, "Are you coming in, then? You and the cold night air," as if it were my fault that the door was standing wide open. Mr. Stirling was the one lingering on the doorstep, doing all the talking. She might have said "Hello" or "Welcome to Orchard House"—don't you agree, diary? I thought of Nettie, and how I used to purse my lips when she called me ducky, and it was the closest I came to crying all day.

Emily Stirling was waiting for her father in the cart. I'd neglected to say goodbye to her when I got out, which was surely forgivable at such a critical moment of my life. She had also neglected to say goodbye to me, which is less forgivable, since she is a fortunate girl with at least one living parent who loves her, and a familiar home (albeit a smelly farmhouse) to go to, and no excuse for self-absorption.

At least Mr. Stirling had the good grace to wish me well, and we even shook hands, although his palm is too rough to be pleasant, and I'm sure there is dirt ingrained in the skin. I could smell it. I wonder how close Willowbrook Farm is to Orchard House, and whether we shall be forced to socialise often.

"You'll be hungry," said Mrs. P. as she closed the front door. The devil in me wanted to say, "No I won't," in a gesture of universal protest against everyone and everything, but the thought of going to bed on an empty stomach was too depressing. She led the way down the stone-flagged passage to the kitchen, and I followed.

"A sandwich will do, I hope?" she inquired, uncovering a plate and setting a tower of thick-cut bread, beef, and mustard before me. Yet again, I'm afraid, my eyes welled up. Beef and mustard! Soft-boiled eggs are my preference, as Cook knew well, or bread and milk, or rice pudding with jam. Only men eat mustard. Pa liked it and so does Frank, but I—in deference to Mamma—despise it. I wouldn't have touched it tonight if I hadn't been famished. With my first bite I thought the inside of my head was going to catch fire, and smoke gush forth from my nose.

Thank goodness Mrs. P. was sufficiently conventional to fill my mug with milk; I half expected a tankard of beer.

While I ate, Mrs. P. sat down on the other side of the table and picked up her knitting, although she didn't work a single stitch. I made her my principal object of study, since I couldn't make much of my surroundings by the light of one candle; all I had was an impression of a cosy, cluttered room, most unlike the big, basement kitchen at 17 Erskine Place.

"What does the 'P' stand for in 'Mrs. P.'?" I asked: a heroic act, though I say so myself, what with the enfeebling effects of homesickness, and the strangulating effects of the mustard, but one of us had to make conversation. She looked up in mild surprise, as if she'd quite forgotten me.

"'P' for Potter."

"Mrs. Potter," I said, and that was all the conversation we had until I'd finished my supper.

I thought all houses were fitted with gas jets in this day and age, but it seems they are not. Mrs. Potter led me to my room by candlelight; I followed behind with a jug of hot water for my washbowl. Having lit a second candle, and placed it in a brass holder by the bed, she bid me goodnight and left me alone.

If it weren't for that single flame, the gloom, like the silence, would have been heavy indeed. There was a fire in the hearth, but it was red and old. I parted the velvet curtains and tried to peer beyond the window. The flash and rumble of London at night, which I had always taken for darkness and quiet, were gone, replaced by a moonless, starless, soulless abyss. I closed the curtains with a shudder.

My new room is neither small nor uncomfortable, but it is the very opposite of girlish. (Not that my London bedroom was girlish exactly, but it had a spindly look, which was halfway there.) The furniture here is sturdy, the colours rich, the ornaments few: a speckled mirror, a framed drawing of a horse, and a brass snuffer to match the candleholder. The bed itself is a four-poster with red drapes, and so high that I'm obliged to use my trunk as a mounting block.

I washed hastily and climbed under the covers, intending to write this long account tomorrow—but sleep refused to come. I could only toss and turn, wondering where Miss Greenaway's room was and trying to distinguish the minuscule sounds inside my head from those outside it. Eventually I sat up and wrote the above.

Now that I have finished today's entry and read it over, I find I am dissatisfied. The narrative fits together too well; it makes too much sense; one thing leads too neatly to another. It's not that I have lied, certainly there were trains caught, and conversations exchanged, and sandwiches consumed, but these incidents were secondary to the true story of the day; to the unruly clash of fears and griefs and speculations taking place inside my head.

Two hours later

Oh good God! I have discovered the answer to Frank's riddle:

Kitty = The Cat

The Cat = THE FELINE

Now I <u>know</u> I shan't sleep.

Three-quarters of an hour later

When Mrs. Potter told Mr. Stirling that Miss Greenaway was ill, I got it into my head that she must resemble Mamma. Not, of course, that she could possess Mamma's angelic qualities, only that she must be similarly fragile, with her hair spread over her pillow-case, and lace cuffs spread over her hands.

Now I know she's The Feline, a most peculiar image keeps invading my brain, and the less I want it, the more it comes. I see Mamma with white fur instead of skin, and whiskers springing from her cheeks, and sharp claws resting on the quilt and, worst of all, a pair of yellow eyes that are by no means human.

Tuesday, 21 March, 1876

I woke this morning, very late, to the sound of kittens mewing. Now you will think me quite, quite mad, and I thought so too for a time. I opened my eyes as wide as they would go and stared into the sleepy dusk of my room, but the mewing continued faintly, from outside. As soon as I felt sure (as sure as possible) that I was awake, I got up and parted the curtains over the big bow window.

Below me, in the keen sunlight, a dark-haired woman was emerging from a hole in the earth with a bucket in her hand. The mewing sounds were coming from the bucket. I thought, at first, I was hallucinating. It made me think of that Greek myth about

Persephone returning from the underworld every spring, except that there is nothing in that myth about a metal pail full of newborn kittens.

"The mother's dead," the woman said, calling to some unseen person in the house. Whoever it was (Mrs. Potter?) must have replied by asking how many kittens there were, because the woman shouted again, "Five. Well, two are dead, so three really. Three little sisters." She scooped a tabby scrap from the bucket and held it up to her face, scrutinising it with interest rather than adoration. I did not trust that look, nor did I like the fact of the bucket and its proximity to a water pump. I ran downstairs and flung open several wrong doors, before bursting into the garden.

"What are you going to do with them?"

To do her credit, the woman responded to my urgent tone of voice rather than my sudden appearance, seeming to understand that this was not the moment for polite introductions.

"Oh . . . !" she said. "Well, Robert Stirling would tell me to drown them. Mrs. P. says she doesn't care what I do, as long as we don't end up with a regiment of cats about the place."

"You can't possibly drown them."

I peered into the bucket as the woman replaced the furry scrap, sliding it gently off her palm. Now there were two black kittens and one grey tabby squirming like a single entity and paddling their legs.

"I left the dead ones in the cellar," the woman explained. "The mother must have sneaked in yesterday when the trapdoor was open. I had it open, you see; I was putting some of the clutter from your room out of the way."

I looked at the woman properly for the first time and asked, "Are you Miss Greenaway?" I was torn between interest in the cats and interest in the dawning possibility that this might, at last, be her. On closer inspection I thought it unlikely. She was heavy-featured to the point of ugliness, her hair was windblown, her skin was tanned, her voice was strong. That is to say, she was neither feline nor frail.

"I am," she replied. "And you are Miss Maude Louise Gower."

She said my name in a curious way, as if it carried more meaning than it did. And the way she looked at me! I don't mean a stare; I mean a piercing flash of a glance. At first I thought she was reproving me for my half-dressed state—I doubt I've ever been outside in my nightdress before, let alone barefoot—but I don't think that was her motive; I don't think she was interested in my outward appearance. How could she be? A woman with such untidy hair, and visible darning in her skirt.

"You want to keep them?" Miss Greenaway indicated the bucket with a nod. It was lucky we had the kittens to talk about, otherwise I don't know what I would have said.

"Yes! Oh, most certainly, yes."

"And if we do, what will you call them? I think they're all girls."

I touched the grey one between the ears and along the curl of its spine. When I looked at the kittens I was almost happy, but when I looked at Miss Greenaway, or the rambling house and garden, or the oversized skies of Cambridgeshire, then I felt—not miserable, exactly, but discomfited.

"Little Dorrit," I said, after some thought, "and Little Nell, and Nancy." I couldn't help smiling a little—at them, though, not at her. Miss Greenaway laughed.

A ground-floor window opened and Mrs. Potter's voice floated out with the scent and sizzle of bacon. "What's going on out there? We're not keeping them."

"I'm afraid we are! Maude's given them names. We can't drown them now they've got names!"

The window slammed shut. Miss Greenaway and I stooped over the bucket while I explained which was which (Little Dorrit and Little Nell were the black ones, Nancy was the grey) and she greeted each of them by name. I almost forgot my scepticism, but suddenly she said, "Your father adored Dickens," which recalled me to myself. I did not wish to discuss Pa with her.

"Thank you," I said. "I know."

Unfortunately, I was shivering so hard that my devastating tone failed to make itself felt.

"Goodness, you're only wearing a nightdress!" Miss Greenaway exclaimed, as if she hadn't noticed before. "You must be half-frozen!"

As you know, dear diary, I am quite accustomed to the cold, but up until this morning I hadn't realised what a variety of guises it has. In Erskine Place the cold comes in gusts, wriggling under doors or round the corners of buildings, smelling of chimneys and railways and cooking and dirt and people. In Sawyer's Fen, the cold comes from far across the fields, in long streamers of wind. (I'm not saying it's preferable to London cold. In fact, I think I'm saying the opposite; I think I'm saying it's more relentless and inhuman.)

"Come inside; let's get some breakfast," she said, and I was glad of that, although a part of me (the Mamma part) disapproved. I thought it must be nearly eleven o'clock, and the kitchen clock proved me right. I ask you, what sort of people think it acceptable to breakfast at eleven o'clock?

The "kitchen" could more accurately be described as a "kitchen, study, library, and snug rolled into one," but at least it was warm, with a roaring range and a mishmash of rag rugs laid over the stone floor. I thought Miss Greenaway might send me upstairs to get dressed before we ate, but she merely moved a pile of books from a chair and invited me to sit before offering her "gardening coat" as an extra layer over my nightdress. "I know it looks odd," she conceded, when she saw the face I was trying not to make, "but if you roll the sleeves up . . ." There were white speckles of mildew on the collar, and crumbs of soil on the cuffs, and I declined.

Miss Greenaway didn't press the point. She was already at the range, wresting the frying pan from Mrs. Potter and ordering her to sit down.

"I'll finish off," she said. "Maybe I'll add some eggs to the pan. Didn't Emily bring some eggs on Friday?"

Mrs. Potter argued back, in a most un-servant-like manner, "Don't be silly, Kitty, you should be the one sitting down. And the eggs are there, in the basket, staring at you."

"Where?"

"There!"

It really is an astonishing household. Can you imagine Ruth or Nettie telling Mamma or Pa not to be silly? In an odd sort of way it upsets me (I don't like it when things are inside out and upside down), but at the same time it makes me want to giggle.

At least the kittens were allowed to go right next to the range, inside a bundle of blankets, which would never have been allowed at 17 Erskine Place. Also, I have never seen, let alone tasted, eggs like the ones Miss Greenaway fried. The yolks were as orange as rising suns.

After breakfast Miss Greenaway procured a pipette, and I fed warm milk to the kittens. They managed pretty well, I think. The milk is creamier here than it was at home, just as the eggs are yellower, but I won't be swayed by their allure. Frank says The Feline is not to be trusted, and I believe him.

Night has fallen now, and I've retired to my room, feeling tired. Miss Greenaway took me for a walk through the fields this afternoon, and we were joined by Mr. Stirling's gun dog (a brown-and-white pointer called Scout). Apparently, this is quite usual. The fields were muddy and Miss Greenaway says I could do with a stouter pair of boots, which may be true, but makes me feel defensive of my present ones. I can't stop thinking how large the skies are (far too large, in my private opinion), but Miss Greenaway says Sawyer's Fen is a good place for stargazing.

We had soup and omelettes for supper and afterwards Miss Greenaway insisted that she and I would wash up while Mrs. Potter rested. There is quite a tussle between the two, as to who is the more fragile: according to Miss G., Mrs. P. must take constant care of her wheezy chest following a bout of pneumonia in November; according to Mrs. P., Miss G. is more delicate than she looks. To the dispassionate eye, the former claim is more believable than the latter, since Mrs. Potter is ancient and breathes like a traction engine while Miss Greenaway is much younger and bounds about like a horse—but it is not for me to say.

I wonder how old she is? Miss Greenaway, I mean. It's hard to tell. Her face is young, except when it creases in a smile; her hair is black, except where there are strands of silver.

I broke a plate while we were washing up. Mrs. Potter (observing proceedings, if you please, from a rocking chair by the range) tutted and rolled her eyes, but Miss Greenaway didn't seem to mind. She said it was good luck, and that the Greeks had a tradition of smashing plates on purpose, when they were celebrating weddings and so on. I asked whether she was referring to the ancient Greeks who invented the myths, but she said she had in mind their modern-day descendants.

Apparently Miss Greenaway has travelled around Greece on a couple of occasions, and witnessed plate smashing at first hand.

Miss Wilson once made me write "I must not entertain rebellious thoughts" one hundred times, every evening, for a whole week. Perhaps I should set myself a similar task, with the line, "I must not trust Miss Kitty Greenaway."

Then again, in my experience it is an ineffective way of fixing facts into heads, and terribly dull, and a waste of paper.

Wednesday, 22 March, 1876

Everything at Orchard House seems to take place at such-and-such a time "or thereabouts." For example, yesterday evening I asked what time I should come down to breakfast and was told, "Nine o'clock, or thereabouts." Part of the problem is the fact that the grandfather clock in the hall is at variance with the kitchen clock by a good ten minutes, but when I pointed this out Miss Greenaway said, "Hmm, I expect you're right," as if it didn't matter much. I have since established that the one in the kitchen actually tells the time, while the grandfather clock is chiefly ornamental.

Miss Greenaway came to see me after breakfast today. She tapped on my door and waited until I called, "Come in!" which makes a favourable contrast to Miss Wilson and her boorish manners. How was it that no one, apart from me, used to shudder at the sound of *her* name? For all Miss Greenaway's eccentricities, I've yet to understand why she should incur such disdain from Frank and The Relatives, when my former governess incurred none at all.

The kittens have their own box, and I'm allowed to keep it in my room. There is a degree of mess and smell involved, but all in all I am glad to have them snug beside my fire. I was tending to them when Miss Greenaway entered with an armful of books.

"Look at these!" she said, dropping them on the bed. "Ever since you christened the kittens I've been wondering where my Dickens set was, and at last I've unearthed it. Goodness knows what these were doing on a shelf with Roman comedies; I really ought to have a better system. All the novels are there, I think, and the Christmas stories, and *Sketches by Boz*."

"They're beautiful." I got up and took a closer look at their tissue-thin pages and red leather bindings. "Did you bring them upstairs because . . . I mean, am I allowed to borrow them?"

"Oh, you can have them, they're yours. I'm sure you'll read them more than I ever will."

I opened the Christmas stories. The inside of the front cover was inscribed, in a strong but fading hand, "K. Greenaway," and a couple of pages on there was an illustration showing Marley's ghost tormented and in chains. I love books with illustrations.

"Thank you," I said, for what else could I say? The Dickens was harder to withstand than the creamy milk and the eggs with golden yolks; it was a gift, personal to me, and I had never owned anything so splendid. (Of course, Pa owned books as fine, or even finer, which I was at liberty to read, but they never belonged to me.)

"I wish I could show these to my brother Frank," I said. "He loves Dickens too; he's read The Old Curiosity Shop three times."

I had a nervous desire to mention my family (although not Pa, not yet) and watch for Miss Greenaway's reaction. Perhaps she might start, or blush, or tremble? Perhaps she might explain what nobody else was willing to mention? In fact, she knelt to inspect the kittens and said, with perfect ease, "I hope I shall meet your brother before too long. What is he like? Does he much resemble you?"

"Oh no, Frank is much more wonderful than me. He is so clever, one of the best in his year at Cambridge, and in a few years he'll be a celebrated physician, and I'll be his housekeeper. And he isn't only clever at medicine, he also reads a great deal, and plays the piano, and writes poetry, and he is ever so witty; the wittiest person you ever met, except—"

I was going to say, "except Pa," but I stumbled to a stop, and in my confusion I spotted you, dear diary, and picked you up off the floor. I flicked through the earliest entries until I alighted on Frank's poem.

"Listen to this," I said, "my brother wrote this; it was published in his college newspaper last spring."

And I proceeded to read "A Lesson for the Ladies" from beginning to end.

"It's very funny," I observed, as soon as I'd finished. (Did I sound over-earnest? I've a suspicion I did.) Miss Greenaway was smiling, but not in the right way, and one of her eyebrows was arched.

"Don't you think so?" I persisted.

She seemed to have difficulty answering. Finally she said, "Did everyone in the Gower household find it funny?" which struck me as an odd question in itself and a most unsatisfactory reply. I cast my mind back to last spring, when Frank had been waving his poem at anyone who would look. Naturally I'd enjoyed it, and Frank must have done or he wouldn't have sent it for publication. I can't claim Mamma laughed when she read it, because Mamma never laughed at anything, but she called Frank her dear, clever boy and showed the college newspaper to Dr. Nesbit, who found it so hilarious that he went purple and nearly choked to death (according to Ruth, who was in the room at the time). I remember Cook reading it out loud in the kitchen and Nettie remarking that Master Frank was "a caution." I forget what Pa said; probably he was away on business when it first appeared in print.

I shrugged. "Yes."

"Hmm." Miss Greenaway stooped over the nest of kittens and scooped up Nancy (the grey tabby). The kitten's ears twitched as she touched their tips with her little finger.

"I think Nancy will always be the smallest," I said, anxious to change the subject. "She doesn't eat as much as the other two. Little Nell is the greediest."

But Miss Greenaway hadn't finished with the subject of Frank's poem. I was beginning to wish I'd never mentioned it.

Miss G.: "You yourself would not wish to be a clever woman?"

Me: "Clever, yes; a scholar, no. They're not synonymous." (You must admit, that was a neat reply! I don't think I have ever used the word "synonymous" in conversation before.)

Miss G.: "True, but I don't see how it can ever be a bad thing to deepen one's understanding? Surely it's better to know more, rather than less, about the ways in which people—people other than yourself—perceive the world?"

Me (quoting Mamma, word for word): "It's right for a lady to have a sprinkling of knowledge, but any more than that is vulgar."

Miss G. (after a long, thoughtful pause): "Tell me, Maude, would you rather be vulgar but interesting, or ladylike but dull?"

Up until then I'd been doing rather well (wouldn't you agree?), but I'd run out of ready replies. I must have looked somewhat stricken because Miss Greenaway told me not to worry, I didn't have to answer, but I might like to mull it over in an idle moment. She appeared to have recovered her sense of humour.

"I ought to warn you," she said, placing Nancy among her sisters again, "that I'm something of a scholar myself. You remember Emily Stirling, whom you met on the train? Well, she comes to Orchard House a couple of times a week for tuition in Greek and Latin. She wants to go to university, you see."

My face went hot and I found myself staring at the floor. I wish I'd had an elegant but icy answer up my sleeve, but I couldn't think of one.

"I suppose you think me dreadfully vulgar?" Miss Greenaway asked with a smile in her voice, at which I was obliged to shake my head.

On reflection, I was <u>not</u> obliged to go on to say, "I suppose you think <u>me</u> very dull?" but I did, which made Miss Greenaway laugh heartily, the way she ought to have laughed at Frank's poem. "Perhaps you were hoping for a 'yes,'" she replied, "but I'm afraid my answer is 'no.' I do not, by any means, find you dull."

I've written today's entry in a rush of inspiration and now, suddenly, I've stopped.

Sometimes it seems such a stupid thing to do: scribbling in a notebook and making a record of all my nonsense. I thought a journal would help my thoughts to become ordered and methodical, but it doesn't invariably work.

Never fear, dear diary: no doubt this is a passing mood.

Thursday, 23 March, 1876

Emily Stirling has come for her Greek lesson this afternoon. Miss Greenaway invited me to join them but I pleaded a headache, to which she replied, "Very well, I suppose there's no harm in a few days' holiday, but we ought to do <u>some</u> lessons next week," as if it went without saying that my illness was a fiction! I am mildly affronted. Surely the idea of big, bony Emily Stirling declaiming Greek poetry with a voice like a bugle is enough to justify a headache? Besides, no one ever spoke to Mamma like that when she was unwell.

In all seriousness, I do not feel myself: my skin is tingly and my vision is too bright and sharply focussed. When I'm up and about, I wish I were in bed with the covers over my head, but as soon as I'm there I am restless and have to get up. When I heard Emily arriving around three o'clock I stayed upstairs, looking out of the window, knowing I ought to go down and say hello.

Frank has referred to Cambridgeshire as a drab county, and I agreed with him when I was sitting in the train with the Stirlings, but the view from my bedroom window is growing on me. I suppose Frank is bound to see things differently, since he is relatively well travelled: he has been to Wales, the Scottish Highlands, France, Switzerland, and Germany, whereas I have never been farther than Leamington Spa. Even so, Cambridgeshire—or this corner of it—feels like a place of unparalleled vividness and growth. I never noticed spring before, except as a lessening of the cold.

The garden below my window is filled with shades of green: dank greens in the shadows; piercing greens in the sunlight; fluttering greens in the wind. There are colours pushing through the long grass, yellow daffodils, purple crocuses, blue hyacinths, and the trees are in bud. I am not sure what their names are, but I think they are fruit trees. Apples, perhaps? Plums? The pantry shelves are full of apple chutneys and jars of plum jam.

Beyond the garden there are meadows dotted with white cows. It is a wide, flat landscape, but not a bleak one, softened as it is by copses and straggly hedgerows and water-filled ditches that reflect the clouds. The only building is a house, half a mile away, which seems to look at us directly and hold us in its gaze. It is much like Orchard House: large and rambling, and made of light, yellow brick. At first I thought it was Mr. Stirling's farmhouse, but when I looked closer I realised it was derelict, with no glass in its windows and a spindly tree growing out of its roof.

I wrote to Frank on Tuesday, avoiding all important topics. I did not refer to Miss Greenaway; I only described the kittens, the layout of the house, the view from my window, and the fact that I was in good health.

I wish I could talk to my brother face to face.

A few minutes ago, I went to the top of the stairs and heard Miss Greenaway and Emily laughing in the study. I wonder what they are laughing about, and whether they have mentioned me at all.

At around four o'clock, if the grandfather clock is to be believed, I was bowled over by a wave of sadness. This happens, every so often, when I am reminded of everything I've lost since the start of the year. I was browsing through the Dickens books when I heard Pa doing his droll voice for the Ghost of Christmas Present (only three months ago! three short months!), and the next thing I knew I was on my knees, hunched and sobbing. I almost called for Miss Greenaway to come, but I didn't. I recovered by myself. As soon as I was finished, I splashed my face with cold water from the wash jug and climbed into bed with Bleak House.

Mrs. Potter brought me a cup of tea shortly afterwards. You'd think that would be a comforting thing, but she set the tray down with a rattle and said, "Tea for your ladyship!" in such a voice that it wasn't.

I replied with an apprehensive "Thank you," but she only snorted.

"You've the mistress to thank, not me. 'Poor Maude is under the weather,' she says, and won't I be a dear and make sure 'poor Maude' is all right, and perhaps take her some tea? She's got too much heart for her own good, that woman; kindness will be the death of her."

This seemed to me an unduly pessimistic forecast, though I didn't dare suggest as much. I didn't dare say anything (not even "thank you") since there's no point being pleasant if the person you're addressing is in a foul mood and determined to think the worst. I sipped my tea and reflected how pitiful it was to be stout, stooping, and ancient, with the eyelids and jowls of a bloodhound. Could any human being look like Mrs. Potter and <u>not</u> be disagreeable? (This was actually a rather charitable thought, although the way I've written it, it comes across as mean.)

"You don't look ill," she went on, surveying my room with her hands on her hips. If she wanted to find fault there, she was thwarted: I'd given the place a thorough tidy this morning, including washing the kittens' box and blankets. Her eyes returned to my face. "Typical Gower: putting your pleasure and convenience first, with never a thought for her."

I think you will agree, dear diary, that this was more than a little unjust given that

a) it was only a cup of tea,

b) I hadn't requested it, and

c) Miss Greenaway herself hadn't had to lift a finger.

In my outrage, I failed to notice the most curious element of Mrs. Potter's remark until it was too late. By the time I'd got round to asking, "What do you mean by 'typical Gower'?" she was halfway downstairs and on her way back to the kitchen.

Monday, 27 March, 1876

I am pleased to report that my intuitions regarding Emily Stirling have been confirmed. She has a low character.

"Pleased?" I hear you say, reprovingly. "Should you not rather be sorry?"

Dear diary, I cannot help it, I am pleased. My judgement has been flawed lately, at odds with itself and unsure of reality, and it's a relief to know I can still be right about something. But let me tell you what happened, and you shall judge for yourself . . .

Miss Greenaway gave me lessons for a couple of hours this morning, in history and mathematics. I can't deny that she makes things interesting: in history we talked about Julius Caesar being murdered, and in mathematics we drew complicated shapes with rulers and compasses. Since I didn't manage to complete all my exercises before lunch, she suggested I bring them to the study later on, while she was tutoring Emily in Latin.

"There's plenty of room for us all at the big table."

"But what shall I do when I've finished my polyhedrons?" I asked. "They'll only take ten minutes."

"Either read your book, or listen to Emily's Latin lesson. It's up to you."

In one of those faulty leaps of logic to which grown-up people are prone, Miss Greenaway thinks Emily and I must feel a friendly interest in one another because we're both young, and both girls.

I decided to bring Bleak House.

When the Stirlings knocked on the front door, Miss Greenaway made me go with her to let them in. First greetings are always mortifying, in my opinion, unless they involve someone you love. I could feel Emily looking me up and down, and Miss Greenaway willing us both to be genial, and Mr. Stirling taking everything in, for despite his blunt appearance he has a sharp pair of eyes.

Miss Greenaway said all the right things with an easy air. ("Come inside, Emily . . . Are you heading off straightaway, Robert? You know you're welcome to come and warm up by the fire . . . Here, Emily, let me take your coat . . . Have you remembered your books this time? . . . Good girl.") Meanwhile, I stood like a blockhead and said nothing at all. I was torn by contradictions: wanting to be clever; wanting to be ladylike; wishing to go unnoticed and wishing to be remarked upon; worrying I was too haughty; worrying I was not haughty enough; trying to be everything at once and failing to be anything at all. No wonder Mr. Stirling glanced at me oddly as he took his leave.

(Incidentally: Mr. Stirling and Miss Greenaway are plainly friends, but are they in love and will they marry? It is, as she might put it, "something to mull over in an idle moment." Mrs. Potter mentioned that he is a widower of several years, and since, between them, they seem to represent the entire village of Sawyer's Fen, barring a row of shops and cottages down the road and a few scattered farms, it feels like a natural plot development. If I had to guess, I'd say Mr. Stirling dwells on the possibility with more interest than Miss Greenaway herself.)

When Mr. Stirling was gone, and we were sitting around the lamplit table in the study, I felt oddly peaceful. I don't know why. I think we all felt it, for a little while. I completed my drawing of a dodecagon while Emily read from Virgil in a not-entirely-dreadful voice, translating as she went with help from Miss Greenaway. Outside, the blossom shivered in the breeze; inside, the coals rustled in the hearth. Sometimes Emily turned a page; sometimes Miss Greenaway leaned back in her chair and stretched like a cat. I opened Bleak House and read a chapter and a half without interruption.

"What was that noise?"

The question was Miss Greenaway's. She shot to her feet at the bang; Emily and I glanced up from our books.

"Maybe it was the wind?" I said. "Maybe it's knocked something over?"

"No," said Emily. "It came from indoors."

I badly wished to contradict her (why does she have to be so definite? oh, I could box her ears with the Latin dictionary!), but I knew she was right. We followed Miss Greenaway into the hall, where Mrs. Potter lay sprawled on the floor, dragging slow, heavy breaths from her lungs. She opened her eyes as we gathered round, and tried to smile at Miss Greenaway.

"Oh! My poor darling!" Miss Greenaway went down on her knees, speaking to the old woman exactly as if she were a small, beloved child.

Mrs. Potter whispered, "No harm done, I'm all right. I had a funny turn and fell over the rug."

I'm afraid I became a blockhead again: standing around, biting my nails, wondering how to be helpful. Emily wasn't much better, although when Miss Greenaway said, "There's a bottle of brandy and a glass in the corner cupboard in the study . . ." she understood, before I did, that one of us was being asked to go and fetch it.

"What shall I do?" I asked.

"I don't want the doctor." Mrs. Potter fixed her eyes on Miss Greenaway, managing to sound firm, despite her weakness. Her face was so pale you'd think she'd bathed it in dust. Emily returned with the brandy and was instructed to pour a couple of inches into the glass.

"We'll see." Miss Greenaway stroked her servant's forehead and helped her to sip. "Perhaps we'll send for him later on, but not just yet." She turned to us. "I can manage here. You girls go back to the study and carry on with what you were doing; I'll join you once Mrs. P. is comfortable in bed. All will be well, I'm sure."

The fire was burning low, and Emily bustled around the study as though she owned it, piling on coals and flapping the bellows. I returned to my chair and read Bleak House—or tried to. It was difficult to concentrate. I felt duty-bound to uphold the honour of . . . someone (myself? the Gower family name? the Anti-Intellectual

Women of England?) by sitting poker-straight and adopting an expression of genteel indifference, which is more distracting than you may suppose. Mr. Dickens may as well have been writing in Latin, for all I fathomed of chapter eighteen.

Once Emily had finished her little display of housewifery, she sat down with a bump and a sigh, and leaned her elbows on the table.

"What are you reading?" she asked, opening Virgil with one hand and propping her chin on the other.

"Bleak House by Charles Dickens."

She replied with a tiny lift of her eyebrows and reached across the table for the dictionary. Now do you understand my dislike? The idea of such an ugly bluestocking making herself out to be so superior! And I couldn't contrive a way to inform her of her mistake without being openly rude, thereby denting my own claim to pre-eminence. Not for the first time, I wished I were Mamma, so that I could know how to behave.

"Annie's head was full of facts / But Annie ended lonely," I thought to myself, remembering Frank's poem, and smiling to myself like someone who is inwardly amused. I promise you, that smile would have stung if she'd seen it, but she didn't look up from her books.

"Have you been a classical scholar for long?" I asked—as one might ask, "Have you been a leper for long?"—but she ignored my tone and answered, neutrally, that she'd been studying the classics "properly" for three years. I expressed my condolences with a nod and we read in silence for a while. Then Emily began to yawn: opening her mouth wide and making sing-song noises, with no attempt to be discreet. I remembered Frank's impression of the yodellers he'd encountered in the Swiss Alps.

Of course, I started yawning then, but I did so silently and behind my hand.

"Did you go to school," Emily asked, as soon as she could speak, "when you lived in London?"

"No, I had a whole string of governesses."

"What were they like?"

"Some were all right. The last one was awful. Uncouth. I had to get rid of her."

Emily stared. "You got rid of her? You mean, your mother and father did?"

I've occasionally wondered what a "silvery" laugh would sound like. Well, now I know, because a silvery laugh was precisely what came out of my mouth in response to Emily's question. I closed my book and sat back in the chair. What with one thing and another, I hadn't thought about my own appearance lately, but all of a sudden I felt pretty again. Emily's hair is too coarse, her limbs are too long, her hands are too large, and she has a crude idea of what cleverness is. Also, her mouth falls open whenever she is concentrating, which makes her appear stupid and bewildered.

I found myself telling the story of Miss Wilson's departure, and telling it well, at least it amused me, especially the part where I forged the love letter to Jack Briggs the butcher's boy, and the part where Frank put his letter to me in the envelope addressed to Miss W., and vice versa. I even managed to inject humour into the coal cellar scene. Obviously, I cut some episodes out; for example I played down my brother's role in the affair. Emily listened without interruption, but she did not laugh as much as she ought.

Some reaction would have been nice, however dull-witted, but the moment I finished, Miss Greenaway entered with tea and muffins on a tray, and began telling us about Mrs. Potter, and how the colour had returned to her cheeks, and how peacefully she was sleeping.

Tuesday, 28 March, 1876

I received my first letter from Frank today. The envelope was lying at my place when I came down to breakfast, and although Miss Greenaway did not ask questions, she kept glancing at me sidelong as she munched her toast, as if to gauge my reaction. Mrs. Potter wasn't there, having been impelled to take her breakfast in bed.

"It's from my brother," I said, partly for Miss Greenaway's information, partly to reassure myself that the familiar handwriting was real.

Miss M. L. Gower
c/o Orchard House
Sawyer's Fen
Cambridgeshire

How strange to see my new address written in Frank's hand. It feels like an impossibility come true; a missive sent by someone in real life to someone in a dream. I put it in my pocket, so that I could open it when I was alone, and we talked about other things: the kittens, and Mrs. Potter's illness, and whether it would be more interesting to visit the equator or the poles. (Miss Greenaway thinks the equator; I think the poles.)

After breakfast I took Frank's letter upstairs, shutting the bedroom door firmly behind me. Nobody disturbed me, even though it got to a quarter to ten, and we'd agreed to start lessons at half past nine each day. For all her unspeakable sins, whatever they may be, Miss Greenaway is sensitive in small matters such as this. I don't suppose it will count for much on the Day of Judgement, but it does make everyday life more pleasant.

Frank wrote that he is missing me and that I must come to Cambridge soon: Why don't I name a day, perhaps a Saturday, and he will look into trains? He wrote at length about an examination he thought he'd failed, but hadn't; and how his friend Henry Simpson had bought a human skeleton at auction and named it Bismarck; and how Hartwell had fallen in love with some actress he'd met in London, and what a bore he'd been ever since. He asked no questions about Orchard House, and told me none of the things I was longing to know about Miss Greenaway. I shouldn't feel surprised, I neither asked nor told very much in my own letter to him, but I wish he would intuit my NEED to know. (I use the word with due consideration. What was once an idle curiosity is now a NEED.)

During lessons today Miss Greenaway and I discussed the novels of Charles Dickens, with special reference to Bleak House, at which point I did most of the talking, as if she were the pupil and I the teacher! We also discussed solids, liquids, and gases and the Tudors. I was quite certain in my own mind that King Henry VI was famous for taking eight wives, but Miss Greenaway said that I was confusing him with King Henry VIII who had married six wives. We studied several interesting books on the subject, and it turns out she was right and I was wrong, but she didn't laugh at me, so I don't mind.

Wednesday, 29 March, 1876

Spring has been coming ever since I arrived at Sawyer's Fen, and today marked the change from wintry spring to summery spring. From early in the morning, the air was scented with grasses, flowers, and sunshine, rather than raw earth and wind. After lessons I told Miss Greenaway I was going for a walk, but I never got as far as the lane because I was distracted by the garden. It's nothing special in the grand scheme of things, and it's never going to win prizes for tidiness, but it has a lush wildness that touches me. Probably it shouldn't, but it does.

There's a tree beside the gate, just coming into leaf, whose branches hang down like ropes and tangle with the grass. The other day I asked Miss Greenaway what it was called, and she said it was a weeping willow. This morning I pushed the branches aside and entered a rippling, luminous cave, with walls that moved with the breeze. The sceptic in me said it was only a tree; only a stick of wood growing out of the ground. There were several such sticks in Erskine Place, and I never paid them any attention.

The clouds kept coming and going across the sun, and the "walls" glowed and dulled all around me in response. I forgot about my proposed walk and sat down, leaning my back against the trunk. When I closed my eyes I found that I could think about Pa, Mamma, and Ebenezer in a hushed way, without having to cry.

While I was sitting there, losing track of time, Miss Greenaway emerged from the kitchen door, doing up the buttons on her gardening coat (so-called, for I have never seen her gardening in it, unless "to garden" is to meander outdoors with a cup of coffee in one's hand, or to peer absent-mindedly at a clump of upcoming bulbs). Meanwhile, Mr. Stirling strode up the lane and pushed open the gate. The dog, Scout, was with him, but he stayed sniffing about in the verge rather than following his master into the garden.

You understand, don't you, that it's not my fault no one knew I was there? I was not hiding in the sneaky sense of the word, and I couldn't know Miss Greenaway and Mr. Stirling would choose that part of the garden for their conversation. Perhaps I ought to have leapt out as soon as they began, crying, "Stop! I can hear you!" but that would have been terribly embarrassing.

"Robert!" Miss Greenaway waved at him. "This is an unexpected pleasure!"

I could only glimpse them in the thin, wavy gaps between the branches, but it was enough. Mr. Stirling seemed unable to speak or smile, and when he removed his hat I saw that his hair was neatly brushed. Naturally I thought he had come to propose marriage, for why else would a single man visit a single lady looking so solemn and smart? The prospect of witnessing their romance made me sick to my stomach, though I still can't decide whether that was a symptom of disgust, or excitement, or something else entirely.

Miss Greenaway's shabby appearance also annoyed me: <u>not</u> because I wished her to accept him (God forbid—imagine having Emily as some species of stepsister!) but because I wished her to refuse with panache. Despite what I wrote about her ugliness, when I first saw her, it turns out that Miss Greenaway can be attractive, in her own peculiar way. Her style is somewhat like the garden's: you would not praise it openly for fear of being laughed at, and perhaps you would not approve it in your conscience, let alone copy it for your own purposes, but still . . . I like the humorous creases at the corners of her eyes, and I love the violet scent she puts on her gloves and handkerchiefs. I want to smell of violets when I'm grown up. If only she would pin her hair properly, arranging it so that the greys don't show, and desist from throwing that awful gardening coat over her dress. The mildew stains on the collar are unmistakable.

Mr. Stirling cleared his throat. "I hope Mrs. Potter continues to recover well."

"Well enough; she came downstairs for breakfast this morning. For goodness' sake, Robert, out with it. Whatever have I done to make you look so cross?"

The back of his neck changed from windburned pink to red.

"You've done nothing, Kitty, except to be your usual, charitable self. I'm not cross with you."

"Who then?"

He held out his arm, inviting her to stroll, but she plunged her hands in her pockets.

"Who?" she said. "Not Mrs. P., since you asked after her straightaway. Maude?"

Mr. Stirling took his hat off and put it on again. Miss Greenaway was the one with the steadfast gaze; he glanced about him like a sulky girl.

"Yes, Maude."

"Why?"

"I've been discussing her with Emily . . ."

"Oh you have, have you?"

". . . and we both think you made a mistake, taking her on."

"Why?"

"She's just . . . oh Kitty, she's a bad apple."

"What's that supposed to mean? You may as well say, 'I don't like her because I don't like her.'"

"Well, I don't like her."

"You mean you didn't like her father!"

Did I gasp at this abrupt mention of Pa? I feel I must have done, and yet all I remember is a stillness that turned me to stone and a desire to listen, listen, listen.

Mr. Stirling shut his eyes and took several long breaths. Up until now I'd thought of his hands as "farmer's hands," because they were so large and muscular, but it occurred to me that "murderer's hands" would be equally appropriate. What would I do if he tried to strangle her? There was no one within earshot, unless you count fat Mrs. Potter with her wheezes and funny turns. If only I'd had a weapon about my person, or something that would do just as well. I thought about unlacing my boots and throwing them at his head, but they are rather small and soft for the purpose.

"Jealousy," Miss Greenaway scoffed. "Pure jealousy."

"Oh, don't be a fool." Mr. Stirling swivelled on his heel and marched to the gate, before thinking better of it and marching back again. "Twenty-odd years ago perhaps, but not anymore. You're not irresistible, you know."

"Very well." Miss Greenaway's colour was up: there were red patches on her cheeks. "Tell me, please, how Maude has offended you."

Mr. Stirling's manner softened. Perhaps he was regretting his "not irresistible" remark, as well he might. I was surprised at Miss Greenaway for letting it pass; if anyone offered me such an insult, I would never speak to him again.

"You know, Kitty, you don't need to leap to her defence with such bulldog tenacity."

"But I don't understand why you've taken against her!"

"My dear, I tell you, there's no call for defensiveness. She's not yours."

"No! No, she is his, and that makes her precious in my eyes."

They were silent, unable to look at one another. For a moment I was afraid that Miss Greenaway had seen me, because she turned her face in my direction, but she was staring at her own thoughts.

"I only meant that you are not answerable for her character," Mr. Stirling resumed. "She's not your blood relative, and you've had no hand in her upbringing, therefore you can't be held responsible for her faults."

The patient tone was costing him some effort; his voice trembled in the same way his arms might have done in lifting a heavy weight. I am sure, as sure as sure can be, that Robert Stirling is a violent man, so don't expect me to be astonished if he ends his days swinging from the hangman's rope.

Miss Greenaway made an impatient movement with her shoulders, as if shrugging off the touch of an unwanted hand.

"Go on," she said. "What are these dreadful faults to which the child is supposedly prey?"

I won't attempt a word-by-word account of what he said next; I couldn't bear to write it all down. Suffice to say, he gave Miss Greenaway the story I'd told Emily on Monday. The Miss Wilson story. It's not that he told it inaccurately, as such, but he made me sound heartless and unamusing, and Miss Wilson came across as a wronged angel. I sat tight against the tree, clutching fistfuls of grass, unable to shut my ears or speak in self-defence.

"A silly, childish prank," said Miss Greenaway promptly, as soon as he'd finished. "A joke."

"I doubt the governess found it amusing."

"Robert, I am defending the sinner, not the sin. You can't expect Maude to have foreseen the consequences in the way you or I might. Besides, for all we know the governess was a monster; she might have deserved it."

"Come now, Kitty." Mr. Stirling shook his head. "The consequences were not trivial. The governess felt forced to resign her position."

"Well—"

"And so far from being repentant, young Miss Gower goes about boasting of her wit and cunning!"

Miss Greenaway folded her arms and frowned. I don't mind admitting, only to you, mind, that it was a painful juncture. I had never seen her with such a severe expression.

"What was Emily's response?"

Mr. Stirling raised his eyebrows. "To begin with, she couldn't decide whether she was more impressed or disgusted by the story."

"'To begin with'? No doubt that means you put her straight."

"Certainly I put her straight. She had a good cry over her own wavering and agreed with me that Maude is a bad apple."

"The metaphor of the day," muttered Miss Greenaway, in parenthesis.

"And now she says she won't continue with her lessons unless Maude is absent from the room."

"Oh, honestly, Robert!" Miss Greenaway blew out her cheeks and pushed her fingers through her hair. Her face is like a pool under a changeable sky: sometimes opaque, sometimes clear. I believe I was able to read it pretty well, just then. I believe she was searching, with delicate care, for the words that might move him.

Ruth used to look like that when she was sorting through her sewing box, selecting threads or buttons for a fancy piece of needlework.

"Maude has suffered a great deal over a very few months," she said. "It would be astonishing if she'd come through entirely unscathed. But she is young and bright and full of promise . . ." Miss Greenaway pointed absently, with her toe, at a crocus that was beginning to show purple. "And as far as accomplishment and character are concerned, she may be Emily's equal in a year or two . . ." I didn't like that, and neither did Mr. Stirling, to judge by the noise he made through his teeth. "Perhaps she will surpass us all in time, who knows? But Robert, she needs the chance to heal. She needs our patience and affection."

"Hmm." Mr. Stirling was unimpressed. "I'm afraid my patience and affection are reserved for Emily, and she is immovable on this matter. She will not share her lessons with Maude."

"Then she will have to do without lessons and get to Cambridge on her own, because I refuse to banish Maude from my study."

The two looked at one another steadily, then Mr. Stirling said, "I see," and Miss Greenaway replied briskly, "I'm glad you see," and that was all. He placed his hat very firmly on his head and went away.

Miss Greenaway returned to the house, and I let many minutes elapse before I followed.

Lunch was a subdued affair, but as she was serving the soup Miss Greenaway remembered to ask whether I'd had a pleasant walk, and I'm afraid I said that I had. I even added that I'd gone as far as the river and thrown some crusts for the ducks (which I did, only that was yesterday rather than today).

Miss Greenaway hardly touched her food, and Mrs. Potter made her go and lie down. Miss G. was resistant, but Mrs. P. can be terribly firm, and in this instance I think she was right, as Miss G. did look pasty. It's all the fault of Mr. Stirling's brutishness, of course. On the one hand I would like to run over to Willowbrook Farm to tell him what he's done and make him feel the full weight of his guilt; on the other hand, I don't want him to know, in case it leads to a reconciliation.

The doctor called to check on Mrs. Potter, this afternoon. At least, he was supposed to be checking on her: in fact he spent more time with Miss Greenaway.

After he'd gone I went to see her, but she was asleep. Her face looked like a child's, lying there on the cotton pillowcase, and I do know that's an odd thing to say of a strong-featured woman who must be forty years old or more. I can't explain it, except that sleep has a habit of making people appear innocent and open to hurt.

I couldn't settle to anything this afternoon. I played with the kittens for a while, and then I wrote a silly letter to Frank, which said "WHY MUST I HATE HER? TELL ME WHY?" in a wild hand, nothing like my own. In fact, it scarcely merits the name "letter," since I neither dated it nor began with "Dear Frank" nor signed my own name at the end. I scrawled it in a sudden rush and put it in an envelope, but fortunately I didn't get as far as posting it. How affected it would have seemed, in the cold light of a Cambridge college room! How hysterical!

I will conduct my own investigations as to why I should hate Miss Greenaway, and if I fail to discover any satisfactory reasons I will write again to my brother, being sure to come across as sensible and proper.

Miss Greenaway was up and about this evening; quite her usual self. After supper she retired to her study to do some work (she is writing a book about the Greeks in Homer's time), and as I was making my way to bed, she called me in. Apparently she had finished writing and was putting together an order for the dressmaker's—did I need anything in the way of clothes? She moved the pens around on her desk in a nervous fashion as we spoke, and when I replied that I would be grateful for a new black dress she said, "Certainly, and have you any preference as regards colour?"

"Black please, while I am still in mourning."

"Oh yes. Yes, you said."

She arranged the pens in a row, rearranged them in a diagonal pattern, studied them for a while and pushed them all apart.

"Try to be kind," she said abruptly, looking up at me. "Won't you, Maude? Always try to be kind to people, even when they don't deserve it."

I knew she was thinking of Miss Wilson, and a dozen indignant replies rose to my lips, but I couldn't say a single one of them out loud without giving myself away.

"I'm glad you're pretty and clever and perceptive and witty, and all the other things you are," she said. "Really, Maude, I mean that. But it's your kindness I value most of all. I'd rather have you dull and kind than witty and cruel."

I nodded without saying a single word in self-defence; she must have thought me stupid indeed! We bid one another an awkward "goodnight," and I went upstairs to bed.

Two thoughts occur to me, in relation to this encounter:

Firstly, how annoying it is that I am unable to defend myself as regards Miss Wilson! I have thought and thought, but as far as I can see, any such attempt would be tantamount to admitting I'd eavesdropped on Miss Greenaway and Mr. Stirling.

Secondly I wonder what kindness she has ever seen in me, in order to say she values it? Perhaps she means my rescue of the kittens? I can't think of anything else.

Saturday, 1 April, 1876

I pledged to find out why Miss Greenaway is hateful, and I meant it, but how does one go about such an investigation?

I've allowed this question to flummox me for three days, but I received a letter from Aunt Judith this morning, which has inspired me to put all doubt aside and begin in earnest.

I shan't transcribe Aunt Judith's letter in its entirety, since much of it comprises an account of her health, and Uncle Talbot's health, and lengthy admonitions to me to be well behaved. As you might expect, she does not mention Miss Greenaway by name, but she does make several references to the "evil atmosphere" and "pernicious influence" with which I am, apparently, surrounded. Most alarmingly, she confesses herself "uneasy" as regards my new circumstances, and tells me that her conscience has been keeping her awake at night.

Dear diary, you see, don't you, why my inquiry must begin at once? Aunt Judith's conscience must be soothed, as a matter of urgency, but how can I write a suitably reassuring letter if I do not know the nature of the "evil" that threatens me? A naive or clumsy response might spell doom, by which I mean several years' dreary sojourn at the Firs, in St. Albans, where Aunt Judith and Uncle Talbot live.

I shall start by marshalling my facts in the form of a list:

Reasons for Hating Miss Greenaway

1. *Miss Greenaway is a female intellectual. There is no denying the truth of this, since she writes academic books and articles, teaches Greek and Latin, has been on archaeological digs in Greece, and promotes university education for women.*

   I do not say that Frank's Sally-and-Annie caricature was wrong, only that there is a mismatch between his and The Relatives' (and my) prejudices, and Miss Greenaway herself. She is not, for example, scornful of non-intellectuals, nor does she have a squint, nor is she lonely. She is eccentric, but I cannot bring myself to think her unlikeable (let alone hateful) on that score. Her conversation is interesting and varied, but I believe that is compatible with being a woman.

In conclusion: if erudition is Miss Greenaway's principal vice, then I think I am equipped to defend her. Surely I am capable of rewording the above in such a way that even Aunt Judith will be persuaded in her favour?

2. Frank and Uncle Talbot refer to her as "The Feline." Why? (NB: They intend the comparison to be derogatory. If I were to liken someone to a cat, I would mean it as a compliment, but that is beside the point.)

The moral defects of cats are said to be: cruelty, indifference, self-interest, slyness. I cannot think of anything else. Laziness, arguably? Cook used to say Ebenezer was lazy.

I have applied my mind to each of those nouns in turn and I cannot see that they apply to Miss Greenaway, except in as far as they apply to all human beings sometimes and to some degree. In fact, Miss G. strikes me as being among the least cruel, indifferent, self-interested, or lazy people I know.

A question hangs over "slyness" since, by definition, a truly sly person may not come across as such. (You see how rational and logical I am!)

Is Miss Greenaway sly?

3. There is something dubious about Miss Greenaway's connection to Pa. For example, when I read back over this diary, I find Frank describing The Feline as a "vicious, predatory beast who lures foolish men to their doom . . . a mighty, insatiable, flesh-eating cat" (17 January). If the "flesh-eating cat" is Miss Greenaway, then presumably, given the context of our conversation, the "foolish men" include Pa. (NB: All cats are flesh-eating because God made them that way. I wish I had pointed that out to Frank at the time.)

Also, Uncle Talbot said he could think of worse ways to die than curled up in a cosy little basket with The Feline (17 January again), which implies that Pa was with Miss Greenaway when he died.

DO THEY SUSPECT MISS GREENAWAY OF MURDERING PA? It would be a better justification for hatred than any of my other ideas! But it's too preposterous. Even The Relatives (even dreadful Cousin Amelia) would not expect me to live under the guardianship of my father's killer. They would be much more likely to inform the police.

Besides, despite her supposed preference for eating people, there is some evidence that Miss Greenaway and Pa were on friendly terms. If this were not so, why would Pa have left me to her care? Why would Miss Greenaway have said, "Maude is his, and that makes her precious in my eyes"? (Conversation with R. Stirling, Wednesday, 29 March.)

4. When the question of my coming to live at Orchard House was first discussed, Frank told The Relatives, "My mother will be turning in her grave." (See 10 March.)

At this point I paused and put my diary away, tired of the whole sordid question. (Searching out reasons to hate someone may be a necessary exercise, but it is also depressing.)

I fetched Pa's tobacco pouch from my folding desk and held it to my nose, but the scent wasn't as strong as it used to be, so I flung it away and ran into the garden. I went and sat under the weeping willow, where nobody could see me. The grass was cold and damp, and it didn't feel much like April, but I can't say I cared.

When I returned to my room, I found Miss Greenaway standing by the fire. She didn't look round when she heard me come in, and I thought she must be angry. For one horrible moment I suspected her of reading you, dear diary, and finding out about my investigation . . . but there was no sign of it, and the drawer where I keep you remained shut. She took a deep breath and wiped her sleeve across her cheeks, and I realised it wasn't anger that kept her standing with her back to me.

"I'm sorry, Maude," she said, trying and failing to sound cheerful. "I only came to talk to you about your homework, but I found this on the floor . . ."

She turned round, and not only was she holding the battered leather pouch but she had a shred of tobacco stuck to her wet cheek.

"The smell of it . . ."

"I know. It smells of my father."

"It's uncanny. It's as if he were here."

I went to the window and looked out across the meadows. A minute went by before I noticed, by the ache in my muscles, that I'd compressed my features into a severe frown. Miss Greenaway came beside me and put her hand on my shoulder. I expect she thought I was indulging sad memories of Pa; she wasn't to know I was pondering the open question of her character.

"That's where he lived," she said, "when he was a boy."

"Who?"

I'd been entranced by the ghost of my own reflection, but Miss Greenaway was indicating the ruined house across the meadow: the brick house with the empty windows and the tree growing out of its roof.

"I don't understand what you're talking about."

"Your father grew up in Sawyer's Fen. But you must have known that . . . mustn't you?"

She paused to give me time to say "yes" or "no," and when I said neither she carried on:

"We used to play together as children: your father and I, and Robert Stirling, and Robert's younger sisters."

I looked up at Miss Greenaway, and back at the ruined house. The world seemed to tilt, as if I'd moved too quickly and made myself dizzy. I waited for it to right itself, but it refused to do so.

I had <u>not</u> known that. Surely my father was London born and bred, like me? I'd never thought otherwise, but I'd never asked the question.

I didn't admit my ignorance, but I'm sure Miss Greenaway guessed at it.

"Let's go for a walk," she said. "It would do us both good. We can take a look at your pa's old house if you like, although it's rather a sad sight . . ."

I nodded.

Miss Greenaway handed me the tobacco pouch. After she'd gone I closed my eyes and pressed it to my face, but Pa wasn't there anymore. All I could smell was old leather and violets.

She was ready first, in her thick boots and her dark green cloak. I'd seen her wear that cloak before, and I'd seen an unknown woman wear it as she followed behind Pa's funeral cortège, but I only made the connection today. It felt like a momentous discovery, and it felt like something I'd known all along, which is nonsensical. I do know that.

"You wore that cloak for my father's burial," I said, as I came down the stairs.

Miss Greenaway gave me a look, half-humorous, half-sad. "You're a sharp one, Maude Gower," she said. "You notice things."

I didn't reply, but I thought about her words as I was lacing my boots. It's true that I notice things. The trouble is (and I wonder whether she realises this?) I never seem to understand what anything means.

As soon as we'd left the protection of the house and garden, we had to huddle against the wind, which made it difficult to talk.

Thanks to Miss Greenaway's remark, I began to notice myself noticing things: the April wind like cold, shiny glass against my bare face; the milky stink of the cows (a good, honest smell or a disgusting one? I doubt I shall ever decide); the birds perched on branches in the copse, swaying and bouncing with every gust of wind, but clinging on.

Pa used to notice things too. "Look at the green in those clouds," he'd say, or, "Stare into the heart of the fire, Maude, and see if you can spot the dragon's cave with its hoard of gold." I wonder, is it good to notice things? Mamma did not notice much at all, and everybody knows she was closer to heaven than Pa. She would sigh, as if he'd pained her, and say, "There's no green in a cloud, George. Clouds are either white or grey."

I was frowning again, and Miss Greenaway kept glancing at me as if she was afraid to speak. When she said, "Your homework was excellent, Maude. You write very well," I was not surprised by her desire to change the subject from Pa.

"Perhaps you'll be an author one day!" she shouted through her scarf, which made me guffaw inside, although I pretended I hadn't heard. Can you imagine the teasing I'd get from Frank if I announced my intention to be a "lady novelist"?

The ruined house is only half a mile from Orchard House, but we went a roundabout way to avoid the staring cows, and what with the wind in our faces and the knotty ground underfoot, it took us a while to get there. Arriving at the front porch, we ducked through a doorway without a door, into an immediate stillness.

Miss Greenaway pulled a handkerchief out of her pocket and blew her nose. I think it was the effect of the wind, because I felt the same, although I'd forgotten my handkerchief and had to sniff.

I stared around.

"Well . . ." said Miss Greenaway.

Well indeed.

The house had no ceilings and barely any roof, and I could see the sky racing between the rafters. Where there ought to have been pretty wallpapers, pictures, and mirrors, the walls were festooned with ivy. The floors were made of rubble and nettles.

"This used to be Pa's house?"

"He was born here. His mother died when he was a baby, and he lived here with his father until he was eighteen. It was a nice house in those days."

"It feels as though nobody's lived here for hundreds of years."

Miss Greenaway nodded. "It is strange, how quickly the place has died."

I didn't question her use of the word "died." It made me think of 17 Erskine Place, and that nightmare I had where it was falling to pieces.

She went on: "There was a terrible storm, the winter after your father left. The roof was badly damaged and never fixed, so I suppose that's partly why. The people who bought it only wanted the land; they never bothered with the house itself."

Pa left Sawyer's Fen when he was eighteen years old. Twenty-five years ago, then. A quarter of a century.

I walked around the room, stepping over the grassy clumps and hidden bricks, searching for evidence of my father. When I failed to find it, I looked for evidence of any human presence, but there wasn't much of that either. The house belonged to nature, and my father to the realms of "once upon a time." There were brambles in the hearth, which struck me as pretty, but also sinister.

"You see that window up there, in the gable?" Miss Greenaway pointed to a hole high up in the wall, with a rotten frame. "That used to be our playroom. It was a box room really, full of dusty old packing cases, but we made it ours. I remember dressing up as pirates with red kerchiefs round our heads and burnt-cork moustaches. Your father was always the captain, and Robert always <u>wanted</u> to be the captain . . ."

She tailed off, and I couldn't tell to what extent this was a nice memory or a sad one.

"Were you and Pa cousins? That's what Uncle Talbot said."

". . . No. No, your father and I weren't related."

When I went on to ask, "Were you and he sweethearts?" I didn't mean to be rude, I simply wanted to know. Miss Greenaway began inspecting the wall beside the door, running her gloved fingertips over cracks in the plaster, like an expert builder with ideas for mending the house. Generally speaking, she is not one to object to questions, so I waited, and in a while she said:

"Your pa wasn't happy in Sawyer's Fen. It was always too small for him. He had no feeling for the land, the way Robert does; he couldn't wait to get away. When he was eighteen, his own father died, and he immediately sold the property and went to London to seek his fame and fortune."

". . . And you?"

"And I was part of his plans, to begin with. But I was living at Orchard House with my grandparents in those days, you see, and they relied on me; I couldn't simply leave. George said he would find a way, or perhaps he said he would wait for me, or . . . I forget exactly what he said."

She had her back to me and I couldn't tell if she meant to carry on, so I said: "Pa met my mother in London. He went to a party at his employer's house, Mr. Hobbs, the publisher, and she was there, as Mr. Hobbs's—"

"Mr. Hobbs's ward. Yes."

A chunk of plaster—a large chunk, at that—came off in Miss Greenaway's hand, showering her skirts with dust. She didn't jump back or brush herself down; she just stared at the lump she was left holding.

"He brought your mother to Sawyer's Fen, a few weeks after their marriage," she said. "I didn't know the first thing about it until we met in the lane. He couldn't look at me, and he introduced her in this strange voice, this rapid, angry voice, so unlike his own. 'I'm a married man, Kitty. Can you believe it? This is my wife. . .'"

"And what did you say?"

The chunk of plaster crumbled some more, turning her black gloves white. The tension in her fingers was not matched by the lightness in her voice.

"Oh, I was as gauche as gauche can be. Your beautiful mother put out her hand and said something, I forget what, but precisely the right thing, while I opened and shut my mouth like a fish."

Miss Greenaway tossed the plaster aside and strode into the adjoining room. She crossed the grassy hallway into another room, and back across the hallway to the first room. I followed in her footsteps like a dog, unsure whether she was trying to shake me off, or lead me on, or whether she had, in fact, forgotten me altogether.

My mind was thronging with questions, but I was too afraid to ask any, in case they made me sound like a baby who understood nothing of the world: Was he wrong to marry Mamma? Did he love you more than her? Was he never truly happy at home, with us? With me?

Also, I confess, I was afraid of the answers.

In the end I asked what seemed to me the best, because the most straightforward, question: "Was Pa with you when he died?"

Miss Greenaway stopped in her tracks and turned, at which point I realised I'd asked the very worst question of all. For a split second her eyes went hard and I thought I'd discerned her cunning at long last, and the evil in her face, and her long-meditated intention to murder me in this desolate ruin. (What a vindication for Aunt Judith et al.)

I thought it was a simple "yes" or "no" question, but Miss Greenaway made it seem like a conundrum with a million and one possible solutions. She searched her mind for a long time—she even appeared to search my mind, before answering, finally, "Yes, he was with me at Orchard House."

I remembered all the times Pa had gone away on business, and the many days and nights I'd missed him. I'd never thought to ask what "on business" meant; I suppose I'd thought it too dull to bother about, and beyond my understanding.

"You wish he'd been with you," said Miss Greenaway, placing her dusty hand on my sleeve. I nodded automatically, though it wasn't true. Imagine watching Pa as his heart stopped! Imagine having to witness his fear, without being able to allay it! Perhaps it's proof of my cowardice, but I didn't (I don't) envy her those privileges.

Miss Greenaway clasped her hands and looked me in the eye. I folded my arms across my chest and did my best to look back, although it was hard. The wind made a low hooting noise where it met the gaps and corners of the house.

"I'm sorry, Maude," she said. "I've wanted to say sorry for a long time, but I didn't know how to broach the subject. I know how shocking it must seem to you; how shocking it is."

I nodded again, whilst disagreeing in secret. Miss Greenaway and Pa were . . . what is the correct word? Adulterers? If only I knew precisely what adultery entailed, but my notions are very dim indeed, and therefore "shocking" is too straightforward a word to describe my feelings. ~~Is adultery just to do with loving somebody who is married, in which case why is it wrong, or does it involve that alarming version of kissing, which Frank and Miss Wils~~

A harsh response seemed appropriate, so I said, "You don't seem very sad about his death." I'd forgotten about the incident with the tobacco pouch. I was thinking about her bright dresses, and her passion for studying, and the cheerful way she is with me and Mrs. Potter.

What a look she gave me! Miss Greenaway has never made me feel childish or ignorant before, but she made me feel it then. You'd think there were whole worlds inside her soul—whole galaxies, invisible to the likes of me. She answered me wearily: "Oh Maude, I've grown so used to losing your pa over the years. What difference does one more parting make?"

I made no reply. I even doubted that Mamma, with her gift for elegant rejoinders, would have found the right words. How does one put on a crisp voice and tell someone as desolate-sounding as Miss Greenaway that she is much to blame for being desolate?

"I loved your father as much as . . ." She flicked her hand impatiently. "Never mind comparisons and figures of speech. It's enough to say I loved him. Was that wrong of me, Maude?"

I unfolded my arms and let them hang at my sides.

"No."

I have worried about my answer ever since. All the time I was walking home, and eating supper, and writing this diary entry, I was thinking about my "No." I meant it sincerely, but I'm afraid I should have said "Yes" instead. "Yes, Miss Greenaway, you were very wrong indeed to love Pa."

That is what Mamma would have said. I try, with every fibre of my being, to think as Mamma would think, but the fibres of my being are in rebellion and won't be told.

Monday, 3 April, 1876

I wrote two letters this morning and posted them this afternoon:

Darling Frank,

I would dearly, dearly love to see you. Would this coming Saturday (eighth) suit? Miss Greenaway keeps a Bradshaw's Guide in the hall drawer, and I see there is a train from Sawyer's Fen that arrives in Cambridge at ten o'clock. If you will engage to meet me at the railway station, we might spend the whole day together!

Of course I wish to see you for your own sake, but I also want to have a serious talk with you about Miss Greenaway. You have dropped so many hints concerning her diabolical character, for example, you refer to her as "The Feline" and describe her as predatory and shameful, but you never say, in precise terms, what she stands accused of. You and The Relatives have treated me like a child in this matter, but I am not a baby anymore. I shall be fourteen this month.

I know, dear Frank, that you only mean to protect me, but I think you are acting unjustly, towards me (for if you will entrust me to the care of a vicious woman, oughtn't I to be the very first person you apprise of the nature of her vice? instead of which, I am the very last!) and towards Miss Greenaway (in case you <u>*are*</u> *mistaken in your judgement of her).*

Having met and come to know Miss Greenaway (as you have not), I believe you are mistaken. However, I do not mean to make a case for her by letter; I would much rather we met, so that I can explain things properly.

Please don't be irritated by this letter. Really, I am not questioning your judgement, only the facts that have been laid before you. Would it not be a happy thing, for all concerned, if I were to be proved right in this one instance, and you wrong?

Next Saturday then, ten o'clock at Cambridge railway station?

Your loving sister,
Maude

Dear Aunt Judith,

Thank you for your letter. I was sorry to hear about your toothache and Uncle Talbot's lumbago. I am quite well. The weather in Cambridgeshire is cold, but bright and springlike, and I hope it is the same for you in Hertfordshire.

Miss Greenaway and I have just come from the village church of St. Jude's, where we laid flowers at her grandparents' graves. The vicar was unlocking the door as we left, and we stopped to exchange a few words with him. Reverend Banks is an elderly gentleman, most cordial, and much respected in the village, and his wife is cousin to the bishop of Peterborough.

I think you would be pleasantly surprised by Sawyer's Fen, Aunt. It has a well-kept air, and its people are modest and respectable. Aside from Willowbrook Farm and the vicarage, Orchard House is the largest and most refined of its houses. If only you could see it, all your anxieties would be allayed in an instant!

This afternoon I intend to bring my sewing box out and finish my mending, and if I have time afterwards, I shall carry on with my watercolour portrait of Mamma.

I lead a very quiet life here in the countryside; you might almost say it was nunlike. There are barely any distractions: far fewer than in London or even, I suspect, St. Albans. Why, I doubt the citizens of Sawyer's Fen have even heard of theatres or concert halls, let alone visited any!

I beg you not to be uneasy on my account.

Your dutiful niece,
Maude Gower

I observed a curious thing as I glanced over my second letter: namely that I'd duplicated Aunt Judith's own handwriting throughout, without intending to do so. I debated whether to copy it out again in my own hand, lest she suspect me of mockery, but I decided against. Aunt Judith probably assumes that all upright people form their letters in the same thin and emphatic way. If she notices the pastiche (which is doubtful), I shouldn't be surprised if she marks it down in my favour!

Tuesday, 4 April, 1876

London skies were always grey. Of course there were gradations: at best, perhaps at dawn on a summer's day, you might call it a "pearly" grey; at worst it was a filthy, suffocating darkness. It was, though, always grey.

Tonight I am sitting in bed as the sky turns from primrose yellow to iris blue. I have left the window open, as well as the curtains, and the cold air washes my face while my body stays warm under the covers. There are birds trilling in the trees, and their notes seem to match the various shades and scents of the evening, as if everything in nature is saying the same beautiful thing, in its own way.

I don't know what that "thing" is, at least, I cannot put it into words, but it has something to do with hope and something to do with peace.

I am pleased by the letters I wrote yesterday, especially the one for Frank. I hope he has received it by now.

Wednesday, 5 April, 1876

I have slept well since I came to Orchard House. Whenever we go on a long, blustery walk together, which we do almost every day, Miss Greenaway is certain to say, "You'll sleep well tonight!" and she is invariably right.

Sometimes I think I sleep too well, too blankly. Those dreadful nightmares, in which stone angels packed my mouth with soil, have vanished, but so have the pleasant dreams I enjoyed before Pa's death.

Last night was so peaceful, with the window wide open and the breeze stirring my hair, that I fully expected a lovely dream. I even anticipated how it might go: the ruined house restored to its former glory, and my father striding over the fields to meet me in Miss Greenaway's garden, and a picnic by the river.

Well, any simpleton knows it's impossible to anticipate dreams, let alone order them to your liking. So far from enjoying a reunion with Pa, I had a nightmare vision of Mamma, which was worse than any dream I've ever had, in all my life. She was in Tower Hamlets cemetery, but the undertakers had laid her face down in her coffin, and she was struggling to roll over in the confined space. She tried and tried, but she couldn't get onto her back. The flesh was coming away from her skull, and with every tiny, effortful movement, her yellow hair fell from her head in clumps.

I thought I'd feel better if I wrote my nightmare down, but I don't. Now that it exists in words, it seems more real.

Thursday, 6 April, 1876

No letter from Frank. If he doesn't answer by tomorrow's post, I shan't know what to do on Saturday, whether to travel to Cambridge or not.

He is annoyed with me; that's what it is. I've just reread my letter to him, and it sounds more indignant than I meant it to.

The strange thing is, I didn't feel angry when I sat down at my desk to write the letter, and I didn't feel angry afterwards when I sealed it up and posted it, but <u>during</u> the writing of it, when I put, "You and The Relatives have treated me like a child in this matter," and "I think you are acting unjustly towards me," and "I believe you *are* mistaken," and so on, something flared up inside me and my pen moved more and more swiftly across the paper, and I *could*, believe me, I *could* have said much worse.

Even so, I'm afraid I overdid it.

Friday, 7 April, 1876

I did overdo it. Frank's letter arrived in this morning's post, and he writes as follows:

> *Dear Maude,*
>
> *This Saturday will not do at all because Hartwell, MacLeod, and I have planned a jaunt to London. The week after will be Holy Saturday; hardly the best time for you to come pleasure seeking. The Saturday after that, the twenty-second, should suit well enough and I'll do my best to keep it clear of other engagements.*
>
> *I confess to being disappointed by the tone and content of your letter. I am used to your being a silly little mouse, but I had never suspected you of being a wrong-headed or, heaven help us, a hard-hearted one. No doubt (**no doubt at all**) Miss Greenaway is all charm and witchery, but whose judgement do you choose to trust, Maude? The brother whom you've known and loved all your life? Or a woman of dubious reputation, with whom you've been acquainted for less than a month?*
>
> *Do not presume to tell me I act unjustly, when you know nothing of the matter in question. Do not demonstrate your childishness by badgering to be treated as an adult. Above all, do not claim*

to understand the ways of the world more thoroughly than your brother who is—need I remind you?—a full nine years older, and a gentleman to boot.

Until the twenty-second.
Frank

Ordinarily I read Frank's letters many times over, but I read this one once, with my cheeks burning.

After I'd returned it to its envelope, put it away in my desk, and walked up and down the room a few times, I confess that I cried.

It was one of those messy, ugly, red-faced weeps to which I'm prone, and yet, as strange as it sounds (and I'd only admit this to you, dear diary), I found myself yearning for Miss Greenaway to come upstairs and discover my graceless collapse. I wanted to drop my forehead on her shoulder, and cry, and cry, and cry, and hear her say, "Poor Maude, don't be sad," and "Everything will be all right."

In fact, I did hear her on the stairs as my sobs were subsiding, and I squeezed a few more tears from my eyes in case she knocked on my door, but she went to her own room instead. She knew I'd just received a letter from my brother, and I suppose she thought it kind to leave me alone with it.

I've written two abjectly apologetic letters to Frank, three furious ones, and one reasonable-sounding one, and thrown them all on the fire.

Wednesday, 12 April, 1876

Mrs. Potter has had another "turn." I didn't witness it; I suppose it happened one night while I was asleep. She looks strange now: a thin, wasted face on top of a fat, weary body. It appears she's given up work altogether; she just sits about in various chairs, wrapped in shawls, her eyes either closed or half-closed.

Miss Greenaway waits on her old servant hand and foot, and when she's not busy doing that, she's reading, or writing, or teaching me, or leading me on long walks. The orderly running of the household, such as it ever was, suffers horribly. For example, today's luncheon consisted of a hunk of cheese squashed inside a lump of bread ("sandwich" is too dignified a name) and an apple, which we ate in the garden sans cutlery, crockery, napkins, tables, or chairs! I sat down on the low wall by the rockery, but Miss Greenaway paced and munched simultaneously, and as soon as she'd finished her apple, she tossed the core into the hedge and wiped her fingers on the grass. I have chills when I imagine what Mamma would say!

Sometimes I think Miss Greenaway and I resemble outlaws in a hideout, with only a few days left to live, and no patience for the more elaborate aspects of civilised life. We manage on food, warmth, and camaraderie, and we're oddly happy.

Thursday, 13 April, 1876

We took our work outside today, which was every bit as distracting as it sounds. The sun may have been warm, but the air was not still, and we had to weigh our papers down with stones, plant pots, and other bits and pieces from the garden. Also, I'd brought the kittens along, because I thought the fresh air might do them good, and it was difficult to concentrate on my book while they were bouncing about and catching at one another's tails. Little Nell, who continues to belie her namesake by growing fat, kept rolling into the long, damp grass and mewing for rescue.

I knelt beside Miss Greenaway on the tartan rug. Mrs. Potter sat in a wicker chair under an apple tree, all but invisible beneath her layers of shawls, watching over us like some ancient and all-knowing prophetess. I wished she would either sleep or speak, but she did neither.

Miss Greenaway was wearing her spectacles, which have the unfortunate effect of making her look crotchety, so that it came as a relief every time she threw me her usual smile. For most of the morning she worked on her book about the ancient Greeks, and towards lunchtime she wrote a letter to one of her friends at Newnham Hall, which is one of the ~~so-called~~ women's ~~"colleges"~~ colleges in Cambridge. Meanwhile, I was supposed to be studying The Iliad in a verse translation by Dryden: an activity I find enjoyable enough when Miss G. is reading it over my shoulder and explaining things, but not so enjoyable when she isn't. I admit, I would rather have spent the morning with Charles Dickens.

One way or another, we were both distracted. Miss Greenaway kept glancing anxiously at Mrs. Potter and leaning over to adjust her coverings or touch her hand, whilst I kept breaking off to ponder The Great Question in Frank's letter ("whose judgement do you choose to trust, Maude?"), much as I have been doing all week. Sometimes I came to the conclusion that it was not so much The Great Question as The Wrong Question, and my only worry was how to present this possibility to Frank without seriously annoying him. At other times I concluded that a loyal sister was duty-bound to reply, "My beloved brother, of course!" and I made an inward pledge to renew my investigations into Miss Greenaway's character.

A dog barked in the distance and we both looked up. Scout often used to bound after us on our walks, or come snuffling round the garden gate, but hadn't done so for a while. This prompted me to say, "It's a long time since we last saw the Stirlings. Has Emily given up her studies?"

It was sly of me, I know, but it was about time I made some mention of the estrangement. Mrs. Potter blinked at me from her cocoon, as if she could read my mind, but I ignored her. Despite her bloodhound looks, she's always had a sphinxlike air (at least she has in the short time I've known her), and her illness exacerbates it.

Miss G.: "I'm afraid Mr. Stirling and I have quarrelled."

Me (all innocence): "Oh?"

Miss G.: "It was nothing important, in fact it was rather silly: just a case of Robert being Robert and me being . . . me."

I bridled at "nothing important" given that they had, in fact, been disputing whether or not I was morally fit to breathe the same air as Mr. Stirling's daughter, but I wasn't supposed to know that, and I didn't let on.

A lengthy pause ensued, during which my eyes ran over and over the same three lines of Dryden and Miss Greenaway gazed abstractedly in the direction of Scout's barking.

"You're quite right, Maude," she said suddenly. "It's ridiculous to let such a quarrel drag on; too petty, especially at our age."

I was about to point out that I hadn't said—or indeed thought—anything of the sort, but she was looking at me so benevolently that I didn't like to. Mrs. Potter had her eye on me too, so I busied myself with the kittens, which was easy enough, since they were full of mischief. I tickled them with a stalk of grass, and they seemed to like the idea of the game, especially Little Dorrit, who rolled onto her back and batted at the grass with all four feet, grabbing at its feathery tip with her jaws.

Miss Greenaway went on: "I'm not so very rich in friends that I can afford to lose one, especially one as loyal as Robert Stirling."

I pretended to be absorbed by the cats, whilst pondering what she'd said. I'd always thought Miss Greenaway unusually well off for friends: she was always writing and receiving letters from Cambridge and London, and even from abroad. But perhaps she meant friends nearby, within walking distance? Locally, she has Mrs. Potter, who would lay down her life for her, and Reverend and Mrs. Banks, who sometimes stop to talk over the garden gate when they're passing, but that's all, as far as I know.

What about me? Can I count myself among her friends? If life were simple, I should be glad to say "yes," but I can't until I've had my all-important talk with Frank.

Whether I include myself or not, I suppose it <u>is</u> a rather small number. When I told Aunt Judith that Orchard House was one of the largest and most refined of the houses in the village, I wasn't exactly lying; I was merely creating the impression that we were much esteemed and visited, which we are not. Orchard House stands apart from the rest of Sawyer's Fen, and not only because the heart of the village is nearly a mile away. None of the ladies pay calls on us, the way they're supposed to,* and we do not call on them. On the rare occasions we venture into the village, Miss Greenaway seems to have to pluck up her courage first, and although most people return her "good morning," there are a few who do not. The woman in the dressmaker's shop served us with a marked coldness last week, though she was affable to her other customers.

Well, whichever way you look at it, Miss Greenaway is wealthier in friends than me. I would never have called Nettie, Ruth, or Cook "friends" when I was with them at Erskine Place, because they were servants and Mamma would not have approved; besides, I doubt I shall ever see them again. Frank is my friend, of course, and so is Ebenezer, if he is still alive, and so are Little Dorrit, Little Nell, and Nancy. Really that is all, unless you count Miss Greenaway.

I shall count her, for the time being, since my tally is otherwise very meagre. If I do not count her, then 80 percent of my friends are cats and 20 percent (i.e., Ebenezer) are likely deceased, which must reflect poorly on me.

* People rarely paid calls on Mamma either, but that was because she was sick, which is a respectable reason for a lady to keep herself to herself.

By the time I'd concluded this train of thought, Miss Greenaway had returned to her letter writing and the conversation was over. Scout barked in the distance, but I was careful not to glance up again or make further mention of the Stirlings.

Saturday, 15 April, 1876

Miss Greenaway went for her usual walk this afternoon, but I said I felt unwell and excused myself from going with her. As it happens,

I do have the beginnings of a cold, although it hasn't troubled me greatly so far; the truth is, Miss G.'s absence provided a welcome opportunity for me to complete my investigation into her character, by thoroughly searching the house. Mrs. Potter was resting in her own room, so I had to move about with the utmost care and quiet. Mrs. P. is frequently deaf, but sometimes, and quite unexpectedly, she is not.

Despite a diligent search through drawers, along shelves, and inside boxes and trunks, I found nothing telling, unless you count a pencil portrait of "George," signed "K. G. June 1849," which stands on Miss Greenaway's dressing table in a pretty silver frame. I would not have known my father immediately, but the name and date gave me the clue I needed to recognise his humorous eyes and mouth, and wide forehead, and the curl of his bright, chestnut hair.

Possibly it is wrong of Miss Greenaway to keep this picture in her bedroom? Wrong to place a tiny vase of violets alongside, as if it were a shrine?

Possibly, but I cannot hate her for it.

There is one more place I must explore, in order that I may say to Frank, "I have done all I can." It only occurred to me this evening, by which time Miss Greenaway was home and Mrs. Potter was up and about. I am referring to the cellar, from which Miss G. emerged with the kittens on my very first morning at Orchard House. She stores things in there: old furniture, broken objects, vegetables and fruit from the garden.

If the house is hiding a guilty secret, the cellar is the place to look. I can see the trapdoor from my window; I have even seen it gaping open, with its stone steps leading into darkness, but I have never ventured down.

PEGGY

September 1945

Downstairs, a noise; a shrill, insistent voice? Peggy looks up from the page. Laurie stirs and murmurs beside her, but doesn't wake. It's the right pitch for a voice, and yet—not quite. The cat has heard it too. It tenses at her feet before clawing its way out of the bed, its tail bristling like a round hairbrush.

When Peggy opens the bedroom door, the cat slips into the darkness without a sound. If she knew its name, she would call it back, in a whisper.

The noise comes in short monotonous bursts. It's the telephone—that's what it is—the telephone ringing in the study. Peggy isn't wearing her watch but it must be late, she's been reading for hours. She runs her hands over the landing walls either side of the door without finding a light switch, and her palms come away with a coating of dust.

Only an idiot would fumble all the way downstairs to answer it. Whoever it is, they're bound to ring off by the time she reaches the study. Peggy looks back through the open door, narrowing her eyes until she's certain she can detect the faint motion of Laurie's breathing. The telephone rings and rings and rings. Peggy begins feeling her way along the landing.

Sure enough, when she's halfway down the stairs, it stops. Peggy stops too, and now there's another noise, like footsteps on stone. *That bloody cat*, she tells herself firmly, but it's not a cat. These are human feet wearing shoes—she can hear the double click of heel and toe within each step—and they are walking rapidly down a flight of stone steps. She curls her naked toes. The actual stairs are wooden, beneath a threadbare runner.

The telephone starts up again, muffling the other noise, which must, after all, have something to do with the cat. Or—Peggy racks her brains, feeling that an urgent answer is demanded of her—or plumbing? Mice? Some electrical fault . . . She carries on more quickly, helped by the wash of moonlight through the open door of the study, and picks up the receiver.

When Frank is connected, and says, "Peggy?" her mouth is too dry to answer.

When he says it again—"*Peggy?*"—she licks her lips and pulls herself together and says, "Yes, yes, it's me."

It's not that he has altered—her father-in-law has always had a young voice—it's only that she can't see him. Her mind is exhausted, and tangled up in the diary, and that's why the man on the telephone sounds blond and boyish.

"What time is it?" she demands, low and brisk. "What do you want?"

She re-creates him in her head: an old man with pale eyes, and thin white hair, and a liver spot on his cheek.

"You asked me whether I believe in ghosts," he says, "and I've decided, I want to tell you that I do."

"I see." Peggy rubs her tired eyes. "Frank, how much have you had to drink? I think you ought to go to bed."

"That house has soaked up evil, over the years, like a dry sponge soaks up water."

Or like you soak up liquor. Peggy doesn't say it, but her irritation is threatening to surface. It may be the fault of the diary; it may be because Frank is tight. She sits down at the desk (Miss Greenaway's desk?) and huddles over the telephone, placing a protective hand on the back of her neck. The study is full of strange shadows. She wouldn't mind a stiff drink herself—not to mention bright lights, and music, and people.

"Frank, listen, it's the middle of the night—"

"Where's Laurie?"

"He's fast asleep."

"As you were when I rang? You haven't been kept awake? I don't trust that house. I don't trust my sister, however dead she may be."

A crackle in the line hides Peggy's failure to reply. She wishes that the curtains were shut, but it's no use trying to reach them while she's on the telephone. Peggy isn't superstitious, but she doesn't like reflections in dark windows, especially when she's alone.

Perhaps it's a fault in the line that makes Frank's voice very loud, all of a sudden.

"Go back to Laurence," he says. "I want you to go, at once, immediately. Keep watch over him; keep him safe."

"He *is* safe! For heaven's sake, Frank, listen: supposing—just supposing—Orchard House is overrun with ghosts, and Aunt Maude is stalking about in a white nightdress, rattling chains . . . why on earth would she wish to hurt Laurie?"

The old man answers without hesitation: "Because she would do anything to hurt me."

The rain has stopped, but the trees and gutters are dripping, and the sound mingles with the fizzing on the line. Peggy wishes she could retract the word "ghost." Naming matters, she thinks. When you name something, you call it into being.

"Go to bed, Frank. We'll talk in the morning."

She hangs up. Any other human voice might have been a comfort tonight, but not Frank's. His is a voice from the diary; a spectre in its own right.

There's that noise again: feet careering down stone steps, a flurry of silk. It must be coming from somewhere. The hall? The parlour? Peggy enters each of the downstairs rooms and forces herself to stand and stare until she's made sense of the shadows. Try as she might, though, she cannot make sense of the sound. It seems to come from below, and she searches under rugs and along walls for an entrance to the cellar. Twice she thinks she's found a likely door—only to lay bare a gargantuan boiler and a broom cupboard. Back in the study she kneels and presses her ear to the floor, and there it is, more vivid now: the sweeping of skirts, the tripping of feet, the rasping of breath. She closes her eyes and tries to un-hear it, but the swishing only grows clearer and the footsteps seem to quicken in time with her own breathing.

An almighty thud from below, and a piping cry from above, and Peggy's eyes flick open. She is disabled, for an instant, by sheer confusion, but the cry comes again, more loudly—"*Mummy!*"—and she scrambles off the floor, tripping over her own feet in her race for the stairs.

There's a figure at the top, waiting. Her heart flickers with a momentary doubt as she pounds up the stairs and folds her arms about it—but it *is* Laurie, of course it is, in his flannel pyjamas, with his hair on end and a smear of dribble on his cheek. He rubs his face against her shirt, and she carries him back to bed, his legs wrapped round her waist and his arms wrapped round her neck.

"You're getting too heavy for this, young man." She staggers into the bedroom and manages to nudge the light on with her elbow, before dropping her son on the bed. (She could have sworn she left the light on? Laurie must have switched it off.) She helps him under the covers, and by the time she's fetched a sweater from her suitcase—the old navy-blue one, which used to be Jonathan's—and pulled it over her head, his eyes are starting to close.

There's no sign of the cat. Peggy clambers into bed and reaches for Maude's diary. God, she could do with a drink.

"Mummy?" Laurie mumbles from the edges of sleep. "Was it you?"

"Me?"

"Before? Was it you, coming towards me, with a candle?"

She opens her mouth and shuts it again. For all Laurie's drowsiness, his question is edged with unease, so rather than say, "It was only dream," she answers, "Yes, it was me."

Laurie's mouth is falling loose and his eyes are closed. He says, "I thought it was a different lady."

Peggy watches him fall asleep, and looks warily around the room. *The shushing of rain is like the rustle of silk*, she reassures herself. *The drip-drip of the gutter is like the click-click of shoes.* She pulls the woollen sleeves over her hands and holds them to her face, breathing the lingering scent of her husband's skin. The war has left everyone bone-tired—herself and Frank as much as anyone. A proper sleep would do them all a world of good.

Yes, that's what she wants: a sleep that lasts months, or years, and brings her, oblivious, to a fresh, new morning.

She sits and pictures it for a while, before draining the cold dregs from her teacup, lighting her last cigarette, and returning to Maude's diary.

Easter Sunday, 16 April, 1876

Miss Greenaway and I went to church this morning; Mrs. Potter was persuaded to stay behind because she is still very weak and breathless.

"Perhaps you could say a prayer for her in your head, during the intercessions," suggested Miss Greenaway, as we set off down the lane.

I nodded, but after a moment's thought I wondered aloud: "Strictly speaking, would you categorise Mrs. Potter among the sick or among the dying? I suppose it doesn't really matter; they're both clumped together, aren't they, in the intercessions?"

Miss Greenaway frowned and looked away over the fields, as if she found my question glib, though I hadn't meant to upset her. Sometimes I feel as if the sudden loss of both my parents gives me the right to be matter-of-fact about the sufferings of others, especially when they involve old and insignificant people like Mrs. P. (forgive me, diary, but you know what I mean). Is that wrong? It doesn't feel wrong when I think it; only when I articulate it.

"It's no simple matter," she said after a while. "Placing people in categories, I mean."

If that was a rebuke, it was a mild one, and our walk to the church was otherwise pleasant.

Despite its many sadnesses, I think I will always remember the chill, yellow light of this particular spring. Inside St. Jude's, the sun came spilling through the stained glass like a shower of jewels, drenching the front pews and the staid ladies and gentlemen who sat in them.

Reverend Banks preached about the joy of resurrection, and I thought about cats, and heaven, and hot cross buns in a pleasant, dreamy, mixed-up way. When I'm with Miss Greenaway, I don't have to worry about whether I'm sitting straight and wearing the right expression. Even when I sniffed during the sermon, which I did a couple of times, on account of my cold, Miss Greenaway fumbled in her pocket and passed me a handkerchief, without so much as a whispered "tut."

Of course, it's because she doesn't care for me as earnestly as Mamma did. That's the only reason. Mamma's standards were ~~laudably~~ ~~implacably~~ high, which is why she would slap me across the wrist if I sniffed in her presence, let alone in God's.

Robert and Emily Stirling were among the congregation; I immediately recognised the hulking shoulders of the one and the ugly hat of the other. (An ostrich feather is all very well in a hat, so long as the bird in question does not appear to have perished through chronic malnourishment and scabies.) It struck me as fortunate that they were sitting at the front, because it meant we would be able to escape without having to meet them. Imagine my discomfiture then, when Miss Greenaway made a point of loitering in the churchyard at the end of the service!

"I think we ought to get back to Mrs. Potter," I said, tugging at her sleeve.

Miss Greenaway bestowed one of her brightest smiles on me, probably thinking I meant to make amends for my earlier blunder. (NB: She is quite, quite beautiful when she smiles, despite her large nose and mouth, and her age, and the various other factors that count against her.) Nevertheless, she continued to stand about and study the gravestones, which long centuries, English weather, and lichen had rendered illegible.

"I need to have a word with someone," she said. "I'll be very quick."

Dear diary, you have guessed correctly: it was Mr. Stirling she wished to see. As soon as he and Emily emerged into the sunshine, Miss Greenaway hurried over. I wanted to stay behind, but she turned and motioned me, so I dragged my feet in her wake.

"Robert? Emily?" she said shyly, her arms outstretched. I presume she was only offering a handshake, but you'd be forgiven for thinking she wished to embrace them both. "Happy Easter!"

If they hadn't been on holy ground, and it hadn't been Easter Day, I suspect they'd have cut her altogether. As it was, they ignored her gesture and barely nodded. Mr. Stirling touched his hat without quite tipping it. Neither smiled.

Poor Miss Greenaway! Her arms dropped to her side as she watched them pass along the gravelled path. It was gratifying to me to find them unequal to her magnanimity, though it was a pity to see her so crestfallen.

This evening I gave her a bunch of daffodils, which I'd picked in the lane, and it seemed to give her genuine pleasure. I longed to point out (although of course I couldn't) what a very different kettle of fish I am from Emily Stirling.

Tuesday, 18 April, 1876

Mrs. Potter wanted to sit in the parlour* this morning because it has a sunny aspect, and because she's sick to death of being in bed. Miss Greenaway, having settled the old woman in an armchair, fell to wondering where the footstool was.

"You know the one I mean," she said. "The tapestried stool that's lost half its stitches. It used to be red and gold, but it's gone a sort of dusky pink with age."

Mrs. Potter closed her eyes and said she was aware of the stool Miss Greenaway meant, but could manage well enough without it.

"I don't want you to 'manage well enough'; I want you to be perfectly comfortable. Besides, I should like to know where it is."

"It used to be in Miss Maude's room," Mrs. P. said. "You probably moved it to the cellar before she arrived."

"Oh, of course." Miss Greenaway smacked herself lightly on the forehead. "That's exactly what I did. I'll fetch it at once."

"<u>I'll</u> fetch it!" I said.

They looked at me in surprise, and Miss Greenaway seemed mildly appalled.

"Goodness!" she said. "I don't expect you to go, Maude, though it's kind of you to offer."

I'm sure she feels sorry for me; she thinks I'm suffering agonies of remorse for the sick-or-dying comment I made on Sunday.

"No, really!" I insisted, warming to the idea in proportion to Miss Greenaway's resistance.

Funnily enough, it was Mrs. P. (Mrs. "I don't need a footstool" P.) who came to my aid.

"Don't fuss the child, Kitty; she's more than capable of going to the cellar and coming out alive."

"I'm not doubting her capability, I'm only . . ."

"Only what?"

"It's very dark in there, and the steps are so steep."

"Then give her a lantern and tell her to be careful."

They exchanged a long look, before turning to me for the final say.

"I don't mind cellars," I said, pressing my nails into my palms. "I like the dark."

* Is it a parlour? At any rate, it's the closest thing Orchard House has, with smarter chairs and fewer heaps of books and papers than the other downstairs rooms.

The trapdoor is a monstrous device, more appropriate to a medieval dungeon than an innocent domestic cellar. I had to set the lantern down in order to unfasten the bolt, grip the metal ring with both hands, haul the door open, and lower its great bulk to the ground without smashing the paving stones (or my toes).

I was afraid Miss Greenaway might come and hover at the top of the steps, impeding my search, but Mrs. Potter had been so sarcastic about "babying" and "mollycoddling" that she had been driven to affect a lack of concern, in self-defence. Also, the postman had just called, bringing a letter from her married friend in America, which provided a welcome distraction.

I went down the steps into smells of dust and vegetables, and crowds of wavering shapes and shadows—treading as cautiously as you may imagine, for the descent was indeed steep and there was only a rope, looped slackly along the wall, by way of a banister. It was just as well Miss Greenaway had given me a lantern: I thought the sunshine would pour through the opening to help me, but the stone-cold darkness seemed to soak it up, the way blotting paper soaks up ink.

It wouldn't be long before she came looking for me, so I swallowed my terror (and this is no mere manner of speaking: it <u>did</u> feel like a lump in my throat) and carried on to the bottom of the steps.

The cellar was divided into four cavernous rooms, walled and floored with bricks, three of which were more or less empty, barring two broken packing cases, a rickety stepladder, and a shelf of cobwebbed bottles.

The fourth—the room at the bottom of the steps—was more cluttered, but not impossibly so. There were wooden racks all along one wall, where apples, onions, potatoes, and other vegetables from the garden were stored. The unwanted furniture was in a higgledy-piggledy pile at the back of the room, but there wasn't much of it and I spotted the tapestried footstool at once. There was little else. A watering can. A pile of dust sheets. A bundle of garden canes. A sink with a dripping tap.

How long had it taken me to discover this much? Perhaps two minutes? I was dying to return to the upper world, but I still had time in hand.

(Time for what?

Time to search.

Search for what?

I DON'T KNOW.)

I poked about among the furniture: sliding my fingers inside ripped upholstery, forcing open a wardrobe, unfolding a portable writing desk.

There was nothing, or almost nothing. Only a little drawer inside the desk, and inside the little drawer a bracelet and a packet of letters.

The silver bracelet was tied to the ribbon that held the letters together, and it took me ages to untangle everything. By the time I'd succeeded I could hear the kitchen door opening and footsteps on the path above.

Crouching in the lantern light, I glanced at the tarnished bracelet, and the inscription engraved on its inner curve. It was in Latin—"Caritas Something Something"—I don't know; I hadn't got time for elaborate lettering, so I slipped it onto my wrist, making sure to hide it under the cuff of my sleeve. I turned my attention to the letters instead, tearing one from its envelope and then another. My hands shook for fear of everything—of the cellar, of the footsteps, of the letters themselves—and consequently it was difficult to take much in. I saw that they were written by my father to his "Beloved Kitty" and that at least one of them was dated November 1875, which is less than half a year ago.

"Maude?" Miss Greenaway's voice was faint, but only because the open air diluted it. She was getting closer.

I tried to read, but my father's handwriting was uneven and feverish. Words slipped away from my eyes as I darted from sheet to sheet, and Miss Greenaway was almost at the top of the steps.

"Maude? Are you all right down there?"

I thrust the letters and the ribbon back inside the desk and ran towards the light. Halfway up I realised I'd forgotten the footstool, so I scurried back to fetch it.

~~If I'd had a pocket, I could have stuffed the letters~~

~~I wish I'd had a pocket in my dress, so that~~

If I were a true detective, inspired by pure curiosity, I would have found a way to smuggle those letters, or at least some of them, out of the cellar. I would be picking them apart now, in the privacy of my own room, and congratulating myself on having found evidence at last.

Clearly, I am not a true detective, because I didn't want to take them, and I don't want them now,* even though I cannot stop thinking about them.

There's not a single sentence I can recall in its entirety. There are only words and phrases that make no sense—or almost no sense—at all.** Things like, "those darling hairs at the nape of your neck," and "with my tongue," and something about "your nakedness." I keep telling myself that shoes have tongues and truth is often naked, yet I'm as sure as can be that my father was not discussing shoes or truth. As for "those darling hairs at the nape of your neck" . . . why would any respectable person write such a thing, in any circumstances, ever?

I can accept that Pa loved her, but I'm not sure I can, or should, accept this. And what is "this," anyway? Is there a word for it? Is it something that normal people would recognise and understand, or is it Pa's own invention? Perhaps he was sick in the head; perhaps that's why he died.

It is not Miss Greenaway's fault if my father wrote ~~horrible~~ ~~deranged~~ ~~insulting~~ strange letters to her, and gave her a bracelet engraved in fancy lettering that reads: "Caritas Omnia Ignoscit" (whatever that means).

Or is it her fault?

She didn't have to tie them up with ribbon and keep them safe in a drawer.

* Perhaps a tiny, microscopic, particle-sized portion of me does, but the rest of me does not.

** It would be better if they made no sense at all.

I went to Miss Greenaway's study this evening, while she was taking her bath. Mrs. Potter was in bed. The Latin dictionary is awfully cumbersome, but I managed to find my way around it, in the end.

Caritas = affection, love, esteem.
Omnia = all things/everything.
Ignoscere is a verb meaning to overlook, forgive, pardon.

So, "Love Forgives Everything," according to the silver bracelet that Pa gave Miss Greenaway.

It's a nice sentiment, except when you reflect that the "Omnia" in question includes Pa's marriage to Mamma and, by extension, my own and my brother's existence.

Pardon me, then, if my heart refuses to melt.

Wednesday, 19 April, 1876

I wish I'd never written yesterday's entry. If I hadn't told you about those letters and the bracelet, they'd still be secrets in the cellar, and only Miss Greenaway would know they existed.

Well, all right, I would know—but not for long. I'd allow the memory to fade. I'd convince myself it had been too dark to read properly, that I'd been hasty and distracted and confused . . . I'm good at making my mind play such tricks on itself. I've done it before and succeeded.

Things become different, once they're written down. Even if I tore these last few pages out and burned them (which I was very, very close to doing last night), I'd notice the ripped edges every time I reached for my diary, and think about the cellar even more than I otherwise might.

I hereby swear that I shall never write or speak about those letters again. If possible, I won't think about them either. I've hidden the bracelet at the back of the drawer where my stockings are kept.

Friday, 21 April, 1876

Miss Greenaway put her head round my door tonight, whilst I was reading in bed. We have fallen into a routine whereby she says,

"Hello, bookworm, isn't it time for sleep?" and I plead for one more chapter, and sometimes I win, and sometimes she wins. These little rituals can be pleasant, but they can easily grow wearisome. For the last few nights, I've extinguished my candle without argument and turned over on my side to sleep, and that's what I did tonight.

Miss Greenaway came and sat down on the bed and asked if I was all right.

"Perfectly all right, thank you."

"You're not sad or worried for any reason?"

It's easy—or easier than normal—to talk about things in the dark, but I was on my guard against that and answered promptly, "No."

"You can tell me anything," she said. "There's nothing you can say that will shock me, Maude; you're free to speak your mind."

I'll admit I was tempted. I couldn't see her, even in outline, and I could barely feel her weight pressing down on the mattress. Her kind voice was the only presence in the room, and it was like having an imaginary friend who would listen, speak, and understand on my command, in whatever way I wished. I stared into the darkness, at the place where I supposed her to be, and tried to catch the rise and fall of her breathing.

She was wrong, of course. I might have been free to say what I liked, but neither of us could guarantee we'd be unchanged by it; that we wouldn't like one another less in the aftermath.

"There's nothing wrong," I told the darkness politely. "Perhaps I'm a little nervous about my visit to Cambridge tomorrow. It feels ever so long since I last saw Frank, although it's only a month."

She let out a sigh and the mattress lilted as she got to her feet. Her voice, when she spoke, was louder and more ordinary.

"I predict that all your shyness will evaporate the moment you see him, as if you'd never been apart."

"Maybe."

I wasn't nervous in the simple way she envisaged, but I could hardly explain that.

"I'm going into Cambridge myself, tomorrow," she added, "so if it's any comfort, you won't be alone on the train."

"Oh . . ."

"Not that I'll be in your way once we're there," she said hastily. "I've plenty to keep me busy, as I'm sure you have too; I only thought you might like a travelling companion."

My reply was too long in coming, because I was trying to think of a civil way to say, "Please, please avoid meeting my brother at the railway station." Eventually I concluded that there is no civil way of saying such a thing, so I asked if Mrs. Potter could keep an eye on the kittens while we were away, and she said she was sure it could be arranged, and we bid one another goodnight.

After she was gone, I relit my candle, read another chapter of Oliver Twist, and wrote this diary entry.

Saturday, 22 April, 1876
(I shall write today's account
as if it were one entry, although
I certainly shan't finish it tonight.
There is a great deal to say and I'm tired.)

I needn't have worried—at least, not to begin with—because Miss Greenaway melted into the crowd when we reached the railway station. She was at my side as we were alighting from our carriage, but in the moment it took me to scan the crowd and exclaim, "There's Frank!" she was gone.

The train had pulled in on time, but Frank said, "Oh, *there* you are," as if I were late. He received my kiss with a patient air, but gave me none in return. I supposed he was still annoyed about my letter, and although I'd been intending to get it out of the way at once, I shrank from broaching the subject.

We walked all the way from the railway station to his college rooms at St. John's, which felt like an awful trek. My brother strode ahead with his hands deep in his pockets, while I trotted and jogged in an effort to keep up. It goes without saying that Cambridge is a smaller and gentler place than London, but it's a city all the same, and the hum and whirl of it felt strange. So many people! Such a racket of horses and wheels and human voices! I'd been looking forward to this visit for weeks, yet all I felt, as we marched along Regent Street, was out of breath and depressed. Have I degenerated into a country mouse already, one month out of London?

I made a few puffing attempts at conversation, but Frank replied rudely, if he deigned to reply at all. For example,

Me: "Have you had a busy week?"

Frank: "I'd like to know what a leisurely week looks like!"

Or,

Me: "How are your friends? Hartwell and MacLeod and the others?"

Frank: "Dull as dishwater, the lot of them. Hartwell is the worst; he's in love—or professing to be—and if he's not gallivanting with his sweetheart, he's talking about her ad nauseam."

He didn't ask how I was faring—not once! I was on the verge of complaining, but I didn't, because that would have led us to the subject of Miss Greenaway.

Shortly after his gripe about Hartwell, Frank asked, "How's that little governess of yours? Whatever-her-name-was who ran away to Brighton. Do the two of you correspond?"

I couldn't think whom or what he meant, to begin with; Miss Wilson was a character from another lifetime, and so irrelevant to my current preoccupations that she might as well have "run away" (if that was the right expression) to the moon as to Brighton.

"Miss Wilson? No, of course we don't correspond. What a peculiar question."

Frank caught at a stone with his foot and kicked it along the pavement.

"She was a good sort; knew how to keep a fellow amused. I've half a mind to invite her up to Cambridge next Saturday, if I'm to be in the business of entertaining female visitors."

I made no reply. Indeed, I turned mute until we arrived at St. John's, to show how offensive I found his remarks, but I don't believe he noticed.

I am pleased to report that my brother was somewhat more cheerful by the time we reached his rooms. I flung myself onto his sofa with a groan, and he procured some milk and biscuits, having observed with a softened manner that I looked "as white as a Lancashire cheese." When I'd drained the glass and eaten the biscuits he said, "All right now, Miss Mouse?" which came as a relief, because he'd addressed me only as "Maude" so far.

I'd visited Frank's rooms on one previous occasion, with Pa. They were old and fine with uneven floors, dark panelled walls, and wavy glass in the windows. Everything smelled of brandy and tobacco (a different make of tobacco from Pa's). I would have said that the rooms were entirely masculine in character, but Frank suddenly asked, "What's it like, then, living at Orchard House?" and I found myself answering, "Much like living here." Well, _I_ know what I meant: Orchard House may not smell of brandy and tobacco, and there are no human skulls on any of the mantelpieces, but it has the same dusty, solid, bookish air as a Cambridge college.

Frank took exception to my reply; I suppose he disliked the idea of an all-female establishment bearing any resemblance to his own. I pointed out that I was only answering his question as best I could, and could hardly be held accountable for Miss Greenaway's taste in furnishings, but he folded his arms, jutted his lower lip, and stared from one of his windows, making me wish I'd never come. My brother is the best person in the world, but he is prone to sulks. I expected a lecture on the iniquities of The Feline, and braced myself, but ten minutes went by in which nothing was said at all. (Ten minutes! I am not exaggerating; there was a clock on the wall, directly opposite the sofa.)

When Frank did break the silence, it was to say, musingly: "I don't especially admire her type of beauty, but it's better than nothing. Anything's better than nothing when you're bored."

"Frank, I have no idea what you're talking about. Are we still discussing Orchard House?"

He glanced at me briefly. "You've put me in mind of that little governess of yours."

"Oh, for goodness' sake!" As much as I love my brother, sometimes I hate him.* "Frank, I did not come all the way into town to reminisce about Miss Wilson!"

He pursed his lips again. Rather than risk an entire day of moody silences, I indulged him so far as to ask, "What's wrong with Miss Wilson's 'type of beauty,' anyway?"

You'd think I'd asked an interesting question, judging by the way he stroked his chin and looked up at the sky.

"I mean no offence," he replied, "but she rather resembles you, in the sense—"

"She does <u>not</u> resemble me!" I bounced off the sofa, and he turned in surprise. It seems I've grown taller over the last month (as a result of breakfasting on all those bright-yolked eggs, perhaps) because we were almost eye to eye. Dear diary, <u>you</u> understand why I balked at the comparison. Miss Wilson (whom I objected to having to think about, let alone talk about, let alone distinguish myself from!) is a coarse-skinned, mud-brown-haired nobody, whilst I, however insignificant in every other respect, am widely acknowledged to have inherited my looks from Mamma.

"No, all right," Frank conceded, "I don't mean she looks like you, but you're both . . . you know . . . "Angel in the House" types. Prim facial features, tidy figures, hair nicely pinned."

(I did not <u>want</u> to recall the dishevelled Miss Wilson whom I'd spied, with Frank, on the landing that January night, but she popped into my head regardless.)

"Rather like Mamma," I said.

"Mamma is above criticism."

"As I am not?"

"Certainly you're not; you're my little sister, and don't you forget it. However, in this instance I don't mean to criticise. I'm only saying that my personal preference, as regards types of female beauty, veers towards the Pre-Raphaelite. Does that mean anything to you?"

"Yes . . ." I sounded more certain than I felt. Pa had taken me to art exhibitions on occasion, some of which involved Pre-Raphaelite paintings, but I can't say I'd liked them as much as the horse pictures by George Stubbs. As I recall, the Pre-Raphaelites painted a great many women plucking at lyres, gazing at fruit, drowning in streams, and so forth—all of them looking bored as bored can be. "You mean you like sleepy women who wear their hair down?"

Frank laughed, although I was trying to be accurate rather than funny.

"This is by no means a suitable topic for young mice," he said, sounding more like himself than he had done all morning.

"Just so," I thought, "and I wish to goodness you hadn't brought it up!" However, I didn't say as much: I was too glad of the thaw, and too conscious of our limited time.

"Come along, Miss Mouse," he said, reaching for his hat. "Let's go and have a look around town and make the most of our day."

Frank helped me on with my coat and hat, which was his way of apologising, so I didn't object. Mind, he made a terrible knot of the ribbons under my chin, and I had to redo them as we walked along.

* I ought not to have written that I hate him; I could never hate my brother. Occasionally he irritates me, which is as much my fault as his, no doubt.

I can't remember all the Cambridge landmarks Frank showed me, and even if I could, I'd never do them justice in writing. My knowledge of history and architecture is scant, and my brother's isn't much better, so you'll be better off with a guidebook if you want to know actual facts about the city. I did gather a whole host of impressions, however, and these I have—so to speak—wrapped in tissue paper and tucked away in the recesses of my mind, to be brought out as and when required, such as at night, when I can't sleep and need something nice or curious to think about. For example:

- The age-mellowed red brick of the huge courtyard at St. John's.
- The Backs, with their majestic trees and lawns, and the great college buildings reflected in the river.
- The ceiling in King's College Chapel, like so many fans flicked open and overlapping. How can stone bear such a resemblance to lace? I stared for so long it's a wonder my head didn't snap off my neck; next time I shall take a mirror.
- Two female students! I presume they were students; at any rate they were carrying some hefty books and I heard one of them use the word "jurisprudence" as they went past. They both appeared healthy, and indeed rather lively. Neither was wearing spectacles. I'm glad Frank didn't spot them, because he would have made a caustic remark, and I wouldn't have known what to think or say.

Frank was in a much kinder mood as we made our tour of the city, yet he wasn't himself. Once or twice he declared that he was sick of studying medicine, and that he was going to give it up. When I asked what he'd do instead, he replied, "Run off to Italy, marry a peasant girl, father a dozen children, and become a painter."

My brother doesn't know one end of a paintbrush from the other, so I told myself not to be overly worried. I suspect everyone indulges dreams of escape, don't they, from time to time?

We had luncheon at a tea shop in Trumpington Street, and it was so busy that we had to wait for a table. I felt a good deal more cheerful than I had done in the morning and I was excited, rather than depressed, by the buzz of voices, the scraping of chairs, the jangle of the bell on the door, and the clatter of crockery and tills. The waiters wove between tightly packed tables and brought us cakes on a tiered stand with tea.

"I'd eat like this every day, if I could," I said, as I bit into my second jam tart and Frank filled his plate with plenty of everything. He affects to prefer manly food, like chops and beefsteaks and so forth, but truth be told, he's partial to a cake stand.

"The Feline not feeding you properly?"

"Oh, yes! She makes lovely meals." I started to tell him about the creamy milk, and the eggs with yolks like rising suns, but he made a great show of apathy, leaning back in his chair, munching pensively on an éclair, studying our fellow diners, until I trailed off. It was the second time we'd touched on The Dreaded Subject of Miss Greenaway and shied away.

Just as I was racking my brains for a more promising topic of conversation, Frank leaned across the table, nearly landing his chin in a cream horn. "There!" he whispered. "Over there! Don't turn round now, but there's a Pre-Raphaelite stunner in the corner by the window. A little older than my ideal, but a stunner all right; just the sort of thing I meant."

I took a slow sip of tea, placed my cup on its saucer, and turned my head. There were any number of women in the shop, but they all had their hair respectably pinned beneath hats, as far as I could see, and none was plucking languorously on a lyre. I gave a start when I spotted Miss Greenaway sitting by the window among friends, her face bright with amusement. She hadn't noticed me. There were six of them, squashed together at a table meant for four, in animated conversation as they waited for their order to arrive.

"Yes, yes, that's the one!" Frank had followed the direction of my stare. "The dark-haired one. Quite the Rossetti, wouldn't you say? That heavy mouth . . . Turn back round, Maude, or she'll catch you staring."

I did turn round, and ate a whole piece of cake without registering what it was.

"Your face is red," said Frank. "It's too hot and crowded in this wretched place. Let's polish off these last éclairs and get out in the fresh air. I'll take you on the river, if you like; I promised I would, didn't I?"

I ought to have told him, "That's not some 'Pre-Raphaelite stunner'; it's Miss Greenaway." I really, truly ought. A part of me wanted to, but Frank was rattling on so, about the cost of hiring boats and whether the weather would hold, that the moment passed.

I glanced over my shoulder as we left the tea shop, to ensure we weren't being followed. It would be just like Miss Greenaway to run after us, and introduce herself to Frank, and slip me an extra shilling for my pocket money. She didn't come, however, and Frank made no further mention of his "stunner." Really, there is no reason why the two of them should ever meet, in which case this curious mix-up will not matter.

It had rained while we were in the tea shop, but the sun came out as we neared the river, and the wet pavements shone. Frank gave me his arm, and I grew calmer. I half persuaded myself that it might not matter much if they did meet. There would be some embarrassment involved for Frank, but only a little, and only I would know about it.

The rowing boat wobbled as the boat-hire man handed me aboard, and it wobbled again when Frank leapt in and fitted the oars into the rowlocks. The water was thick and green, like pea soup, and I didn't dare ask how deep it was, for fear of the answer. The man pushed us away with his foot, and we glided into the river.

"To Grantchester, then?" said Frank, subduing the oars into a rhythmic dip and pull.

"Grantchester . . . yes."

I thought of trailing my fingers in the water, but it was too clouded, and I was afraid of what might lurk beneath. A swan paddled alongside us, followed by two cygnets, its fierce beak on a level with my face.

I studied my brother's expression before I spoke again.

"Frank? May I talk to you now about . . . about Orchard House?"

He read my hesitation correctly.

"I think you mean 'about The Feline,' don't you?"

"About Miss Greenaway."

Frank rowed on in leisurely fashion. I counted two strokes, three strokes, and took it for permission to speak, but just as I was drawing breath, my brother got in first.

"Listen, Maude. Let me tell you a thing or two regarding Miss Greenaway."

I suppose I should have been grateful that he kept his temper and used her proper name, but I shuddered like a cat when someone strokes its fur in the wrong direction.

"Oh, yes," I said. "Do please tell me all about her; you must understand her so well, having never met her." My sarcasm was wasted on Frank. He continued to row upstream, as placid as the swan.

"You know the Greek myths, don't you?" he asked. "You know the tale of Odysseus and the sirens?"

"Vaguely." I had a confused picture of mermaids and shipwrecks in my head, but I'd forgotten how the story went.

"All right. Well, when you get back to Orchard House I suggest you look it up, and as you read, remember this: the sirens represent The Feline, and the doomed sailors represent Pa."

"The doomed sailors . . ."

"Exactly so. That's my final word on the subject of that woman, and it's all you need to know."

The swan eyed me malevolently, and I eyed it right back. I couldn't look Frank in the face while I replied, in case I gave in to impulse and pulled his nose. My voice shook—that's how angry I was.

"You think you're so grown up and mysterious, Frank, but you're not as clever as you think, and you don't need to turn real life into Greek myths out of some foolish desire to protect me!"

It was frightening, the feeling that if I didn't press down hard on the monster inside myself, there was no knowing what it might do. It might scream and roar. It might lash out. It might have us both in the river. In all my life, up until now, I'd only ever been playfully cross with Frank.

"Anyway," I went on, "I do know why you hate Miss Greenaway. It's because Pa loved her more than he loved Mamma."

Ha! That gave him pause! His whole face fell slack. They (by whom I mean not only my brother but The Relatives) thought they'd flummoxed me, little baby Maude, with their winks and nudges, and their coded words.

"Well?" Frank recovered himself hastily. "Isn't that reason enough to hate her?"

"It's not Miss Greenaway's fault if somebody loves her who shouldn't."

"It is her fault if she encourages it. It is her fault, if she loves that somebody back."

"And why should she not love Pa? You and I loved him, and she knew him ever so much longer than we did."

I know it's a naive argument, but I think there is some truth in it too. Frank smirked, of course, and said, "What a child you are."

The sky had been darkening in unison with our quarrel, and now another shower arrived, freckling the surface of the river. Frank tugged roughly at the oars and manoeuvred the boat into the shade of a willow tree, but not before we'd got a thorough soaking. My hat was heavy and limp on my head, and when I removed it I discovered that the dye had started to run. (It was the pale straw bonnet I bought last summer, which I coloured black when Pa died. So far, I've only ever worn it in fine weather.) Amidst the confusion of my thoughts, I was conscious of an urgent longing to go home, but when I asked myself what I meant by "home," I discovered it was neither 17 Erskine Place nor Orchard House. "Home" was an unreal picture in my mind's eye, which embraced Pa, Miss Greenaway, a bright fireside, a set of Dickens novels, and all the cats I've ever known and loved.

"I'm not a child," I said, as we sheltered among the shivering fronds of willow. Frank wedged the boat among the reeds, so that we couldn't drift off without shoving the oar against the bank.

"Oh well, you're bound to say that. You've been telling me you're not a child ever since you were old enough to talk."

"No, but Frank, I do understand the sort of love you mean. I know Pa didn't feel for Miss Greenaway in the same way he felt for us."

"I'll say!" He raised his eyebrows at some imaginary interlocutor. James Hartwell, perhaps, or another of his friends, and I saw them all laughing, later on this evening, at Frank's account of our conversation. My blood, which had lowered to a simmer, rolled back to the boil. What was it he'd told me, not so long ago, in one of his letters? "Henry Simpson says you are a comic genius and one of the other fellows thinks I ought to put you on the stage."

~~I blush to~~

~~The unforgivable things I said next~~

~~I don't know what came over~~

I will tell you what I said next, without commentary, for better or worse. I know I behaved shockingly, but I'm not sure what to think about it: whether to justify myself, or make excuses, or wallow in remorse. Doubtless I shall regret committing it to the page, just as I've regretted previous diary entries, but the urge to confess is irresistible.

"Why shouldn't Pa enjoy a love like that?" I demanded of Frank. "Other men do."

"Yes, but, forgive me, are they not encouraged to enjoy it with their lawful wedded wives?"

"Oh, but Pa's lawful wedded wife was Mamma, which is as much as to say he was married to a stone. A stone angel, no doubt, but still a stone."

"Maude!"

"It's all very well for you; you were her darling boy; you could do no wrong. You never suffered from her . . . from her perfection."

Frank spluttered.

"Her perfection? How can one suffer from another person's perfection?"

"One can, when that perfection is lofty and loveless! You wouldn't know, Frank; you were never made wretched for accidentally using a vulgar word, or wiping your nose on your hand. You were never sneered at, or locked in the coal cellar . . ."

"Maude!" Frank raised his voice above the seething rain, but I went on:

"You never felt it, but I did, and Pa did, and meanwhile Miss Greenaway was loving him with all the warmth—"

"Stop! Maude! No more!"

Frank's tone checked my flow of words. He sounded as if he was going to cry. I wrapped my arms around my legs and buried my face into my knees, and when I tried to say "I'm sorry," it came out as a moan.

If I'd blurted everything silently, to myself, it would have been bad enough, but to say these things out loud, to Frank . . . I thought of the punishing dreams in store for me; of Mamma coming to my bedside dressed in white, with her angel's wings, and the soil beneath her fingernails.

We never did reach Grantchester. The showery weather made a plausible excuse for the boat-hire man, and we were wet and chilled, but that wasn't the real reason we returned early. Our hearts weren't in it anymore.

Oddly enough, as soon as Frank said, "No more!" and I tried to say "Sorry," our anger dwindled to nothing. Frank even asked me if I was all right, and put his coat round my shoulders, saying he didn't need it while he was rowing. (The coat in question was sweat-soaked, rain-soaked, and altogether unpleasant, but I appreciated the tenderness of the gesture.) Instead of being angry, we grew careful and withdrawn, and if we talked at all it was about neutral matters. Sometimes I felt sure Frank was pondering the accusations I'd hurled at Mamma, and I felt a strange, you might say perverse, pride in the idea of my brother taking me seriously. He never actually voiced his thoughts, however, so I may be mistaken.

During a broken exchange about the novels of Mr. Disraeli (none of which I've read), I said, "Frank? I want you to know that I do love Mamma very dearly."

"Yes, yes." He turned his face away, as if he needed to keep an urgent eye on the ribbon of weed dripping from his right-hand oar. I'm sure he only said "Yes, yes," in order to move me off the topic, and not because he believed me. He thought I was trying to restore his peace of mind and placate any eavesdropping ghosts.

There is only one train to Sawyer's Fen after four o'clock on Saturdays, so I had little hope of catching a different one from Miss Greenaway, unless she'd cut her day very short indeed. Even so, it was not inevitable that she and Frank would come face to face, and I blame myself for the fact that they did. I was so patently eager to shake him off and send him back to college that he grew suspicious, thinking I planned to miss the train on purpose, and insisted on coming into the station to wave me off.

"Poor Mousey," he said. "I'm sorry we have to part, but really, we must. I can't have a girl in my rooms overnight, even if she is my sister."

I made no answer because at that moment I spotted Miss Greenaway, and she spotted me.

Her face lit up and she managed to wave, despite an armful of parcels. My face did not light up in response, nor did I wave, and she noticed that. Then she noticed Frank. She hesitated for a fraction of a second, before hastening towards us through the crowded ticket hall.

"Maude!" She kissed me on the cheek. "I see the rain caught you out—I should have armed you with an umbrella—but I trust you've had a lovely day, all the same. This must be Francis?" (Offering her hand to Frank.) "Pleased to meet you at last."

I was standing alongside my brother, so I couldn't see his face without turning round and making a show of my curiosity. There was an awkward moment when he neither took her hand nor spoke, followed by an almost equally awkward moment when he did take her hand but remained silent. It suddenly occurred to me that he might be feeling, among other things, confused—after all, as far as he was concerned, this was the "stunner" from the tea shop—so I glared at the ground and muttered, "It's Miss Greenaway."

Frank retrieved his hand, although not, thank goodness, in the rude, snatching way I'd feared.

"Miss Greenaway," he echoed.

If she was embarrassed by his manner (the manner of a person suffering symptoms of concussion), she didn't show it but asked cordially about his studies, and his college life, and how he liked Cambridge. To my brother's credit answered all her questions, albeit briefly, and the encounter did not deteriorate into A Scene. I know he was blushing, though; I could feel it like the glow from a hot coal. Frank, like me, is a great one for turning red at the least little thing.

Miss Greenaway glanced at the station clock and exclaimed, "Look at the time!" at which we hurried out of the ticket hall and onto the platform.

"Francis?" she shouted over the hiss of the engine. "You must come and see us at Sawyer's Fen. We'd love that, wouldn't we, Maude? Come next Saturday, if you're free, and stay for the day!"

Given all the hullabaloo, it's my belief that this proposal did not absolutely demand an answer. The engine whooshed and whistled; carriage doors slammed all along the train; Frank could, so easily, have let it drop. Instead, he shouted back: "Very well, I will! I'll come on the early train!"

Why did he have to sound so belligerent, the silly boy, as if Miss Greenaway had issued a challenge, rather than an invitation? It crossed my mind that he'd agreed to come, against his better judgement, because next Saturday is my fourteenth birthday, but on reflection this seems unlikely. Frank never remembers my birthday, even at the best of times, and he and I are not living through the best of times.

The rest of the day was pleasant, a hot bath, dry clothes, supper with Miss G., bed and a book, but not sufficiently interesting to be recorded in detail.

Monday, 24 April, 1876

I knew I'd be punished with horrible dreams, but I didn't expect them to be this bad. I anticipated visions of a wrathful Mamma, accusing me of all manner of crimes (namely: describing my own mother as a stone, condoning Pa's sin against marriage, and quarrelling in a public place with dye dripping off my hat), but it's worse than that. Last night and the night before, I experienced . . . how to describe it? . . . something more real than a vision. It was as if Mamma's sorrow had come to life, climbed into bed, and lain down beside me in the dark.

I suppose it was a dream, although the scenery was my bedroom, so it's hard to say. My pillow seemed to be sloping oddly, as if someone else's head were pressing down behind mine, and I felt cold breath on my neck, and a clinging arm around my waist. Very well: you will tell me that my pillow needed plumping, that there was a draught, that my bedclothes were awry, that I'd been worrying over the things I said to Frank . . . and that everything conjoined in a nightmare. Perhaps. Oh, but the sadness! The sadness was real and heavy, as if that ghostly arm had stolen inside my rib cage, plucked out my heart, and replaced it with a rock.

"Mamma!" I pleaded into the darkness, but I don't think she heard. Or perhaps she did, but my appeal left her cold.

Tuesday, 25 April, 1876

The same thing happened last night, only I must have screamed for help in my sleep because Miss Greenaway burst in, wielding a lighted candle and a small ivory shoehorn, shouting, "It's all right, Maude!" and "Lay your hands off her this instant!" and "I'm carrying a gun!"

It was all very confusing until we managed to establish that there were no housebreakers in my room, and that I'd merely (merely!) been dreaming. Miss Greenaway collapsed onto my bed with a laugh, and I tried to join in, but couldn't. Despite her amusement, which I believe was genuine, Miss Greenaway's legs were trembling. I could feel them through the mattress.

"I'm sorry you had a bad dream," she said, wiping her eyes.

"It wasn't a dream," I replied. "It was real."

"Oh?"

"I don't mean 'real' in the way a burglar is real . . ."

If Mamma's spirit was watching and listening from a dark corner of the room, then confiding in Miss G. was the last thing I ought to do. I knew it, but I kept talking. Truth be told, I didn't want Miss Greenaway to leave just yet.

"There was a person in my room. I don't mean a man, I mean . . . I mean someone I used to know. A ghost."

Miss Greenaway took my hand. The candlelight turned her skin to gold, and her hair was blacker than ever by comparison.

"Someone you loved?"

"Someone I . . . yes."

"Well . . ." She took a deep breath, and I expected her to tell me that there were no such things as ghosts. What she actually said was: "Perhaps the ghost doesn't mean to frighten you. Have you thought of that?"

"But . . ."

"If *I* were a ghost, and took it into my head to visit someone I loved, I'd want that person to be glad. I'd want them to sit with me all night long, and tell me what's happening in their world, and then I'd tell them what it's like being dead. We'd have the most marvellous chat, and when morning came we'd be sorry to part."

I smiled faintly.

"But Miss Greenaway, what if you were a ghost and the person you used to love, who used to love you, had done something terrible, deserving of punishment? Perhaps they'd been vulgar, or disloyal, or cruel. Wouldn't you make yourself as frightening as possible, so as to put them in their place?"

Miss Greenaway squeezed my hand.

"I don't believe you are really a cruel person, Maude."

"But just supposing . . . ?"

She lowered her eyes and meditated on my hand again. I'd say she was like a fortune teller, only she was reading my knuckles instead of my palm.

"Maude, if I were a ghost, I do believe I'd forgive the people who'd hurt me. I simply couldn't be doing with petty resentments once I was dead, could you? They'd be among the first things I'd rejoice to give up, along with worrying about bills and darning stockings."

I smiled, so as not to hurt her feelings, but after she'd kissed me goodnight and gone away the lightness went too. She was trying to be kind, but I'd rather she understood what I meant.

Wednesday, 26 April, 1876

Dear diary, you will scarcely believe what happened today. As if the nightmares weren't sufficient proof, now I know I am a creature of ill omen. I'm like the raven from Edgar Allan Poe's poem, and all the more unsettling for inhabiting the form of a golden-haired girl.

Up until yesterday, the year 1876 had entailed the deaths of two people intimately related to me (three, if you count Ebenezer), but I'd never actually witnessed anyone breathe their last breath. Pa died away from home; Mamma during the night; Ebenezer . . . who knows what became of Ebenezer, except the odious Miss Wilson? Today, though, shortly before lunchtime, I saw death happen. I was there. Can you imagine?

An electric thrill goes through me now, when I say the name "Mrs. Potter."

The effect is even more pronounced when I write it.

Mrs. Potter.

Mrs. Potter.

Mrs. Potter.

I was in the study when I heard her cry out. She'd been bed-bound for a couple of days, and knowing how much she disliked me, and not knowing how to talk to her, I'd avoided her in all that time. Doubtless I ought to have rushed upstairs when I heard her cry, but I thought Miss Greenaway was in earshot.

I meandered around the shelves, flipping through various books, while Mrs. Potter shouted out three times, in a tone of ever-increasing urgency. When the noise came for the fourth time, I returned my present volume to the shelf and went to the window. Miss Greenaway was at the other end of the garden, strolling around the flower beds, steam trailing from her coffee cup. She drinks it thick and black—disgustingly so, in fact—and she likes to drift away with her thoughts while she sips. It's my belief she prefers to be left alone with her late-morning coffee, though she's never said as much.

When Mrs. Potter cried out a fifth time, I accepted my duty to act. It wasn't merely the number of times she'd called that prompted me in the end, but the sound that was coming from her mouth: neither "Kitty" nor "Help!" nor any proper word. I hardly know how to describe the sound: I have considered the words "howl" and "groan" and "wail," but although they are not quite wrong, they are not quite right either.

I ought to have fetched Miss Greenaway at once, and I wish to goodness I had, but she looked so tranquil, brushing through the long grass with her deep thoughts and her coffee, that I traipsed upstairs in her stead. It wasn't Mrs. P.'s sharp tongue I feared, since she's been taken so poorly she's said little to either of us, and least of all to me. I was much more anxious that she'd demand something horrible of me (i.e., the kind of intimate task required of a nurse).

As soon as I poked my head round the door, the word "death" occurred to me so clearly, I almost said it out loud. (I assure you, however, I did not; I may be tactless on occasion, but I am not as bad as all that.) Mrs. Potter was changed in some mysterious way since I last saw her. Was it the fishy quality of her skin, or the way her lungs wheezed like a broken accordion? But these symptoms had become commonplace over the last couple of weeks. It might have been the slackness of her posture, the way she lolled, like the marionette Pa gave me one Christmas, whose strings I cut, because I wanted it for a doll. I don't know. Perhaps it was something altogether more mystical.

I had mustered a few conversational openings as I was climbing the stairs, but they deserted me the moment I saw her. (If "Death" would have counted as a tactless exclamation, then so too, in its own way, would, "How are you, Mrs. P.?") I approached the bed, staring, but before I could turn and run, she'd got hold of my wrist.

"Oh, do let me go!" I stammered. "I ought to fetch Miss Greenaway."

Mrs. Potter did not turn her head at the sound of my voice. Her eyes were open, but unseeing. Only her lips and tongue were working, twisting, yearning to form words.

I waited.

"Don't trust her," she managed, eventually. "Not one inch. She'll . . . she'll . . . do for you."

I shivered as surely as if someone had touched my neck with a cold blade and glanced round, half expecting to see Death himself at the door, scythe in hand. (If it had been midnight, rather than midday, you may be sure I wouldn't have dared look.) There was no one there, however, and through the open window I could hear birdsong filling the trees, and a cart clattering along the lane.

"Surely . . ." My normal voice was too loud for the listening house, so I lowered it to a whisper. "Surely I can trust Miss Greenaway?"

~~Then she died~~

I don't know when Mrs. Potter died; there wasn't a clear-cut moment. I stood at the bedside for a while, waiting for her reply, surprised by the strength of her grasp. Gradually it occurred to me that her hand was not imbued with strength so much as weight, and I wriggled free, upon which it dropped like a stone to the quilt. I noticed her eyes, too: earlier, they'd seemed fixed on scenes from a distant world, and now they were fixed on nothing at all. How strange, the minute degree of difference, in hands, in eyes, in the lines of the body, that told me she'd changed from a dying old woman to a dead one.

I observed all these things in the split second before I ran to tell Miss Greenaway. Afterwards, I wondered whether I should have tried to close Mrs. Potter's eyes, but I was glad I hadn't thought of it. While she was dying I felt sorry for her because she was so ugly,* but once she was dead I felt terribly respectful and afraid, and the idea of touching her corpse was unbearable.

* I hope I'm still young and beautiful when I'm on my deathbed, with lots of people looking at me tenderly and weeping their hearts out. Most people would prefer to live to a ripe old age, but I am not most people, and I think there are worse things than dying in one's prime.

Breaking the news of a death is exciting, as well as sad. I know it's wrong to admit that, but it's true, and I felt superior to my usual self as I ran across the grass shouting, "Miss Greenaway! Oh, Miss Greenaway, come at once!"

Miss Greenaway did not drop her coffee cup, or faint away in the flower beds, when I told her what had happened. She hurried back to the house with me, but it was a businesslike hurry, not a hysterical one.

"Did she say anything at the end?" That was her only question, and I answered, "No." It was a lie, but I justified it on the grounds that Mrs. Potter would not wish to be remembered by Miss Greenaway for a few confused mumblings.

The rest of the day was spent on an endless series of practical tasks: the doctor, the vicar, and the undertaker were sent for and received; letters were written and posted; food was eaten on the move; endless cups of tea were poured and neglected.

All day long, Miss Greenaway was remarkably composed. She never shed a tear, and when Reverend Banks made a mild witticism, she smiled. I'm not even referring to one of those sad smiles, which are almost as ladylike as tears, but a real one that showed her teeth.

Thursday, 27 April, 1876

I ought to have guessed it was only the daylight that kept Miss Greenaway going. During the night, when I was drowsing and warding off dreams, I heard someone moving about the house. At one point the someone approached my door, and my skin prickled, but the footsteps were too rapid and heavy to belong to a ghost. (To any ghost, but least of all Mamma's.)

As soon as I was fully awake, I realised who it must be, so I lit my candle and went to find her. She was sitting on the stairs, sobbing with her face in her hands. By the sound of it, and from what I could see of her slippery fingers and face, they were not genteel, Mamma-like tears, to be dabbed away on the corner of a handkerchief. They were Maude-like tears, and I ought to have been disgusted by such an exhibition, but funnily enough I felt softened. I sat down on the stairs and put my arm round her, and I didn't mind when she leaned her heavy head on my shoulder, even though her hair tickled my nose.

"I know she was old," Miss Greenaway explained between racking hiccoughs, "and it wasn't unexpected, but she's been my friend for as long as I can remember. She nursed me when I was a baby, and kept house, first for my grandparents and then for me, and I loved her."

Since she seemed to want to talk, I came up with a few sympathetic questions, such as "Did she always live with you at Orchard House?" (yes, always) and "Was there a Mr. Potter?" (no, she never married, "Mrs." was an honorary designation). Partly because Miss Greenaway seized on my interest so eagerly, and partly because her posture was shrunken and stooped, it felt as though we'd switched roles: that she was now the child and I the grown-up.

I waited until she was calm before offering a handkerchief (yes! I, Maude the Unprepared, had a clean handkerchief in the cuff of my nightgown!), with which she mopped her face and blew her nose.

"Now then," I said, consciously mimicking Cook's manner whenever I was sick or upset. "A cup of hot milk and a good sleep, and everything will look better in the morning." I barely refrained from calling her "young miss."

The range had gone out, so we made do with cold milk and oat biscuits, but it was still pleasant to serve things nicely in matching cups and saucers, and to see how meekly she ate and drank. "Thank you, Maude," she said, more than once. "This is very kind of you. I'm sorry for spoiling your sleep."

It's nice to be in charge of someone. Of course, it's not an entirely novel experience, since I'm used to looking after the kittens, but they don't make me feel important in quite the same way.

When she was in bed, I plumped her pillows and arranged her blankets, promising to stay until she was asleep.

After a while she dozed, but I stayed on. The window was ajar and there was a chill in the leaf-scented air, warning of rain. I wrapped myself up in Miss Greenaway's shawl, but it was a square of light, summery cotton, and no use to my icy feet. The grandfather clock struck one, and I thought of my own cold bed.

Finally, I climbed under her covers too, as cautious as could be for fear of waking her. I nodded off, huddled inside the curl of her body, and dreamed a happy dream that I can't, for the life of me, recall.

Miss Greenaway is terribly striking in her black dress, like Mary Queen of Scots, or Dido, or some other tragic figure. When she came into the kitchen for breakfast, I remarked, "Oh! You are wearing black for Mrs. Potter!", as much as to say, "You didn't wear it for Pa."

"I'm wearing it because it suits my mood," she replied sleepily, spooning tea into the pot. "Not in deference to convention."

This sounds simple, but if you think about it properly, you will see how impossibly muddling it is. I keep asking myself whether her attitude is

a) excessively nonchalant, because surely "black clothes for mourning" is a law of nature rather than a convention? Certainly it is not a question of mood. Or,
b) excessively fastidious, because nobody goes into mourning for a servant. Therefore,
c) why were my instincts offended on Pa's behalf? If no decent woman goes into mourning for a servant, still less does she do so for an unrelated man who is married to another.

Rather than confess these difficulties I drank my tea and said, "Black suits you," which indeed it does.

Friday, 28 April, 1876

Miss Greenaway wore light blue today and I made no remark, even to myself.

Saturday, 29 April, 1876

As I was getting up I heard the morning train pull into Sawyer's Fen, and noticed its white plume over the treetops, but thought nothing of it. The spectacle of Mr. Stirling striding along the lane was much more interesting, especially when he turned in at our gate. He was relatively well dressed today (i.e., at the gentleman-farmer end of the spectrum, as opposed to the hired-labourer end) and carrying a bunch of purple flowers.

I was still fastening the buttons on my bodice as I ran downstairs to warn Miss Greenaway, but she must have spotted his approach through the study window, because she was already opening the front door. She was in black again. I lurked on the stairs where he couldn't see me.

"Kitty, I'm so sorry." Mr. Stirling began speaking before the door was fully open. His voice is usually deep and rough, but he'd gentled it to suit the occasion.

Miss Greenaway was curt. "Sorry for your behaviour on Easter Sunday?"

"Sorry for your loss," he clarified. "But sorry for that too. I've been a fool."

"A very great fool," she agreed, and although her tone had not yet softened, I could tell she was on the brink. The flowers rustled as they changed hands, and she said a clipped "Thank you." I'm certain she was about to ask him in, when the latch clicked on the garden gate and a familiar voice rang out: "This is Orchard House, isn't it? And I've got the right day?"

I leapt down the stairs and rounded the corner into the hall. Miss Greenaway and Mr. Stirling were framed in the doorway like figures in a picture: she with her bouquet, he with his head bowed and his hat in his hands. Both squinted into the sunshine as Frank came sauntering up the garden path. My brother had acquired a silver-topped cane, although he carried it tucked up under his arm and seemed to be walking well enough without it. His crimson waistcoat was also new.

Halfway across the garden Frank paused and tapped the silver knob against his chin. I wanted to rush out and rearrange him; to urge him to stop acting like a player in a third-rate melodrama. Why wasn't he being himself? I could have shaken him when he exclaimed, "But I am interrupting a tête-à-tête! I fear the presence of a third party is unwelcome!" If he had prefaced it with, "Behold!" or "Alas and alack!" or "Zounds!" it would have been perfectly in keeping with his manner.

Miss Greenaway and Mr. Stirling regarded him blankly. I rushed between them, into the garden.

"Frank! I had quite forgotten you were coming today. We've had such a dreadful week."

I flung my arms around his neck, as if I'd joined him on stage, before seizing the silver-topped cane with a playful air I didn't feel.

"You look quite the dandy!" I cried. "What's this new affectation? A walking stick?"

He seized it back without answering, and it crossed my mind to wonder what sort of play this was.

Miss Greenaway rubbed her forehead and said, "Francis . . . Frank . . . you'll have to forgive us, we're at sixes and sevens this week."

After that, nobody seemed capable of doing anything in the right way. It was as though every member of the cast had forgotten their lines, and begun to improvise desperately. Mr. Stirling seemed disproportionately embarrassed after he introduced himself to Frank, and Frank reminded him they'd already met. Miss Greenaway tried to tell my brother what had happened since we saw him last Saturday, but he only understood that a servant had died ("Deuced inconvenient!") and failed to grasp the central fact that Mrs. Potter's death was a matter of genuine grief. Meanwhile I hopped from foot to foot, desperate for Mr. Stirling to pipe down, and for Frank to like Miss Greenaway, and for Miss Greenaway to forgive Frank's tactlessness, and for everyone to understand everyone else in a proper light.

"I think it's time I wished you all a good day," said Mr. Stirling, breaking through the confusion at last.

Miss Greenaway nodded distractedly.

There was a scattering of purple petals around her feet, because she had been plucking at the flowers while we talked, and half the stalks were bare. If I hadn't disliked Mr. Stirling so much, I'd have felt sorry for him. He whistled for Scout, who was waiting obediently by the gate, and walked away.

Miss Greenaway ushered us all indoors, and as we were entering the parlour, Frank said, "He's a good friend of yours, is he? This 'Stirling'?"

"A fair-weather friend," she replied, with an uncharacteristic lack of logic or justice, which I declined to draw attention to. Far be it from me to defend Robert Stirling.

"No," she added a moment later, as I'd half suspected she would, "that was a shabby thing to say." She gestured for Frank to take the armchair and sat beside me on the sofa. "Robert is a good friend, and I'm out of sorts. Everything's been upside down this week, and that includes my humour. I haven't even offered you any tea."

Having observed the omission, Miss Greenaway did nothing to rectify it, which is quite funny when you think about it, although at the time it didn't seem right to laugh. Frank sprawled amongst the velvet cushions like a man of the world, and I'd have said he was entirely at his ease, were it not for the way his fingers kept twiddling and tapping.

"That's quite all right, Kitty," he said. "I'm not in any hurry for tea."

Kitty, indeed! Who did he think he was? Uncle Talbot? I shot my brother a look, but Miss Greenaway seemed unaware that he'd spoken. She was all alone inside herself this morning: a dark woman in a dark dress, full of sad thoughts. If it weren't for Frank's attentive stare, I might have reached for her hand, but under his eyes it would become a bigger gesture than I meant it to be.

The silence stretched. Mrs. Potter's knitting lay on the arm of the sofa—a ball of grey wool, two needles, and a few inches of stocking stitch—and Miss Greenaway took it onto her lap. Frank sprawled and stared. I said, "I must show Frank the kittens!" at which Miss Greenaway smiled vaguely in my direction. Nobody reacted when I cleared my throat. If I were Frank, I would have apologised for coming at such an awkward moment, or asked after our health, or, at the very least, made banal remarks about the weather. I didn't understand him today. I haven't properly understood him since Pa died.

The floor flickered with shadows, as the trees moved in the sunshine. Miss Greenaway sighed. I knew she'd slept badly last night, and wondered whether I ought to say so, but it didn't seem right to conjure an image of her in a nightgown.

"It's my fourteenth birthday today."

Heavens, I only said it for want of anything better! How was I to know it would bring them round? They began talking over one another.

Miss Greenaway: "Are you really? Fourteen today! I ought to have known!"

Frank: "Oh Lord, Mousey, I've forgotten again. I always forget your birthday. It beats me why anyone would choose to be born on such an unmemorable date as the twenty-ninth of the month."

This was better!

"Really, it doesn't matter!"

I was glad to see Miss Greenaway coming out of herself, and Frank behaving somewhat more naturally, but I didn't want either of them to get in a fluster about my birthday. I'm not being martyr-like; I mean it. My previous birthdays felt significant, and I would have been hurt if they'd gone unnoticed, but that was the old time. Everything was different now. What could I possibly desire in the way of gifts? Neither Pa nor Mamma nor Ebenezer would come back to life for the asking, so what was the good of presents and party games?

I tried to express this, and Frank appeared willing to let the matter drop, but Miss Greenaway was less easily appeased.

"Maude, I feel dreadful. The next time I'm in Cambridge I shall buy you a present, and in the meantime you must choose a volume—any one you like—from among my books. And you must have a treat for tea. Let me see, I could try to bake a cake . . ."

I began to protest, but Frank interrupted.

"Maude always has a lemon cake on her birthday."

It wasn't so much what he said, as the way he said it, that made him the very picture of insolence: his long legs stretched out and crossed at the ankles, his arms dangling over the sides of the chair, his head thrown back.

"Not always!" I exclaimed. It's true that I've had a lemon cake for my last two birthdays, but on my eleventh Cook made a ginger cake, and on my tenth she made a cherry cake. I don't remember any further back.

Miss G. (anxiously): "I don't believe I have any lemons."

Frank: "Lemon cake is Maude's birthday tradition."

Me: "No it's not! Oh Frank, stop being silly."

Miss G.: "There's plenty of plum jam in the larder. What about a cake sandwiched with jam?"

Frank: "Oh, I don't think plum jam is really—"

Miss G. (sharply): "Can you bake, Frank?"

Frank: "Can I . . . ?"

Miss G.: "Can you bake? I'm not awfully good at it; Mrs. Potter was the baker in this house. Maude shows promise, she made a batch of scones by herself the other day, but we can hardly expect her to make her own birthday cake."

Frank: "But—"

Miss G.: "Don't you agree?"

Frank: "Well—"

Miss G.: "Really, Frank, a man of science like you ought to be able to concoct a simple cake. I shall help, of course."

Frank (sulkily): "If there aren't any lemons—"

Miss G.: "Perhaps you will teach me how to conjure lemons out of thin air? Or, failing that, we may take a look at the plum jam."

Throughout this exchange, Frank's manner had subtly altered. He began as Mr. Worldly Wiseman, lounging among the cushions, and ended as a chastened, blushing boy sitting forwards in his seat. The silver-topped cane toppled over and rolled beneath the chair, where I hoped it would stay.

"Come along!" Miss Greenaway was inflexible, though not humourless. If she'd been choosing what to wear for that particular moment, I doubt it would have been deep black. When she held out her hand, my brother glanced at it, as if he might like to bite it. I felt myself blush, in anticipation of his rude retort, but he didn't say a word. Of course, he didn't take her outstretched hand either, but he did get to his feet and follow her from the room.

I hardly knew what to do with myself once they'd gone away, not because I minded the solitude but because my nerves were on the rack. How would they—how could they—get along? When I thought of all the terrible things Frank has said about her in the past ("insatiable, flesh-eating cat," etc., etc.), I feared their endeavours in the kitchen were more likely to result in murder than cake.

I took myself off to my bedroom. The upstairs feels heavily silent now that Mrs. Potter is dead. Every time I pass her room I force myself to stop and stare at the door, with my fingers on the handle, and count to ten in my head. By this means I aim to cure myself of the horrors for this particular part of the house. Goodness knows whether it will work, but it's worth a try. It's bad enough having Mamma's ghost slide into bed with me every night; the last thing I need is Mrs. Potter clambering in on the other side and whispering poison in my ear.

Once I'd finished writing up the morning's events, I distracted myself with the cats: Little Nell (no doubt with her sisters' connivance) had set to work unravelling yet another woollen blanket, so I mended it hastily. Once that was done, and my already tidy room was tidied, I could bear the suspense no longer and sidled downstairs.

For some time I sat on the top step, unable to hear anything outside my own drumming fear, but when I finally lifted my head from the protecting circle of my arms, I heard the placid murmur of voices and the rattle of baking tins. I sat still for a while, thinking and listening, and at one point, by some miracle, I caught the sound of my brother's laughter.

The cake was an extravagant triumph, bulging with jam and cream and sugar. I suspect Miss Greenaway had more to do with it than Frank, but it was he who bore it into the parlour when it was ready, his new waistcoat smudged with flour.

It seems perverse in me to have tasted pure happiness, on this birthday of all birthdays, but I can't deny that I did. Not that it lasted all day. I was not in high spirits this morning, when Frank first arrived, or in the evening when my mind was weighed with fresh troubles, but there was an instant, just before I cut the cake, when we all looked at one another, and Frank laughed for no reason, and Miss Greenaway pressed my hand and said, "Happy birthday, Maude," in a certain way she has.

I don't know why that particular moment in time flared up like a tongue of fire, conspicuous among the million moments of light and shade through which I've lived. I can only tell you that it did. Even as it happened I wished I could preserve it, and knew I could not.

Miss Greenaway has given me a book called The Illustrated Greek Myths. I didn't exactly ask for it, that would have been greedy, since it is one of the finest and heaviest volumes in her collection, but she said she noticed the covetous way in which I kept glancing at it, and that I was to consider it mine.

Frank invited himself to stay overnight, since he does not need to be in Cambridge until Monday. I told him he had a cheek; Miss Greenaway said, "You're welcome at Orchard House for as long as you like." Of course I am pleased, only I wish he would mend his manners and stop calling her "Kitty," and I wish he wouldn't laugh at everything she says, even when she's not trying to be funny.

"She will tire of you," I warned, as I was putting sheets on the bed in the spare room. "She will, you know, unless you start treating her like an ordinary human being."

"But she's not an ordinary human being."

I thought about that, as I tugged the cotton covers over the pillows. Of course, in some ways he is right.

"All the same, I think she would appreciate it if you treated her like one."

Frank inspected his waistcoat for any traces of flour, dusted himself down, and said, "Don't you worry your little head, Miss Mouse," which is what he always says when he's tired of my chatter.

Sunday, 30 April, 1876

When Miss Greenaway called us in for supper last night, Frank asked, "Do you take all your meals in the kitchen?" He didn't say it with a sneer, but humorously, as if we were exotic creatures whose manners and customs he found charming. I had forgotten that eating in the kitchen is an odd thing to do, for people of our sort.

"We tend to," Miss Greenaway replied. "It seems pointless laying everything out formally in the dining room, when there's nobody to serve us."

Miss Greenaway once told me that she loves to eat at the bare, scrubbed table in the kitchen, with the stove at her back; apparently it improves the flavour of the food and the conversation. I do know what she means. Even when Pa was at home, there was something about the dining room at 17 Erskine Place, the chill air, the high ceiling, the mahogany table bristling with cutlery, which made me feel as though pleasure was the least of my concerns. I enjoy Miss Greenaway's policy more, but I feel anxious when I remember the sort of person I was brought up to be. Mamma once caught me standing by the fire while I ate a piece of toast, and she said I was a pig, and that I rightly belonged in a sty.

The doorbell rang when we were halfway through our soup, and Miss Greenaway went to answer it. We heard her say something, though we couldn't catch her words, and a masculine voice replied. A moment later she hurried back and lifted her scruffy coat off its hook by the back door.

"Robert Stirling again," she whispered, shrugging on the coat. "I suppose I ought to speak to him. We'll go for a stroll in the garden and he can say what he needs to say there, without bothering you two. Please carry on; I'll finish mine later."

We watched her leave, and I resumed eating, but Frank set his soup spoon down with a clang.

"How uncivil!" he complained.

"Who? Miss Greenaway?"

"Him! This Stirling fellow! Making a social call as we're eating."

"We have allowed it to get rather late," I pointed out. "He probably thought we'd finished."

My sensible suggestion did nothing to appease Frank. He placed his side plate over the top of Miss Greenaway's bowl, to keep the heat in, and stared from it, to the clock, to the door, for a good five minutes. When she still didn't return, he stood up with a "tut" and poured her soup back into the saucepan, before sitting down, picking up his spoon, putting it down again, getting up from the table, and adding his soup to the pan as well.

"Heavens, Frank, don't fuss so! Being at Orchard House is not like being at home. She wouldn't expect you—"

Apparently Frank was indifferent to my opinion of what Miss Greenaway would or would not expect, because he scraped back his chair, threw his napkin down, and stalked off. I folded my own napkin and followed. It didn't seem right to let him wander the house on his own.

I found him in the study, standing by the open window.

"Shall I fetch a light?" I asked, knowing full well that a light was the last thing he'd want. Sure enough he raised his palm for quiet.

Miss Greenaway and Mr. Stirling were crossing the lawn at an idle, conversational pace. It was too dark to tell whether they were arm in arm, but they might have been. Occasional words reached us, as they dawdled among the sketchy shapes of trees and flower beds: I heard "Emily" and "understand" and "in justice to." The sky dropped from one depth of blue to a darker depth, and then a darker still.

I suppressed an urge to enlighten my brother as to the subject of their discussion. No doubt he'd think it hilarious that my ill-advised bragging about Miss Wilson had caused such a furore, and he'd consider it his duty to report the whole sorry saga to his cronies, back at college. I'd never hear the end of it.

Frank said, "You never told me she had a lover on the go." ("On the go"? I did not like that expression, but I was too busy setting facts straight to say so.)

Me: "She doesn't. He isn't."

Frank (gesturing in the direction of the garden): "Well, what do you call that, then?"

I do understand why my brother drew this false conclusion. Of course I do. Everything I've ever gleaned about relations between the sexes (mostly from novels and poetry) has led me—as it has doubtless led him—to understand that a man and woman walking together in close conference, on a balmy summer's evening with a curl of moon in the sky, signifies Romance with a capital "R."

<u>But</u>. But, but, but:

1. *Although they were not conversing loudly, neither had they lowered their voices to that particular degree of softness which would indicate Love.*
2. *Aside from their main topic of conversation, I'm almost certain I heard Mr. Stirling mention that one of his hens had stopped laying. It's difficult to see how anyone could take Maude Gower's Moral Turpitude and The Ailments of Poultry as one's subjects, and be sentimental at the same time.*
3. *Having observed Miss Greenaway and Mr. Stirling together in the past, and knowing what I know about the state of her heart vis-à-vis Pa, I cannot believe a Romance is indicated.*

"I really do think they are friends," I said, "in just the way you and Hartwell are friends, or you and MacLeod."

Frank folded his arms across his chest. When he made no reply, I risked adding, "They quarrelled a few weeks ago. I think Mrs. Potter's death may have put things in a new perspective, and that's why they've decided to let bygones be bygones."

Frank watched them a little longer and drew a breath, as if he was about to speak. I thought we were about to have a proper, confidential talk in the twilight, and I was startled when he turned to me and said, "You really know nothing, do you?"

His scornful tone seemed out of all proportion to anything I'd said, and I didn't see why I should stand for that. I promptly left him and went upstairs, half expecting that he'd run after me and apologise, but he didn't.

Later—much later, after I'd gone to bed and turned off the light—I heard Miss Greenaway say, "Goodnight, Frank," as she crossed the hall, and moments later he came bounding into my bedroom like a puppy, and collapsed across the end of my bed.

"What's happened?" I was glad to see his mood so improved, but I didn't like having my feet crushed.

"What's happened?" he echoed, rolling onto his side and rucking up my blankets. "Nothing has happened and everything has happened."

Sometimes I am in the mood for picking over a riddle, but sometimes they bore me to death. Before I had chance to say so, Miss Greenaway knocked on the door and said, "Goodnight, Maude. Oh, are you there, Frank? Well, goodnight again to you."

I replied in the usual way, but Frank whispered, "Goodnight, goodnight," so softly, she couldn't possibly have heard. I thought it rather rude, but decided to let it pass, since I am tired of being at odds with him.

That was last night; today is Sunday. Frank was supposed to be travelling back to Cambridge today, but at breakfast he announced that the first train tomorrow morning would do just as well. In other words, he has spontaneously expanded a polite visit of several hours into two whole days and nights! I asked what he would do for clean clothes, articles for shaving, etc., pointing out that he was already sprouting a beard, but he stroked his chin and said that he would manage.

"I don't expect you to understand," he added. "You ladies are such complicated creatures; you can't survive half an hour without your paraphernalia."

I bristled. "What paraphernalia?"

Frank waved his toast vaguely. "Oh, you know what I mean . . . your bonnets and crinolines and whatnot."

Miss Greenaway sipped her tea and reached for the newspaper.

"Crinolines!" I snorted. "Who do you know who wears a crinoline? Goodness, Frank, you are ignorant!"

Why did I feel so het up? Why should I care whether or not Frank is up to date in the matter of ladies' fashions? I looked at Miss Greenaway expectantly, as did my brother, and in a moment she glanced up.

"You're welcome to stay another night, Frank," she said, "but bring some luggage next time."

I thought she might have said something playful about our crinolines dispute, but she ignored it altogether and returned to her newspaper. What does this mean? Does it mean she finds us silly, or that she wasn't listening?

Either way, my brother was not discomfited. "Ah ha!" he said. "Next time! And when shall 'next time' be?"

With which, lo and behold, he secured himself an invitation not only for tonight, but for next Friday too!

We spent the rest of the day happily enough. I took Frank for a walk across the fields, to show him the dilapidated house where Pa grew up, although he wasn't as interested in it as I'd have liked. When I said how strange it was to imagine our father roaming these rooms as a boy, Frank said, "Hmm. Poor old Pa, but I can't really picture it, can you? It's just an old ruin."

He's right, in a way. I can't picture it either: with its grass carpets and sky ceilings, the house might have been lifeless for centuries; but at least I regard this as a failure on my part. Frank made it sound like a matter of indifference.

Monday, 1 May, 1876

Frank departed after an early breakfast. As soon as the front door had closed behind him, Miss Greenaway let out a loud sigh, and I turned to her and asked whether or not she'd liked my brother. It was rather direct of me, but I was worried by her sigh, because I didn't know what it implied. She usually encourages questions, but she seemed embarrassed by this one, and she turned away whilst sorting through the newly arrived post.

"Of course!" she said. "Look, here's a letter for you."

I would have been glad to carry the discussion further, but Miss Greenaway retreated to the study with her own letters. I took mine to my bedroom. It turned out to be a species of birthday greeting from one of the aunts—that bringer of joy known to the wider world as Miss Janet Gower:

Dear Maude,

By the time you receive this letter you will have turned fourteen. Over the years, I have not made it my custom to take heed of your birthdays, but the deaths of your parents have sharpened our connection somewhat, and I feel duty-bound to mark this milestone.

I discussed the matter with your aunt Judith last Sunday—she and Talbot having kindly invited me for dinner—and we agreed that we would not give you anything material by way of a gift, since you are well enough provided with worldly things, but would send, instead, a few words of wisdom and sound advice, which will be of more value to a pure-hearted girl than any trinket. For what good will trinkets be, when you stand alone at the dreadful Day of Judgement? Whereas a few choice words from your elders and betters may save you from an eternity of sorrow. I said as much, while Talbot was carving the pork joint, and Judith agreed with me. (Your uncle Talbot had nothing helpful to say, but he has always been prone to flippancy.)

Of course, I have seen the letter you wrote to your aunt Judith in early April. She showed it to me the day after it arrived, and for some time we allowed ourselves to be reassured by your words: after all, it is comforting to know that you are on cordial terms with the vicar of St. Jude's, and that you live quietly at Sawyer's Fen, and that you have been cultivating the memory of your dear mamma by making a portrait of her in watercolours. God would appear to have been kind to you thus far; He has been your rod and your staff as you pass through the valley of the shadow of death (Psalm 23:4).

Nevertheless, I have had several weeks in which to ponder your letter, and I find that my fears, though soothed, are not entirely quashed. What causes me to tremble—and I said as much to your aunt Judith as we started on our sago pudding—is the absolute naivete of your tone. Your manner is not so much courageous as oblivious; you refer to "Orchard House" as if it were an entirely respectable abode; in short, I do not think you recognise the valley of the shadow of death for what it is, even whilst you are walking about in it and making your home there! Now, this may be the result of mere childish ignorance: let us hope so. On the other hand, it may be that Satan is whispering in your ear, urging you to believe that bad is good, and wrong is right, and that the person who shall remain nameless—coarser minds have referred to her as The Feline, but I shall call her The Whited Sepulchre—is deserving of esteem.

Resist! *This is my gift to you, Maude, on your fourteenth birthday: an admonition to resist! Meditate on the image of the whited sepulchre: the burial chamber that is comely and fair without, but hellish within, its air thick and foul with the stench of rotting flesh.*

"But Aunt, she is kind to me!" you will say, and I will ever reply, in the solemn voice of Truth: "She is a whited sepulchre."

It is difficult to prove inward corruption, and you ought not to ask for proof. I tremble at the thought of detailing her crimes, and I cannot open her out and show you the colour of her soul. Nevertheless, you are fourteen years old and on the brink of womanhood, and your aunt Judith and I agree that you may be given a Grain of Evidence for the sake of preserving your innocence.

Well then: if you are ever inclined to doubt my exhortation to Resist, and the blandishments of The Whited Sepulchre become too strong, then OBSERVE HER EFFECT ON MEN. Do members of the stronger sex grow foolish and weak beneath her gaze? Do they smile and laugh when they should be stern? Do they begin to show a preference for sentiment over duty? If the answer to any of these questions is "yes," then, niece, you have your proof.

"Let not thine heart decline to her ways, go not astray in her paths. For she hath cast down many wounded: yea, many strong men have been slain by her. Her house is the way to hell, going down to the chambers of death" (Proverbs 7:25–27).

Your aunt,
Janet Gower

When I went downstairs to begin lessons, Miss Greenaway looked round from the bookshelf and said, "Oh dear. One of the aunts?" It wasn't so much the question that irritated me, as the sympathetic grimace. Aunt Janet is my relation, not Miss Greenaway's, so I'll be the one to make faces when she writes tiresome letters.

"It was a letter from my aunt Janet," I said, and Miss G. seemed to understand that she'd overstepped the mark (she <u>is</u> awfully good at noticing things like that) because she immediately began to talk about what we might study this week, and how there'd be no lessons on Thursday because that was the day of Mrs. P.'s funeral, and the fact that Emily would be resuming her Greek and Latin classes on Monday.

"I hope you don't mind? About Emily, I mean."

"No, I don't mind."

I opened the nearest book and pretended to read, although it turned out to be in Greek. I had said I didn't mind, and it might have been true. How could I tell? I was depressed in such a general way that it seemed unfair to pin all the blame on Emily.

Miss Greenaway studied me thoughtfully. "I was going to suggest a debate of some sort," she said. "Politics, or ethics . . . I hadn't decided. I don't think you're in the mood for talking, though. Am I right?"

I shrugged.

"Very well then. Why not spend some time with your new Greek myths book? Have a browse through the stories, and when you're tired of reading, put the book aside and write out your favourite one, in your own words, with all the descriptive power you can muster. Will you do that?"

I nodded.

"Does it sound like a congenial way to spend the morning?"

I nodded again.

"Good." She pulled her fingertip along the bookshelf, making a line in the dust. "I shall condemn myself to a few hours of housework before lunch. Poor old me. The place will go to the dogs without Mrs. Potter pottering about, poking at things with her duster."

I found it difficult to concentrate on the Greek myths, what with Miss Greenaway's broom knocking against the hall skirting boards, and the feather duster rattling between the banisters, and Aunt Janet's letter echoing round my head. Perhaps it was because of the letter that I remembered Frank's reference to Odysseus and the sirens, when we were in our Cambridge rowing boat, so I chose that one.

The sirens: alluring bird-women whose songs lure sailors to their deaths. Odysseus: the hero who lashes himself to the mast so that he may listen in safety as the ship sails by.

"Look it up," Frank had said, "and as you read, remember this: the sirens represent The Feline, and the doomed sailors represent Pa."

Of course, that was before Frank knew Miss Greenaway; he may have changed his views now that he's met her.

Or maybe he thinks he's Odysseus?

Tuesday, 2 May, 1876

I have just reread yesterday's entry. What a dreadful mood I was in!

Today was much better. I helped Miss Greenaway clean the parlour, because she is expecting guests after Mrs. Potter's funeral on Thursday. I asked whether she required me to attend the service itself, and she replied, "Naturally, you are welcome to come, but I don't require it. You must do whatever you wish." This was a great relief, and I told her I would stay at home. A coffin being lowered into a hole and showered with clods of earth is a sight I never wish to see.

It took us a long time to clean the parlour. There were cobwebs on the cornice and along the curtain rails, which Mrs. Potter hadn't been able to reach for a long time, and the hearth was sootier than it should have been. What a dreadful substance soot is! It rises in great, greasy clouds when you brush it, and settles on everything.

Afterwards we had a short mathematics lesson and made a shopping list for Thursday's "party." For supper I made Welsh rarebit all by myself, following a recipe in Mrs. Beeton's Book of Household Management. Miss Greenaway pronounced it delicious and, I must admit, it was.

Thursday, 4 May, 1876

Apparently my brother did not think it necessary to warn anyone of his intention to attend Mrs. Potter's funeral, so he caught me by surprise when I went to answer the door this afternoon. He has bought himself a new valise, and yet more new clothes—a glossy top hat and a black silk cravat—which is strange on several counts, not least the fact that neither of us is well off.

"Frank! What are you doing here?"

"That's a nice way to say hello!"

I began protesting that I hadn't meant to sound unfriendly, but he interrupted.

"Never mind all that, where's Kitty?"

He barged past me and began prying through the downstairs rooms, as if she was likely to be hiding beneath a table or behind a door.

"Miss Greenaway has gone to Mrs. Potter's funeral," I replied. "I should think the service will be starting in a few minutes, if it hasn't started by now."

"She's already at church?" He wheeled round. "Why, what's the time? It's not half past . . . Oh, dash it, Maude!" I thought he was going to illustrate his feelings by dashing his hat on the floor, but he seemed to remember its brand-newness in time, and forbore. "I knew I should have caught the earlier train! Damn, damn, damn!"

I wanted to know why on earth he was here, in such a state, and shouldn't he be in lectures, and had he told Miss G. he was coming, but I knew better than to ask. He wouldn't give straight answers until he'd been soothed.

"It doesn't matter, does it? You can wait here until they come back, and in the meantime I'll make you a cup of tea and we can make believe it's our house, and we're—"

"Which way is the church?" Frank interrupted, slamming his hat back on his head.

"Oh, but—"

"If I run all the way—"

"If you run all the way you'll arrive red-faced and panting, and the congregation will take you for the lunatic that I begin to fear you are."

My brother did not hear the second half of my speech, for he was already halfway across the garden.

"Which way?" he called from the gate, and as tempting as it was to send him left into the deepest, darkest countryside, I answered, "Right at the end of the lane and straight on for a mile."

I'd been having such a peaceful time of it, before Frank came: setting out plates and teacups in the parlour and tending to the fire. Once he'd gone I would have welcomed an occupation, but I'd left myself with nothing to do. I rearranged the teaspoons, poked the fire, bit a loose nail off my thumb, and went upstairs to check on the kittens, who were shut away in my bedroom for the afternoon.

Do you remember the oath that Frank signed in his own blood? I keep it in the chest of drawers, hidden beneath a bundle of stockings, along with this diary, and the silver bracelet from the cellar. When I'd finished talking to the kittens (who were in a sleepy frame of mind, for once), I brought it out and reread it.

> *I, Francis George Henry Gower, hereby swear that nothing shall ever divide me from my sister, Maude Louise Gower. She shall always be first in my thoughts, as I am always first in hers.*
> *Signed*—F. G. H. Gower

You will think me stupid, but until this afternoon it never occurred to me to think of oaths as mere collections of words. I see it clearly now: oaths are only words, and words are only collections of letters, and letters are only scratches and splotches, which human beings have invented for their own convenience.

Paper is merely paper, ink is merely ink, and even blood is only meaningful if people agree, amongst themselves, that it is.

Is this self-evident? I suppose it is. I suppose I have been very childish up until now.

Pa made the usual oaths to Mamma on their marriage but presently he wished he hadn't, so he (and Miss Greenaway) declared them null and void. The two of them pointed at all those solemn-sounding, inconvenient vows and said, "Look! Nothing but words!"

What I'm trying to say is that my brother's "oath," this piece of paper, which I've kept so carefully at the bottom of my stockings drawer, is worth precisely nothing.

Perhaps this sounds like a statement of the obvious to you, but it comes as a shock to me.

Only a handful of people came to the house after the funeral, but it was still strange to see them. Any manner of social event would feel strange at Orchard House. People in black stood around talking, while Miss Greenaway and I passed cups of tea and plates of sandwiches. Frank was sweaty and awry, following his mad dash to the church, and his hair was sticking up at all angles. I was about to say he resembled a Romantic poet, but that would be unduly generous. It may be terribly Byronic to stand about, staring wildly at nothing in particular, but one ought not to devour shortbread biscuits, rapidly and by the handful, at the same time; it spoils the effect. People were not inclined to talk to him (nor he to them), and at one point Mr. Stirling looked at him with something like contempt. Only Miss Greenaway pretended that he was behaving normally, and kept his teacup replenished. I am sure Frank drank three times as much tea as anyone else.

Emily crossed the room to say hello to me; I suppose she had been told to. I managed, "Good afternoon" and "I hope you are in good health," but I couldn't think of anything else that would not sound false or rude. Neither, it appeared, could she, so we stood side by side sipping tea. Occasionally Emily said, "Hmm," or "Well." At last I have found something that Emily Stirling and I have in common, viz. an inability to make polite conversation with individuals whom we find obnoxious. (I almost pointed this out, by way of filling the silence, but upon reflection I decided it would make matters worse.)

Isn't it surprising, and really rather contemptible, the way people converse lightly in the wake of a funeral? I hardly knew Mrs. Potter, let alone liked her, but at least Death commands my respect. How can the citizens of Sawyer's Fen stand about discussing the best way to grow cucumbers, and the likelihood of rain on Saturday, when he (Death) is the reason for their gathering? I shivered as I pictured him in the parlour, lurking in the folds of the curtains, hiding his laughter inside the shadow of his black hood.

"I want to be like Miss Greenaway when I'm grown up," said Emily.

"In what way?"

"Oh, you know. Clever and beautiful and modern. I'm glad I'm tall and dark like her. As frivolous as it may sound, I do think that the fairer and more delicate a woman is, the less she is taken seriously." Emily paused and blushed. "Present company excepted, of course. Anyway it's the fault of the judgemental world, not of the woman herself."

What utter rot Emily Stirling talks. "Present company excepted" indeed! As for calling herself tall and dark like Miss Greenaway, dear, oh dear! Emily Stirling bears as much resemblance to Miss Greenaway as a Shetland pony to an Arabian horse.

I turned to the mirror over the fireplace by way of reassurance, but my heart refused to lift. Studying my own reflection used to be a straightforward affair. It was one of the surest comforts in life: to look at myself, and to judge correctly what I saw, and to feel pleased about it. Now I look, and I'm unsure what I'm seeing. I recognise the blue eyes and the yellow hair, and the firm little chin, and the pale lips, but I don't know what they signify, and I feel more afraid than glad.

I watched Miss Greenaway's reflection cross the parlour in the looking-glass world and remembered how her features seemed ugly and masculine to me, at first. I glanced from face to face in the mirror and noticed how everyone's attention seemed to turn, covertly or overtly, on her.

Friday, 5 May, 1876

Frank brought a valise with him, this time; apparently he doesn't need to be back in Cambridge until Monday morning. When I expressed my concern ("How will you learn to be a doctor if you fritter your time away here?"), he demanded to know what on earth I knew about it, and said that if "Kitty" was content for him to stay, that was good enough for him.

"Kitty" was not a witness to this conversation, which took place in my bedroom on Thursday evening, after the guests had left.

I seized my brother by the sleeve, as he made to leave the room, and tried to lower my voice.

"Frank, listen! I read that story about Odysseus and the sirens."

He gave an almighty shrug of his arm, but I hung on.

"You told me to read it! You said she was a siren."

He snorted, and I'm sure it crossed his mind to deny it.

"You know you did," I insisted, before he could try.

"Well, if I did, I was wrong."

"But that's just what you would say if you'd been driven mad by a siren! You must see that? Odysseus thought he'd been wrong too, while he was listening to them sing, but he turned out to be right. That's the point of the story."

Frank laughed in an unfriendly way. "It's awfully sweet of you,

Maude, to liken me to a hero of Greek mythology."

"You were the one who brought mythology into it, in the first place."

"Well, that was before!" He finally succeeded in shaking himself free. "Now I've met Kitty, and I can see that she is no more a monster than I am a helmet-wearing, spear-wielding hero of Homeric legend. We are agreed about her, at last, you and I: I will even concede that I was in the wrong, and you were in the right."

"But you know that she and Pa—"

"I know that evil-minded people stoked rumours that distressed Mamma . . ."

"Frank, I don't think they were mere rumours. I believe—"

"THAT DISTRESSED MAMMA, AND WERE UNTRUE."

"Frank!" In my exasperation I tried to grab his arm again, and caught him across the back of the hand with my fingernails. I didn't really hurt him, there was no mark, but in that moment he hated me.

"Why can't you be glad?" he thundered, pushing me so hard that I stumbled backwards. "I've admitted you were in the right, haven't I?"

He stormed out and bumped into Miss Greenaway on the landing. I heard her surprised "Oh!" and the whisk of her skirts as she followed him down the stairs.

Whether it was something she said, or whether it was all down to me, I don't know, but Frank left the following morning (i.e., today, Friday). He caught the early train, and I wasn't awake in time to say goodbye.

Monday, 8 May, 1876

I'd not given Emily Stirling much thought since the funeral on Thursday; I'd forgotten she was resuming her lessons today. However, there she was at the table when I walked in, her Greek and Latin books in a neat stack and her notebook open at a fresh page. We bid one another a cold good morning.

In fact, I was surprised to note, and I am sure she would have been surprised to learn, how little I begrudged her return. There are times when I would do anything to keep Miss Greenaway to myself, but having spent an entire weekend pondering my quarrel with Frank, I was glad of a third party today.

Miss Greenaway herself seemed happy: she even admitted as much, and claimed it was because we were together again. "We've missed you, Emily!" she said, in response to which I observed, in myself, only the faintest twinge of pique. By way of celebration, she provided a plate of biscuits and a pot of coffee with three cups, though it was only ten o'clock and not long since breakfast. I do think she might have noticed, by now, that I am not fond of coffee.

While Miss Greenaway poured, Emily opened her Virgil, and I, having forgotten to bring a book, reached for <u>Roget's Thesaurus</u>.

I love <u>Roget's Thesaurus</u>. I love the way the words are laid out like buttons in a haberdasher's, or jars in a sweet shop, inviting you to linger and ponder and choose the ones that suit you best. Today I looked up "delicate," because it was the term with which Emily disparaged me the other day, and it struck me as odd at the time, since I am used to thinking of delicacy as an attractive quality. To my surprise, Mr. Roget only deepened the contradiction. Is it not strange that equivalent words for "delicate" include "artificial," "gracious," "puny," "womanly," "vulnerable," and "fine," among others? With so many variations, the word almost ceases to have meaning at all.

I was about to look up another word, but Miss Greenaway had finished distributing the cups and biscuits and was ready to begin.

"Will you join us, Maude, and learn a little Latin?"

"Thank you, no. The classics aren't for me; I don't find them interesting."

There was a savage satisfaction in saying it, followed by a pang of regret. I wasn't looking at her face, but I can imagine her reaction well enough: the sharp glance, the almost-smile, the lift of the eyebrows. The pang faded, as pangs do.

"Very well," she said. "You have my permission to think up something interesting to do, so long as you are able to give a good account of yourself by the end of the morning. You may not simply yawn and browse through the thesaurus."

I said I'd write a story, for want of any better idea, and provided myself with ink, pen, and paper. I made a stab at an opening paragraph, but was too busy eavesdropping on the other two, Miss Greenaway and deserving, studious, eager-to-please Emily, to create anything good. The most enjoyable part of the exercise was the loud scoring noise that my pen made, as I crossed everything out, line by line.

"It's heavenly to be in your study again," said the golden child. "Much pleasanter than working at home."

"It's wonderful to have you back," said Miss Greenaway (forgetting, I suppose, that she'd already said as much twice or three times), "but you manage well enough at home, don't you, as far as your studies are concerned? I'm sure your father gives you encouragement?"

"Oh yes," said Emily, "it's not his fault that the farm is busy. I try to work at the kitchen table, but it's always so restless, with people coming in and out, and doors banging, and the dog barking."

Miss Greenaway leaned back in the chair and sipped her coffee. "What you need is your own desk," she mused. "A small foldaway desk that you can carry to your room, or wherever you wish to be."

I thought of the dark cellars beneath our feet, and the packet of letters I'd sworn never to mention again, and the words entered my head a moment before Miss Greenaway spoke them:

"I've got a portable desk."

We both looked up—Emily had an acquisitive gleam in her eye—as Miss Greenaway went on, "You may have it, if you like. It's rather nice, rosewood . . . I used it a lot when I was a girl, but not anymore."

"You do use it," I thought. "You use it to keep letters in, and you'll want to make very sure it's empty before you bring it into the light of day and hand it over to Miss Stirling."

Emily went home at lunchtime and Miss Greenaway asked to look at my story. I gave it to her with some trepidation, because it was called "The Deathbed" and it described the last moments of Mrs. Potter's life, when I had gone to her, and she had spoken those terrible words. I'd taken the precaution of disguising names and places, but I still hoped for—and feared—some telling reaction.

"You enjoyed writing this, in the end," Miss Greenaway said, smiling. It's true: once I'd hit upon my subject, I'd hardly looked up from the page.

I watched her closely as she read, but failed to spot any flashes of apprehension or guilt. Perhaps I'd disguised everything too heavily: the dying slave (Mrs. Potter), the captive princess (me), the sultan's favourite wife (Miss Greenaway), and the Arabian palace (Orchard

House). I thought the bit where the dying slave grabs the princess's hand and says, "Don't trust her! Not one inch. She'll do for you," might give it away, because I can't imagine those words in anyone's voice but Mrs. Potter's, but Miss Greenaway didn't turn a hair. If anything, she seemed puzzled, and her only comment was: "You write well, line by line, but the story lacks shape. I don't entirely understand it; it feels like the middle part of something more involved. Am I right? Is there a longer story inside your head?"

"Maybe."

I suppose there is, in a sense, although I don't yet know the ending, and I wouldn't say it was confined entirely to my head.

I forgot to tell you that before Emily left, she came upstairs to look at the kittens. (Only because Miss Greenaway had said, "You must see Maude's cats, they are adorable," to which Little Miss Simpering Amiability had replied, "Oh yes, please!")

To do Emily justice, she was properly appreciative: sinking onto her knees beside the box where they were sleeping, and talking to them in syrupy whispers. They rolled over lazily, blinked at her, and went back to sleep in unison, as much as to say, "What a supremely uninteresting person you appear to be."

Ha.

Tuesday, 9 May, 1876

Orchard House feels strange without Mrs. Potter, and on the whole I like it, although I suppose I shouldn't.

When I say "I suppose I shouldn't," I'm not indulging in false piety: I didn't like Mrs. P. when she was alive, and I feel no compulsion to pretend I miss her, now she's dead. I only mean that the house feels even more disordered in her absence than it did in her illness. Meals are plentiful but more haphazard than ever. This morning for example, my stomach grumbled during a mid-morning French lesson, and rather than politely ignore the noise, Miss Greenaway said, "Ah yes, what a good idea, let's make some toast," which we promptly did. (Actually she said, "Ah oui, quelle bonne idée, faisons du pain grillé.")

When the weather is fine, we take our supper outside. Yesterday it started raining just as we'd settled ourselves, but rather than come indoors, we removed ourselves and our sandwiches to the weeping willow, and ate in its shelter! The rain hissed all around us, pattering on the leaves, but we hardly got wet at all.

Unless one is a man, and an explorer/adventurer at that, one should surely find this an unsatisfactory mode of living? I like it, though; I can't seem to help it, however hard I try. After we'd finished our picnic Miss Greenaway spoke vaguely about advertising for a housekeeper, and I said, "Oh no!" with much too much vehemence. Before I had time to retract my words, Miss G. smiled and said, "You're right; there's no rush. We manage pretty well together, don't we, you and I?"

Following which, I went upstairs and gave my bedroom a rather frenzied clean, to prove to myself that I'm not a barbarian.

There was only one letter in the post today, and it was addressed to

Miss Greenaway. She read it whilst eating her breakfast—fork in one hand, a sheet of expensive-looking notepaper in the other—and as she did so, her face went perfectly pink. Of course, I longed to know who it was from, and what they could possibly have written to make her blush so violently. I very nearly asked, but then I remembered the sorts of things that letters to Miss G. have been known to contain in the past (you understand what I'm referring to), and I stayed silent.

I pushed the last of my scrambled eggs to the side of my plate and left them, which is most unlike me, though Mamma used to do it all the time. Miss Greenaway disapproves of such waste.

Thursday, 11 May, 1876

I'll tell you exactly who wrote that letter—it was Frank! I went to the study this evening, in search of Miss G., but she wasn't there, and as I was leaving I spotted the envelope on her desk. It was recognisable at once by the thick, creamy quality of the paper, and on picking it up I saw it was addressed to "Miss K. Greenaway" in my brother's hand. He never uses such nice stationery when he writes to me; usually he tears a page from one of his notebooks. (On one occasion, last year, he accidentally included two pages of lecture notes on the musculature of the lower arm, and I had to arrange for them to be posted back.)

I felt duty-bound to learn what he had written, as part of my investigation into the truth about Miss Greenaway's character. On the other hand, the prospect of reading it made me dizzy with dread, and I wasn't wholly sorry when her footsteps approached the study door, forcing me to replace it, unopened.

Friday, 12 May, 1876

I revisited Miss G.'s study first thing, but the letter was nowhere to be seen. Now, of course, I am wholly sorry and quite desperate to read it.

Saturday, 13 May, 1876

I am finding it difficult to think about anything other than letters. In April I swore to put Pa's letters out of my mind, as if I'd never seen them, but having half glimpsed (less than half glimpsed!) Frank's missive, I feel my resolve crumbling. It's not so bad during the day, when I'm busy, but it's terrible at night. I lie there, either awake and thinking over the fragmented sentences I uncovered in the cellar ("those darling hairs at the nape of your neck"); or else having the most peculiar dreams about them; or else, despite myself, inventing even more awful things that Pa and/or Frank might have written to her.

Last night an urgent voice (Mamma's voice?) woke me and told me to venture to the cellar <u>at once</u> with a candle, in order to fetch the letters and read them through. I tried to obey, but got only as far as the landing, where I bumped into an occasional table, stubbed my toe, and shattered a vase. Miss Greenaway emerged from her room, bleary-eyed, and whispered, "Oh, poor Maude, I believe you're sleepwalking," before leading me back to bed.

The whole incident is somewhat indistinct in my mind (perhaps I was not as awake as I thought), but I do remember one part clearly. As I was climbing into bed, I murmured, "Would you have married Pa, if he'd asked?" hoping against hope that she'd reply, with a degree of disgust, "Certainly not! You have misunderstood the nature of my feeling for your pa; it was never that sort of love" (i.e., nothing to do with napes of necks, etc.). As it was, she tucked the sheets around me, kissed my forehead, and said, "It's just as well he married your mamma, in the end, otherwise you wouldn't have been born, would you? Which would be a pity."

This was a flagrant evasion of the question, which means that my investigation is no further advanced than before. Indeed, the puzzle is only complicated by the fact (can it really be a fact?) of her regard for me.

Wednesday, 17 May, 1876

I don't know why the days pass so quickly, unless it is a consequence of their being so full. We are either studying, or gardening, or walking, or cleaning, or cooking . . . The last few nights I have fallen asleep the moment my head touched the pillow, and I've not been greatly troubled by dreams.

Yesterday Miss Greenaway asked me whether I would like to have a dog, to which the honest answer is "yes," although I said "no" out of consideration for the cats. I often make believe that Mr. Stirling's pointer, Scout, belongs to me: he still accompanies us on many of our walks, and is good at coming when I call.

Being busy resembles being happy. Occasionally I start to suspect I am happy, but then something happens to destroy the illusion. For example, when we were strolling in the garden this evening, Miss G. said, ever so casually, "I'm thinking of going up to Cambridge, one day next week," and I knew—by her nonchalant tone, and because she didn't mention his name, and because she didn't invite me—I knew there was some scheme afoot, involving her and Frank and their secret correspondence.

"Can I come with you?" I said, at once.

"Of course, although I expect your brother will be busy on a weekday."

"I don't especially wish to see Frank; I'd like to see Cambridge with you."

"But I'll be visiting friends, rather than shopping or sightseeing. I'm afraid you'll be bored."

"No, I won't, not at all," I insisted, at which she smiled and said all right then, if I was sure, and that her friends would certainly be glad to meet me.

I am, or rather, I was at the time, sure I'd acted promptly to foil a siren plot. However, I must acknowledge the possibility that I have foiled nothing, and have merely lumbered myself with a dull expedition to the blue-stockinged backwaters of Cambridge.

Wednesday, 24 May, 1876

Well, Miss Greenaway and I visited Cambridge today. As to whether I have, or have not, foiled a Frank-related scheme, I am none the wiser.

We arrived around noon and made our way to a tea shop on King's Parade, where we met some of Miss G.'s friends from the "Association for Promoting the Higher Education of Women in Cambridge." (Later, on the train home, I suggested the abbreviation APHEWC, but Miss G. said that sounded like a messy sneeze, which made us both laugh harder than was strictly necessary.) Her friends consisted of three ladies and a gentleman, and they greeted me cordially enough, but as their efforts to draw me out consisted largely in asking questions to which the answer was "no": Had I ever visited an archaeological dig? Was I learning Greek? Perhaps mathematics was more my passion than classics? Or moral sciences? Or natural sciences? In the end, they left me alone.

I am fairly certain that Frank spends his Wednesday afternoons at Addenbrooke's Hospital, but "fairly certain" is not "wholly certain," and every time the door jangled I felt strongly tempted to dive under the table, just in case. My hat (a belated birthday present from Miss Greenaway) is small and narrow-brimmed, and not at all concealing. If Frank discovered I'd come to Cambridge without telling him, things would be bad enough, but if he espied me breaking bread with a gang of Radicals, I would never hear the end of it.

After lunch we said farewell to the gentleman and one of the ladies, and the four of us walked to Newnham College a journey that took us over the river and away from the direction of St. John's, which (irrationally, since F. probably wasn't even in college) made me breathe a little more easily. Newnham is one of the two new ladies' colleges—the other is in the village of Girton, north-west of Cambridge—and Miss Greenaway is somehow mixed up in its establishment. Emily is ambitious to study there, as you know, but it seems she must pass an examination called the "Higher Local" first. ("Which she will—easily," said Miss Greenaway to one of the other ladies, at which I felt the most stupid pang of envy. I have no business feeling pangs of envy over Emily Stirling.)

Newnham College is a grand house, with tall chimneys and lots of windows, including oval-shaped ones in some of the gables. I say "grand," but there are pigs and chickens in the garden, which takes it down a peg or two and makes it smell like a farm. (Imagine pigs and chickens in the hallowed quads of St. John's!) How comforting to think that Emily will feel at home in at least one respect.

Unlike St. John's, and the other men's colleges, Newnham has the raw, unsettled feel of a brand-new site: parts of the garden have only recently been seeded with grass, and the freshly painted window frames are startlingly white against the red brick walls. The interior is sparse and echoey, with no carpets on the floors, only bare wooden boards or tiles. There was a smell of fresh paint everywhere, and in one of the rooms (a dining room?) I saw men on stepladders hanging dark, flowery wallpaper.

Once we'd been admitted, Miss Greenaway led the way down the corridor and knocked on a door marked "Miss A. J. Clough. Head of College." My imagination ran riot: What on earth would Frank say, what would Mamma have said, if they knew I was about to meet the head of Newnham College, one of the chiefs of the bluestockings? I expected Miss Clough to have scales and a forked tongue, at the very least, and when we entered the room, I'm not sure whether I was more relieved or disappointed to see a conventionally dressed, calm-mannered, grey-haired old woman standing up to welcome us. Her eyes—deep-set in shadowy sockets, and indubitably clever—were her most interesting feature, but people's eyes are nearly always their most interesting feature, so that's not saying much.

"This must be the famous Miss Emily Stirling! But you're younger than I thought . . ." she said, having greeted the other three by name. Miss Greenaway hastened to correct her, and I wanted to say something tart like, "I'm awfully sorry to disappoint," but I was too nervous to say anything much. In fact, Miss

Clough was polite to the point of kindness, and managed not to look crestfallen as she was introduced to the (not at all famous, positively inconsequential) Miss Maude Gower.

Naturally, Miss Clough felt obliged to ask me variations on the usual questions, by way of setting me at my ease (had "dear Kitty" made a classicist of me yet? etc., etc.), and for all her cordiality, her interest in me palpably waned with each stuttered "No, ma'am," and "I'm afraid not, ma'am." I ought to have felt especially feminine and lovely in the presence of these women (a "Sally" amid a coven of "Annies," to reference Frank's infamous poem), and it was unsettling to feel like a mere disappointment. When Miss Greenaway came to my rescue, saying, "I shouldn't be surprised if Maude was a famous writer, one day, or an expert on English and French literature; she reads and writes extraordinarily well," I could have wept, despite the preposterousness of the claim, for gratitude.

What a chameleon I am! If Miss G. had praised me in the same terms to Frank, or The Relatives, or Mamma, I would have been mortified.

The rest of the time they talked about dull things, such as money and proposed new building works. On the upside, Miss Clough gave us tea and biscuits, and before we left we all walked around the garden, and I was allowed to feed the chickens with seed from a tin.

I went to bed straight after supper, in order to write this, and to think.

I think and think and think, but never make any progress at all. I seem to live and move inside a great fog of doubt, and I don't know how to disperse it. If I write to my aunts, they will say, "Be assured, she is a devil"; if I write to Frank, he will say, "Be assured, she is an angel"; but neither answer rings true, and I don't know who else to ask.

Friday, 26 May, 1876

An excessively dull morning in the study. Emily wanted to hear about our trip to Cambridge, and Miss Greenaway was more than happy to oblige. Newnham, Newnham, Newnham, all morning, on and on and on! Also, when Miss Greenaway told how Miss Clough had mistaken me for "the famous Miss Stirling," Emily laughed in a way that I didn't quite like.

I was trying to read a book about the Reformation, but I couldn't concentrate, so I went upstairs to see the cats instead. Miss Greenaway called after me, "You know you can move on to something else, Maude, if you've had enough history for one day?" but I pretended not to hear.

Sunday, 28 May, 1876

The apple trees blossomed a few weeks ago, but that's all over now, and the branches are thick with green, summery leaves. I tried to sketch the orchard in April, when it was at its whitest and gauziest, but failed dismally in the attempt. Fleeting things are always the hardest to draw or paint, I think, blossoms blowing in a breeze, the sky itself, people's facial expressions, though they are also the subjects I most incline towards. Miss Wilson always had me drawing fruit bowls and flower arrangements, which are easier but less interesting.

As if I didn't already see far too much of Emily Stirling, yesterday we bumped into her (and Scout) on our evening walk through the fields, and when Miss Greenaway politely invited her to join us, she agreed! I, for one, think that's rude. I had been hoping to talk to Miss G. about La Belle et La Bête by Madame de Villeneuve, which I have just started reading in French, and also Little Dorrit (the book, not the cat).

Incidentally, Emily seems to feature in this diary, and, by extension, in my life, rather too often, at the moment. When I remarked on this to Miss Greenaway earlier, she said, "Do you know, Maude, I think you might learn a lot from Emily . . ." which sounded like a telling off, or the start of one, so I refrained from making any retort and let the matter rest.

Yesterday evening was warm, going on hot, and the muddy patches around the five-bar gates were set in hard, dusty ruts. We ambled slowly, even Scout, and chatted about summer heat in the countryside versus summer heat in London. Nobody knew about the London side of things as well as I did, so I was able to speak with authority for some time, which made a nice change. At one point Emily said, "I suppose Cambridge—" but I cut her off with a description of the Thames in August, and a trip I took with Pa on a steamboat, when I was quite small.

After a while the path dipped down a steep bank to the stream, and Scout took great pleasure in dipping his belly in the water and having a long, sloppy drink. Ordinarily we would cross via the six flat stepping stones and carry on, but this time we stopped. Emily said, "Lucky old Scout," and Miss Greenaway replied, "Yes, isn't he?" and they both stood gazing at the slow current. I was right in the middle of describing the view of Richmond from the Thames steamboat, so I said, "I'm sorry if I'm boring you," but nobody replied.

When Miss Greenaway removed her hat (an ugly, floppy straw affair) and deployed it as a fan, Emily did the same. When Miss Greenaway crouched down at the water's edge, dipped her hands, and splashed her face . . . Emily did the same.

Miss G.: "Lovely!"

Emily: "Yes, lovely!"

Miss G.: "My feet feel so wretchedly hot and confined in these boots."

Emily: "So do mine!"

Miss G.: "Shall we go for a paddle?"

Emily: "Oh yes! Shall we . . . ?"

Miss G. (casting one of her "siren" looks in my direction): "What do you think, Maude? There's nobody watching . . ."

I smiled a tight smile and said, "I'm all right as I am, thank you," because how did they know someone wouldn't appear—a man, a total stranger—while they were rolling their stockings down their legs, or hitching their skirts round their knees? It didn't seem right, in a public place. It <u>wasn't</u> right. I looked away until I heard their first, sloshing steps and their sharp intakes of breath.

"Goodness, it's icy!" Miss G.'s voice was unnaturally high, and full of laughter. "Won't you join us Maude? Please join us!"

I shook my head and watched them pick their way across the pebbly stream bed, from ankle depth to calf depth, while Scout plunged about, barking excitedly and soaking them with spray. The water was a shifting mosaic of glassy browns and golds, and I _did_ want to touch it, if only to dabble my fingers, but it was too late for a change of heart. If I'd been on my own with Miss Greenaway I might have allowed myself to be persuaded, but Emily would smirk and think me shilly-shallying.

What a sober, tidy, silent figure I must have cut, to anyone passing by—standing at the top of the bank in my black dress and gazing down at the stream. Nobody did pass by, however.

Emily took no notice of me, but Miss Greenaway pestered: "Oh, do come and cool your feet, Maude! . . . Won't you come? . . . It's so lovely . . . We shan't splash you . . ." The more she pleaded, and the longer I said "no," the more impossible it was to change my mind, and the more I longed to do precisely that. In fact, shall I tell you what I wanted? I wanted to fling my dress off and sit down in the deepest part of the stream. I wanted to lie right back so that my head went under, and to roll around in it and lap it up with my tongue, like Scout.

But I carried on shaking my prim little head, saying, "No," and "no," and "no" again, until even Miss Greenaway gave up.

This happened yesterday—hours and hours ago—but it still makes me want to weep with frustration. _Why??_ You would think I had missed out on some never-to-be-repeated adventure of unparalleled beauty, rather than an undignified paddle in a sluggish stream, with people I'm not certain I like.

All the same: if there were a potion that banished shame forever, I would drink it. Sometimes I feel as though shame is the only thing keeping me (just) on the side of the angels, but sometimes (when I think about yesterday, for example) I feel it's the only thing barring my way to happiness.

Thursday, 1 June, 1876

Frank has written a letter to Miss Greenaway again. I spotted his handwriting on the front of an envelope when the post arrived, and assumed it was for me, but it wasn't. It was for her.

I have been waiting all day for Miss G. to mention it, but she hasn't said a word.

Monday, 5 June, 1876

Another letter today. I said, "Oh, is that from Frank?" and asked outright if I could read it, but she said, "No," in an irritable tone of voice.

Wednesday, 7 June, 1876

Another letter.

Friday, 9 June, 1876

Another one, <u>and</u> he's proposing to visit again tomorrow.

Tuesday, 13 June, 1876

I brought the letters to the breakfast table this morning. My manner was studiously casual, as though I'd not noticed that among the half dozen envelopes addressed to Miss Greenaway there was another one from Frank! She said nothing, and slipped it into her pocket with a positively furtive air. We talked of other things over breakfast: or rather, she talked and I pushed scraps of bacon round my plate.

Feeling unhappy on a bright summer's day is so much worse than feeling unhappy on a drizzling winter's day. People complain about London fog, but it comes into its own when one is downcast. After breakfast I dawdled about the garden and into the meadow across the lane, and my feelings were by no means improved by the pure blue of the sky, or the unclouded sun, or the flowering hedgerows. I simply felt, as I looked at them, that the big, wide world has no interest in me at all (which is only the truth, although I think it unkind of the big, wide world to insist upon the fact so forcefully).

Every now and then I looked back at the house, in case I could see Miss Greenaway opening Frank's letter, since it is her habit to stand at the study window when she is reading. I couldn't make anything out, however. The dazzling light had the effect of making the windows opaque, as if they'd been fitted with black glass.

Thursday, 15 June, 1876

Another letter to Miss G., from Frank.

Friday, 16 June, 1876

I stole it! I stole one of Frank's letters and it's here in front of me, and my hands are shaking so much I can hardly hold my pen.

On further examination, I appear to have taken only half a letter. Bother. That's what comes of being flustered, although it could not have been a more straightforward theft: I gave the study door a cursory knock, marched in, saw she wasn't there, opened the bureau, spotted Frank's handwriting, grabbed, and ran. Where would we be if she'd caught me? I don't know . . . but she didn't, so it doesn't matter.

"Fortune favours the brave," Pa used to say.

Here it is:

St. John's College
Cambridge
13 June, 1876

Darling Kitty (since you have not absolutely forbidden me to address you thus),

I shan't reproach you for failing to write, since "only" three days have passed since you saw me, and "only" two since you received my last letter, and in the ordinary world, where ordinary mortals dwell, that is not such a long time to wait for a letter. I used to be a citizen of that world, and I used to think nothing of waiting three days—or even longer—for a reply. Even in my delirium, I remember the humdrum state I inhabited before I knew you!

You think I'm raving mad (indeed, I am, but whose fault is that? You turn your eyes on me—the eyes of Rossetti's demonic goddesses—and dare to blame me for losing my mind?), but I will prove that I retain a germ of sanity. I have come up with a marvellous plan, which will allow us to be together—unwatched, unchecked—all summer.

Brighton! Why should we not visit Brighton in July or August, perhaps staying on into September? Perhaps staying on forever! My college friend Henry Simpson has an aunt who owns a boarding house in Wimborne Street, and he is sure she would be willing to let rooms at a reasonable rate (forgive me for stooping to such grubby particulars, but it proves—does it not?—that I'm capable of rational thought!). You will have your own rooms at my expense, and I shall leave you in peace as much as you like, and shan't burden you with unending protestations of love (at least, not unless you permit me to).

It is only fair that I should be allowed to know you more closely—my own sister having enjoyed that privilege for months—and what better place to become acquainted than Brighton, where we may stroll the promenade and inhale freedom with every breath?

The only fly in the ointment is Maude (forgive me the unbrotherly sentiment, yet understand me too!), or so I thought, to begin with. However, on reflection, Brighton

The page ends here and I am sorry I stole it—so sorry I could cry.

I have nothing to say, except that grown-up people disgust me altogether.

Wednesday, 21 June, 1876

"However, on reflection, Brighton . . ." <u>????????</u>

I stole into Miss Greenaway's study while she was in the garden with her morning coffee, but I couldn't find the rest of Frank's letter, or any of his others. Several of the bureau drawers are locked.

She is wearing black again today and looks like a witch.

Thursday, 22 June, 1876

"However, on reflection, Brighton . . ."

I keep trying to finish the sentence, but my mind's a blank.

Friday, 23 June, 1876

Frank is here again. We haven't met since early May, and yet I couldn't feel pleased to see him, which is a heart-rending admission to make. I said hello, how are you, etc.—of necessity—but other than that I have kept to my room or taken myself off on solitary walks.

Saturday, 24 June, 1876

I lie awake, long past midnight, knowing that Frank can't sleep either.

As long as he's lying still, thinking his thoughts, I don't mind too much, but how can I tell? The idea of him walking about the house is torture. Sometimes I'm on the brink of getting up to check, but then I remember seeing him and Miss Wilson eating one another alive on the landing at Erskine Place, and I daren't. I bury my head under the blankets and whisper my prayers, so that I won't hear the night-time creaks and bumps of the house, which are probably—hopefully—caused by the wind.

Thursday, 6 July, 1876

You will wonder at my silence, nearly two weeks have gone by since I last wrote, but I have nothing to say. Life goes on as usual, but everything seems to happen at a far remove from my real thoughts. I can't bring myself to care that July is a wondrous month in the countryside. I don't mind what I read, or eat, or do. I still talk to Miss Greenaway, because if I'm too quiet she quizzes me, but I avoid her whenever I can.

Emily comes every day for her lessons. She has taken to arriving early, leaving late, and completing double the amount of homework Miss Greenaway set the day before. Today she sported a pair of steel-rimmed spectacles, which precisely resemble Miss Greenaway's, and are presumably meant to lend her an intellectual air. Oh, but she is self-absorbed! You'd think the sky was going to fall in should she fail to win a place to read classics at Newnham. Never mind spectacles; she ought to wear blinkers. (NB: Blinkers would have the additional benefit of suiting her horse-like face.)

This morning, for example, when Miss Greenaway left the room for a few minutes, Emily looked up from her dictionary and whispered, "Maude!"

For a brief moment I thought she'd understood something that actually mattered—such was the conspiratorial gleam in her eye—but when I leaned forwards to listen, do you know what she said?

"Maude, do you remember that foldaway desk Miss Greenaway mentioned, weeks and weeks ago?"

"Yes?"

"The one she said I could have?"

"Yes?"

"Well . . . it's just . . . I really want it, but I think she's forgotten, and I feel shy to mention it. I thought perhaps if you were to remind her . . ."

I got up and left the room without replying. She must have thought she'd angered me in some way, but she hadn't. Indeed, I should like to feel anger: it is, at least, an enlivening emotion.

No. What drove me from the study, and up the stairs, and had me staring dull-eyed from my bedroom window with my nose and forehead pressed against the glass, was Disappointment. Disappointment in Emily's question; disappointment in the littleness of life; disappointment in everything that's ever failed to live up to its promise.

Nancy mewed at me, and tried to lean her front paws on my skirt. Normally I'd have picked her up, but today I looked down at her coldly, as if we were strangers, and said, "What?"

Sunday, 9 July, 1876

What about:

> *However, on reflection, Brighton, with its crowds, is a good place to lose a superfluous sibling.*

Or, perhaps:

> *However, on reflection, Brighton, with its piers, is a good place to push an uncongenial sister into the sea and watch her drown.*

I am being facetious. (Obviously.)

Friday, 14 July, 1876

Miss Greenaway still comes to say goodnight to me, every night. I wish she'd stop. Of course I pretend to be asleep, but however quietly I lie, and however gently I breathe, somehow I know she doesn't believe me. She whispers my name, and when she gets no answer she sits down on the bed, and I know that she is looking at me by the light of her candle.

It brings to mind all the dreams and ghosts that I've feared over the years—only this is worse because Miss Greenaway is emphatically real. Even daylight won't banish her.

Last night she touched my head before she left, and brushed the hair away from my face.

Tuesday, 18 July, 1876

I have a slight summer cold, which caused me to sneeze when she was saying "goodnight" last night, so I couldn't pretend to be asleep. (People don't sneeze in their sleep, do they? I don't think they do.) Besides, she'd brought me a cup of hot honey and lemon, and although it gave me shivers to accept a cup from Miss Greenaway's hands, and made me think of all the fools from fairy tales who are bested by witches and their potions, I admit I was glad of it, and it soothed my sore throat.

"Why didn't Frank come on Friday?" I asked, since we had to talk about something.

"Because I expressly asked him not to."

"Why?"

"Because, as welcome as he is—I think he's been too much

absent from Cambridge lately."

The drink did appear to be working like a potion, not only on my cold but on my heart as well. I told myself not to trust her, yet with every sip, my heart yearned a little more, and a little more in her direction. I observed the sharp lights and shadows that the candle made of her face, and thought of Frank's line about "Rossetti's demonic goddesses." I do think Miss Greenaway beautiful, the realisation has grown on me, but I feel her beauty must mean something, and I don't know what the meaning is. Mamma used to refer to people (women, anyway) as attractive "in the right way" or "in the wrong way," but I never understood what it meant. I wish I'd had the courage to ask.

"My brother's company must be refreshing for you," I said ~~slyly~~ truthfully. "He's so witty and clever . . ." (I was going to add "and handsome" but lost my nerve.)

"Is he?" She sounded surprised. "That is, I'm sorry if that sounds rude; of course, he's as clever as the next man. I only meant that you shouldn't be overawed by him. As far as intelligence goes, you are certainly Frank's equal and probably his superior."

Which can't possibly be true, of course, since Frank is a man, and so much older and worldlier than me, but I permitted myself to savour the moment. To be called intelligent by Miss Greenaway is decidedly flattering. Also, in the circumstances, I was not sorry to hear her disparage my brother.

I sipped at the cup, but just as my heart was lifting, Miss Greenaway said: "Once the university term ends, he'll be free to come and go as he pleases. In fact, he has a scheme for August, has he mentioned it to you?"

"A scheme? No."

"He wants the three of us to spend a week or two in Brighton. I gather you've never seen the sea?"

I took a too-hot gulp of the potion, but my heart continued to drop to new depths.

"Brighton," I said. "Goodness."

"I hope I was right to tell you."

"Certainly."

"These last few months have been an unhappy time for you, Maude; a seaside holiday might do you the world of good."

I put the cup away from me, unfinished.

"So you do still wish to see my brother?" I spoke as lightly as I could. "You're not inclined to banish him forever?"

"Banish him?" She laughed. "Of course not."

"Of course not," I thought. "You mean to play with him, for your own amusement, because that is what you were born to do."

Feline. Siren. Witch.

Thursday, 20 July, 1876

I am much clearer-headed today. I feel clever, like someone who is capable of devising and executing a plan. This evening I walked across the fields to Pa's ruined house, and lay on my back in the long grass with my hands behind my head. It was strange to imagine Pa once walking about, or sitting down to read, or eating his dinner in the very spot where I lay.

I can't stop seeing symbols at the moment: for example, in the fact that Pa's house is a ruin while Orchard House is in fine fettle, or in the fact that Little Dorrit tortured and ate a moth, earlier on. ("Cats will be cats," as Miss Greenaway aptly remarked.) This evening, lying under pink mackerel skies, and picking apart a grass stalk, I was comforted by the thought that there is pattern everywhere, if only one notices it, and that pattern equals order, and that order equals meaning.

Why am I so rational and collected today Well, I will tell you.

I haven't mentioned Mamma's ghost lately, but I think you know it has troubled me, for many weeks, sliding into bed when the lights are out and breathing chills down my neck. Well, up until now I have bunched myself up under the sheets and willed it away, but last night I was desperate enough to change tack. I opened my eyes wide and said, loudly enough that the ghost might hear, but not so loudly that Miss Greenaway would, "What shall I do?" and then, lest there be any doubt as to whom I was addressing, "Please, help me, Mamma."

I don't say she replied out loud, but all of a sudden I thought, "Don't blame Frank," and I am perfectly sure that Mamma put those three words into my mind, because they were so clear and so immediate. Afterwards, I fell into a half-asleep, half-awake dream in which Mamma was lying in her bed at home, neither a ghost nor a corpse but as lovely as she ever was, with a pair of immense white swan's wings that swept over the edges of the bed and touched the carpet. My brother was there too, kneeling at the bedside with his face in his arms, but although Mamma rested her hand on his head, she rested her eyes on me.

She is right, of course. None of this is Frank's fault. Nobody blames Odysseus for being wounded by the sirens' song, any more than if he'd been struck by an arrow, or an illness, or a mighty wave. My brother is diseased, and it's my duty to tear him from the source of the infection, even if that makes him hate me for a while, just as Odysseus must have hated the sailors who roped him to the mast. He will understand, in time. One day we will sit together in our own house, playing backgammon by the fire and talking about cheerful things, and I will know by his tone, and glance, and gentle humour, that he is well again, and grateful to be so.

Friday, 21 July, 1876

I woke early and lazed in bed, leafing through this diary. Perhaps it was Mamma who directed my eyes to the pertinent page; at any rate I sat up, reread it half a dozen times, and cursed myself out loud for a forgetful fool. I've since discovered that this volume contains a total of <u>four</u> references to the fact that Miss Wilson moved to Brighton after her abrupt departure from Erskine Place! (See the twenty-fifth, twenty-sixth, and thirtieth of January and the twenty-second of April.)

Well, it all makes sense now. Surely I can guess how Frank's tantalising letter continues?

> *However, on reflection, Brighton is the home of Maude's former governess, Miss Wilson, with whom I am on the most excellent terms. She can be persuaded to chaperone Maude, I am sure, if I speak to her very nicely and offer her a generous fee. With my sister out of the way, we two will be free . . . etc.*

This, or something like it, is certainly what he wrote. Otherwise, why Brighton of all places? We have no special connection to Brighton. I have consulted the map, and if distance were the only consideration it would make much better sense for us to stay somewhere on the East Anglian coast: Great Yarmouth, for example, or Lowestoft.

I am trying hard to remember that none of this is Frank's fault, but he makes it difficult when he involves Miss Wilson. However, I shall stay true to him, even when he is untrue to me, and all shall be well in the end.

He is here, by the way. He arrived about an hour ago, on the early train.

Saturday, 22 July, 1876

It has been raining hard all day. Miss Greenaway is shut in her study, writing letters and working on her book, which would be a satisfactory state of affairs, were it not designed to torment Frank. When she first tried to retreat, shortly after he arrived, he stuck his foot in the door and told her she mustn't work on a Saturday, at which she smiled politely and thanked him, and said she would do her own work, in her own house, on any day she pleased. He began to reply, but somehow she contrived, foot or no foot, to close the door. I was sitting on the stairs; they didn't know I was watching.

Frank hung around the hall for a minute or two. It was very dark, and the rain was making shadows that streamed down the walls, so you can imagine my consternation when he threw open the front door and marched into the deluge without coat or hat.

I hesitated to follow, but I could feel Mamma's eyes on me, and it crossed my mind that he might do himself some harm, so I seized the large green umbrella from the stand and set off in pursuit.

He was striding so briskly down the lane that it was all I could do to keep him in view. I hadn't got my outdoor boots on, so the puddles soaked through my shoes and sloshed up my ankles, and the pale mud spattered my black dress (which was clean when I put it on this morning). What with that, and the way the umbrella kept clipping me round the ear as I ran, I confess that I struggled to maintain an appropriately stoical spirit. After all, I asked myself, what harm could Frank possibly do to himself in Sawyer's Fen? There are no great heights to jump off, no express trains to throw oneself under (indeed, no trains of any description for the next two and a half hours), and the river is so shallow and sluggish that one would have to be very determined indeed in order to drown in it.

All in all, I was more cross than anxious by the time he heard my footsteps and wheeled round, and I wasn't much mollified by the way his face fell.

"Oh. It's you."

"What are you doing, Frank? Where are you going?"

He ran his fingers through his dripping hair and shrugged. The cynical Maude whispered, "Byronic posturing," but the kinder Maude—the version of myself that I must and will take care to nurture—diagnosed genuine suffering. His skin was pasty and his eyes pink with tiredness.

I lifted the umbrella so that it covered him too. "Won't you come back to the house with me?" I said.

A cart came clopping round the corner, the Stirlings' cart, driven by Mr. Stirling himself, in a voluminous, waterproofed cape, and slowed as it passed us by. We stepped aside to avoid getting splashed, and I was proud of the gracious-yet-unsmiling nod with which I returned Mr. Stirling's stare. I suppose we did look strange, my brother and I, but he needn't have declared it so plainly.

"I hate that man," Frank said, when he was barely out of earshot.

I am not fond of Mr. Stirling myself, as you know, and wasn't inclined to leap to his defence. Still, it was my duty to soothe Frank's agitated temper, not stoke it, so I said nothing.

"I can't stand those brutish, brainless, man-of-the-soil types," Frank continued. "I don't know how anyone can."

I took my brother by the arm and turned him in the direction of ~~home~~ Orchard House. I considered making another straightforward plea ("Oh Frank, look at your beloved 'Kitty' with eyes wide open, and see her for what she is!"), but I'd already tried that without success, and the last thing I wanted was to anger and alienate him. I furled the umbrella, since it was serving little purpose and making my arm ache, and we set off through the downpour. If you had seen his face, so distant and careworn, you would have agreed with me that my only hope now lay in guile.

"I hear we're going to the seaside," I said, affecting good cheer.

"She told you?" Frank looked at me with something like interest. "She must really mean to come, if she told you. Good. That's good."

My hair was plastered over my face by now, and my shoes were squelching. I took a deep breath and maintained an easy-going air.

"I'm excited to see Brighton," I said. "Perhaps I will find Ebenezer there."

"Yes . . . what? Who's Ebenezer?"

Frank was gazing towards the house with a distracted air, and not evincing much interest in his own question. I answered it anyway.

"Ebenezer! My cat! The one Miss Wilson stole. I suspect she killed him, but she may have taken him to Brighton."

I glanced at him sidelong, but he didn't acknowledge my reference to Miss Wilson; he simply muttered, "Brighton. Yes, Brighton." Then he stopped walking and said, "You shan't mind if you're not always with us, shall you, Maude? You know I'm fond of you, but you can't be hanging round us all the time. You understand that, don't you?"

He strode off again before I'd had a chance to answer, and in my hurry to catch up I tripped on a rut and fell over, begriming my hands and clothes. He didn't notice, not even when I cried out for him to wait! God forgive me, it was as much as I could do not to run up from behind and thwack the umbrella across his addled pate, but I remembered my pledge to Mamma.

It is not his fault, it is not his fault, it is <u>not his fault</u>.

"When do we go?" I asked, as we turned in at the garden gate.

"What?"

"When do we leave for Brighton?"

"Brighton . . . oh . . . the eighteenth of August. Friday the eighteenth of August."

A good sister would have fussed over him once we were inside, bringing him tea and towels and so forth. I'm afraid my tolerance had run out by then: I will rescue my brother from dire peril, but not from wet hosiery. Not today, at any rate. I went upstairs to peel off my own sodden clothes and light my bedroom fire.

One day, when all this is over, I will be Frank's perfect sister, and I will have patience for the little things.

Tuesday, 25 July, 1876

<u>~~Plan to Prevent The Siren from Coming with Us to Brighton~~</u>

Plan to Rid Frank's Mind of the Pernicious Influence of The Siren

(Because whilst Brighton is the moment of crisis upon which my energies are focussed, my aims are in fact higher and wider.)

. . . I wonder whether it's wise to commit my plan to the page, in case Miss G. goes through my chest of drawers and finds it? Even now, my intuition contends that she'll do nothing of the sort, but I have learnt to distrust my intuition over the last few months. Who knows what such a woman might do? She stole my pa, only to begin work on my brother: she will hardly balk at poking about among my stockings and reading my diary.

On the other hand, if she has no reason to suspect me, she will have no reason to poke about, and I am making very sure she suspects nothing, by being as friendly and co-operative as ever I was (which is to say, neither too much nor too little). Yesterday we even shared a brief exchange on the subject of Frank—that's how self-possessed I am! It was after supper, when Miss Greenaway said, "Your brother seems to get by on very little work," and I replied, "Ah well, it's amazing how far quick wits and charm will take a man," at which she sighed and said, "Too true," and we both of us laughed a little ruefully (though why she should be rueful, I don't know). Fortunately I was busy with my mending at the time, and able to bow my head over my sewing box, rather than meet her eye.

In short: I have decided that I will detail my plan in this book. My thoughts flow best in ink, and whatever is not fixed on the page will not, I fear, be fixed in my brain.

Even so, can you believe that I am setting all this down in Miss Greenaway's study, during class, at the very table where she and Emily are poring over their Homer? A risky enterprise indeed! I was speedy with my real morning's work (geography and history), and Miss G. said I could do whatever I liked until lunch, so I said I would do some private writing (slipping in the word "private" without too much emphasis). I fetched this diary from upstairs, and what should I, what could I, write about, besides my scheme to rescue Frank?

Miss G. and Emily are absorbed in their translation work: pencils poised, brows puckered, heads all but touching. Emily has charge of the dictionary. They are not the least interested in me, but I'm shielding the page with my arm all the same.

The Siren caught my eye just now and smiled, and I smiled straight back, because even now she has the power to make me do so. Henceforth I'll keep my eyes on the page and my mind on my work. It's only by putting Will before Instinct that I can resist falling in much the same way as my brother.

So to the matter in hand:

Plan to Rid Frank's Mind of The Siren's Pernicious Influence

Initial thoughts:

- My brother must be persuaded that The Siren is unworthy of his affections.
- However, it is not in my power to convince him of this truth. In fact, the harder I press my case, the more he resists (see conversation Friday, 5 May).

- Is there anyone in the world who might succeed where I have failed? Mamma might have done it (she could persuade Frank to anything), but Mamma isn't here. Who else? The Siren herself, but I can hardly co-opt her!
- This appears to be an intractable problem . . . but I think it is not. It is intractable only when I attempt to deal with it head-on. What if I were to put honesty aside, and bring cunning into play?
- What if I were to "become" The Siren, and forge a letter to Frank purporting to be from her? A letter that demonstrated to my brother (but how?) the essential rottenness of his beloved's heart? If I, as his sister*

But now I've lost my train of thought. A moment ago Miss Greenaway slammed her book shut and exclaimed, "Enough!" and I thought my heart would stop.

In fact, she had not divined my thoughts; she'd merely been assailed by hunger pangs. "It's no good," she declared. "Homer has just made mention of cheese again, and it's more than I can bear. Maude, I don't suppose you'd make your heavenly Welsh rarebit for lunch . . . ?"

The upshot is, I have to stop writing in a moment and take myself off to the kitchen (although not before I've run upstairs and hidden this book in its drawer!).

After lunch

* If I, as his sister, were to say, "Frank, you are playing with fire!" he would retort, "You are mistaken," and I couldn't prove otherwise.

Whereas if I, as Miss Greenaway, were to open up his hand, place a hot coal on his palm, and fold his fingers around it . . .

Saturday, 5 August, 1876

I have been practising hard at The Siren's handwriting: she has a slanting, speedy style, full of dashes and angles, which is difficult to master. Unfortunately, she has never written to me at length, so I possess only tiny samples, such as the comments on my classwork ("Good"; "Very imaginative!"; "Learn 'vouloir' and 'aller' before Monday's lesson"; etc.). At some point I shall have to purloin a lengthier specimen from her desk. Also—and even more importantly—I shall have to decide what she (I) is (am) going to write in this projected letter.

In a little less than two weeks I will execute my plan, and the life I've led at Sawyer's Fen since March will be over. Everything will change. Perhaps Frank will insist on my coming to live with him, in Cambridge? Is that really so impossible? I can't see there's any alternative if I absolutely and positively refuse to live with The Relatives.

Monday, 7 August, 1876

We did our lessons outside today, since the weather was hot. If I hadn't felt so strange, I'd say it was delightful. We sat among the fruit trees with the sunlight dappling our pages, making it hard to concentrate; at least, I thought so, but nothing distracts Emily, who powers through books like a steam engine, and would continue to do so if the orchard caught fire and burned her to a crisp.

(Ha ha, can't you just picture her sitting there, a blackened skeleton with a pencil lead between her teeth and the charred remains of a Latin dictionary in her lap? I can.) Miss Greenaway reclined in a garden chair and sorted through the post. Presumably there were no letters from Frank, since he had left only this morning.

It was a scene of perfect happiness, the sunlight, the fruit trees, the books, the chirruping birds, and yet it wasn't, because it was on the verge of ending. I sat apart from it and felt its eeriness, as if it were accompanied by a piece of music in a minor key, which only I could hear.

Miss Greenaway said, "Have you finished that chapter, Maude?" and the ease with which she said it seemed so normal, and therefore so terrifying and moving, that I burst into tears. When she slid from her chair and dropped to her knees beside me, begging to know what the matter was, I almost told her everything. The temptation was stronger than it's ever been.

"I don't know," I lied, as soon as I could speak. She stroked my back for a while, before suggesting I drink some cold water and have a lie-down on my bed.

If you think this proves I am weak-willed, you can think again. As soon as I reached the house I went straight to the study, opened a desk drawer (the key was in the lock this time), and snatched a bundle of papers filled with Miss Greenaway's handwriting. They are only throwaway notes and scrawls, so the chances are she won't miss them: for example, the top page comprises a list of housekeeping jobs and a draft advertisement for a housekeeper. I brought them upstairs and hid them with the diary; I shall practise from them later.

I might have been quaking with sobs as I did it, but my actions were admirably cool-headed, don't you think so?

Wednesday, 9 August, 1876

The Plan is clear in my mind now, and although there is room for error (which is as much as to say, utter disaster), I hope and believe it will work.

Whenever I think of it, my heart flips and I find myself biting my knuckles. Miss Greenaway saw me doing this yesterday, when we were deadheading the roses, and she said, "Are you excited about Brighton?" as if I were four, rather than fourteen, years old. However, I was able to answer with an honest "Yes!" and since the conversation had turned that way quite naturally, I was able to check on the details of our itinerary without sounding in the least suspicious.

"We're not going via Cambridge this time, are we?"

"No, your brother has decided we're going to catch the slow train to Liverpool Street station, instead. It stops at Sawyer's Fen around half past nine in the morning. Frank has arranged to be on it, so we can travel to London together, and then on to Brighton."

"And when we get to Brighton," I asked, "where will we be staying?"

The question was artful, dear diary; designed to test Miss G.'s memory, or lack thereof. Thanks to Frank's letter, I already knew that we were staying with Henry Simpson's aunt on Wimborne Street. Pleasingly, she replied:

"That I couldn't tell you, I'm afraid. Your brother has arranged our accommodation through some university friend of his. He did tell me, but I've forgotten what he wrote, and I've managed to mislay the letter."

I snipped at another flower—I was in charge of the white, scented rose that grows round the front door—and dropped it in my basket. Miss Greenaway said, "Oh, be careful, Maude, that one was still in bloom."

"So it was," I said. "I'm sorry."

Really and truly though, I have no room in my head for gardening.

<u>The Definitive Plan</u>

1. *On the morning of our departure, as we're about to leave for the station, I shall come running into the house, out of breath, and tell Miss Greenaway that she is desperately needed at Willowbrook Farm. She will ask, "Why? What for?"*

Me: "I'm not sure. Mr. Stirling rode away so quickly; I only know it's urgent."

Miss G.: "Is Emily ill?"

Me: "I don't know . . . Perhaps . . ."

2. *Miss Greenaway will, inevitably, rush to her darling Robert and Emily's side, but she'll also fret about missing our train. I'll reassure her: "Don't worry, I'll run down to the station and tell Frank what's happened. The three of us can catch tomorrow's train. I'm sure Frank will understand."*

3. *As soon as Miss Greenaway has gone to the farm, I'll place a letter on the kitchen table, in such a way that she will notice it*

straightaway on her return. It will say that I have particular reasons for no longer wanting to live with her, and that I'm going to live with my brother instead. I will tell her not to follow me, or to contact me ever again. I don't think I need make my reasons explicit; she knows who and what she is.

4. *Next I shall sprint to the station and join Frank on the train. (Please God the train is not late.) Of course, he will be full of consternation—"Where is darling Kitty?" etc., etc.—but I shall say she's been unavoidably delayed, that she wants us to carry on to Brighton, and that she will join us at the earliest opportunity. If he is still inclined to disembark, I will hand him the first of two forged letters:*

Frank—I insist you travel to Brighton now, with your sister, and I promise to join you at the very earliest opportunity. Make no mistake: if you disobey me in this I shall not come at all. Your affectionate Kitty.

(If this doesn't do the trick, my plans are well and truly wrecked—as am I.)

5. *Once we are safe in Brighton, at Henry Simpson's aunt's boarding house, I will hand Frank—in all innocence—a second letter from Miss Greenaway. ("She told me not to give it to you until we'd arrived.") I have worked on this letter for many hours, scrupulously burning each draft as I went along, and this is my final version:*

Francis,

I have been patient with you over the last few weeks, and patient with your sister for much longer, but I find I have reached the limit of my endurance. Enjoy your little holiday in Brighton, but do not expect me to join you there. I am hard-pressed to imagine a duller way to spend the summer, than taking care of two children at the seaside.

You are a sweet boy, with your shiny little waistcoats and your silver-topped canes, and you have afforded me a great deal of amusement, but you are too much like your milksop mamma to inspire real affection. I never liked her at all. I liked your pa well enough—he really was diverting, for a while—but it was rude of him to die in my bed, and I cannot quite forgive him for that.

If it comes as any comfort, I esteem your dreary sister Maude even less than I esteem you. Oh, how she adores you! How earnestly she prates about her scintillating destiny . . . as your housekeeper! What an unbounded joy it will be for her, to fetch your supper and warm your slippers by the fire and tidy up after you, etc., etc., etc. . . .

At first I hoped to change her—to corrupt her, as you would have it—but I have tried and failed to make her my creature, and I admit defeat. Do <u>not</u> send her back when your holiday is over, or it will go very hard with her indeed. I don't want Maude, any more than I want you. Only the other day I asked Robert Stirling whether he could think of a more boring and useless object under the sun than a member of the Gower family? He suggested a spent match, but then retracted it, which made us both laugh.

Do you understand, now, the kind of woman you have tried to love? I am not for you, and you are not for me, little Frank. Skip away, into your sunny future, and never try, or wish, or hope to see me again.

K. Greenaway

6. *If, by some hideous chance, Frank and Miss Greenaway were to come together in the wake of this letter, discuss it, and puzzle out its true origin . . . then I am in more trouble than I can possibly imagine. However, having given it much thought, I believe I am safe. What man alive could bear to look at the (supposed) author of such a letter, let alone launch into an explanatory conversation with her?*

Saturday, 12 August, 1876

The kittens are five months old now, and quite the loveliest and wickedest creatures you ever saw. Little Dorrit has taken to scaling curtains at every opportunity, and this morning I was standing on a wobbly chair, trying to encourage her down from the curtain rail in the parlour, when Miss Greenaway came in.

"Be careful you don't tip over and break your neck," she said. "Oh, that reminds me, I meant to tell you: Emily will look after them while we're away."

Little Dorrit had just placed an experimental paw on my outstretched arm, otherwise I'd have swung round and toppled off the chair.

"Emily will have the cats?" I did my best to exclaim softly, so as not to discourage L. D.'s tentative progress. "Why? Who says so?"

Miss Greenaway seemed taken aback. "I asked her yesterday, and she agreed to do it. Was that wrong? But somebody has to care for them while we're in Brighton, and I take it you've made no other arrangements?"

I held my tongue as L. D. mewed, dug her claws into my sleeve, and found her balance. If Emily has the kittens while we are in Brighton, Emily will end up having them forever. Once I've cut all ties with Orchard House, I will scarcely be in a position to return and fetch them. I had planned to pack everything I needed in one bag on Friday and count the surplus as lost; I'd forgotten about the kittens. Miss Greenaway could hardly have hurt me more if she'd kicked the chair from under my feet.

"Emily to have my cats!" I clambered down, with Little Dorrit draped about my neck. "No!"

The last thing I wanted was to weep, or shout, or appear the least bit feeble, but my voice betrayed me. Miss Greenaway stared. I suppose, in her eyes, this was a trivial matter.

"Why ever not? She will look after them perfectly well!"

"Who knows what Emily Stirling might do?" I retorted wildly. "She might change their names and let them loose on the farm, so that they're good for nothing but killing mice and rats. She might"—I lost my breath and caught it again—"she might drown them."

"For heaven's sake!" Miss Greenaway put one hand on her hip and pushed the other through her hair. I believe she has it in her to storm and rage—once or twice I've braced myself—but she always draws back from the brink. She has a way of closing her eyes, compressing her lips, and taking a deep breath through her nose.

"You're making a spectacle of yourself, Maude. The cats will need food and water while we're away, will they not? You would not wish to come home from Brighton to find them dead?"

I merely stared at her, but she proceeded as if I'd nodded my assent.

"Well then. Emily has kindly offered to look after them, in order that you and I can enjoy our holiday. Rather than indulging yourself in a"—she waved her hand, searching for the word—"in a tantrum, which would shame a child half your age, you ought, by rights, to be setting off to Willowbrook Farm to thank her."

When I made no response she added, "I'm disappointed in you, Maude."

I thought: "Well, that is nothing—NOTHING—to how disappointed I am in you." If I hadn't had my plan so perfectly in place, I would have said so too.

Little Dorrit twisted round my shoulders, nudging and purring, but I plucked her off and dropped her. You remember, I have mentioned it several times before—that I'm unable to cry prettily. Well, this was the worst performance of my life so far: I could feel my face burning, and my nose streaming as profusely as my eyes, and yet, forgive me, Mamma, I did not feel ashamed. I exulted in my degradation. I let the tears flow, even though they seeped inside my mouth and made bubbles when I talked. I didn't wipe them away. It was a matter of dark satisfaction to know Miss Greenaway hated me, because it proved how right I was to hate her.

"Emily does not understand cats," I wept.

"Oh, what nonsense. Emily knows more about animals than you and I put together. She's grown up on a farm."

I did my best to sneer, although my facial expression was not mine to command. "Yes, precisely, she's a farm girl. How can a bumpkin like Emily Stirling hope to know anything about anything?"

I thought Miss Greenaway would either slap me, or burst out laughing, or both. In the end she did neither.

"Maude Gower, you are the most outrageous snob!"

"Very well, I'm a snob. It's not my fault if I'm better than her."

"How are you better than her?"

If I paused, it was because the question was stupid, and not because I lacked a ready answer.

"I'm prettier and I grew up in London and my father was a gentleman."

If my retort seems shallow, that's only because I was forced to spell it out. Some truths are more potent when they are implied, rather than expressed.

Miss Greenaway really did laugh this time. She also spun round on her heel, as if she couldn't stand the sight of me.

"Go to your room," she said. "This conversation is futile. You are not behaving like the rational and well-intentioned person I believe you to be, and I don't wish to see you again until you are."

I tried to scoop up Little Dorrit and take her with me, but she was in one of her darting moods and wouldn't come. I left her embarking on a fresh ascent of the parlour curtains; I hope she didn't fall off when I crashed the door shut behind me.

I haven't seen Miss Greenaway since. I thought she might bring me some lunch on a tray, by way of a peace offering, but she didn't, and aside from the fact that I'm hungry, I am glad, glad, glad.

If I didn't already know where I stood, apropos The Siren, I do now.

Monday, 14 August, 1876

You may think it a simple matter, to stay angry with someone who has done you wrong, but you've never had to deal with Miss

Greenaway. I've told you countless times how manipulative she is, and now I have further proof.

Yesterday her tactics consisted of pretending that nothing had happened (except that she said, "Better now?" as she brought the boiled eggs to the breakfast table). She talked to me as if all were well; as if my silences and monosyllables and faraway looks were adequate responses to her conversational gambits. During the day she dragged me off on our usual walks, and tossed book recommendations at me, along with her usual fanciful ideas and nuggets of gossip. It was very hard to remain where I wished to be, namely far away, inside myself.

Today her manner has been more impatient; for example when she showed me a funny cartoon in the newspaper, and I did not smile or laugh, she said, "Come now, Maude, don't sulk."

She is in the wrong, because my anger is legitimate, and yet how can I maintain a dead-eyed hauteur (and enjoy it) knowing that she judges such behaviour childishness?

I took a second look at the cartoon and raised my lips in the ghost of a smile, although I'm not convinced that improved matters, for either of us.

Tuesday, 15 August, 1876

Miss Greenaway tapped on my door when I was preparing for bed, so I called out, "Wait! I'm getting undressed!"

"That's all right," she said. "I don't need to come in."

I opened the door an inch to find out what she wanted, since her voice was quieter than usual, and our eyes met in the twilight. It's strange, isn't it, how you can feel a look, even when the other person's features are in shadow, and you can hardly see her at all?

It had crossed Miss Greenaway's mind to ask, if you please, whether I had started bleeding yet, and if not, whether I knew to expect it? She went on about how it's nothing to be ashamed or frightened of, and that as far as practical measures were concerned, she could supply me . . . etc., etc., etc. You don't need to know all that.

She means The Curse. Cook told me about it when I was twelve, so I was able to answer, "Yes, I know about it, and no, I haven't been afflicted yet." I thanked her, so that I couldn't be accused of sullenness, wished her goodnight, and slammed the door.

Thursday, 17 August, 1876

I have got Miss Greenaway's handwriting to perfection. If I were not destined to be Frank's housekeeper, I might make a career as an expert forger! The letters are written and safely stowed in my coat pocket.

Just think: by this time tomorrow it will be over, and my brother shall be saved!*

I must have gone over The Plan a thousand times in my head; I could execute each step in my sleep. So long as the train arrives on time, and Frank is pliable . . . but I am optimistic, on both counts. I have been listening for the 9:36 every morning since I made The Plan, and it has been punctual for over a week. As for Frank: I cannot see him disobeying The Siren's note. The combination of sharpness ("if you disobey me in this") with softness ("Your affectionate Kitty") was a masterstroke on my part, if you will forgive the note of self-congratulation.

* And so shall I.

I have bidden farewell to my beloved cats. This afternoon I staggered over to Willowbrook Farm with the three of them in a wicker basket. It's just as well the lid was tied down, for they buffeted and nudged it all the way, mewing to be let out.

Emily met me at the door and took me into the farmhouse kitchen. She was not unpleasant. We knelt to undo the straps on the basket, and she asked me to remind her of their names. I was alert for any smirks, but she looked positively solemn in her effort to remember.

"Little Dorrit is the smaller black one," she repeated after me. "Little Nell is the plumper black one. Nancy is the grey tabby."

As I left, Emily was trailing a length of brown wool across the floor and the three kittens were tumbling over one another in their eagerness to reach it. Emily glanced up and waved when I said, "Goodbye," but the cats took no notice.

Miss Greenaway knocked on my door <u>again</u> tonight. I don't know what the time was, but it was fully dark. I was lying awake, too hot, my bedsheets twisted round my legs.

"Are you asleep?" she whispered, as she came in. I thought she wanted to talk about The Curse again; in fact she wanted me to come outside and look at the stars.

"I have seen the stars before," I remarked drily.

"Yes, but it's a glorious night, and we're neither of us sleepy. Won't you come?" She held out my coat.

I couldn't find my shoes or slippers, but Miss Greenaway said not to worry, so I followed her outside with bare feet. She was carrying a blanket over one arm. We bent our heads back to take in the sky, and when our necks began to ache she spread the blanket on the grass, and we lay down for a better view.

"You don't see skies like this in London," she said, and I had to admit that we did not.

When you stare straight up at the night sky, with nothing in your line of sight, no trees or chimneys or gables, then you become untethered from the earth. At least, that's what it felt like to me. I wasn't gazing from the ground, at those clouds of silver-blue dust and diamond shards, I was floating among them, and the unending darkness was as much my element as theirs. It was thrilling, at first, like a dream of flying, but after a while I lost all sense of perspective and felt myself tumbling off the earth, into the void. In that split second of horror it was a relief to feel Miss Greenaway touch my arm, and to see the outline of her hand pointing at the sky, and to hear her talking about the different constellations.

Mind you, anyone's presence would have been a comfort at that moment; it didn't have to be her.

She knocked one last time, when I thought she'd gone to bed, and whispered, "Goodnight!" She must have been holding a candle, because a line of light appeared beneath my door.

"Goodnight!" I whispered back.

"Maude? Are we friends again?"

I crossed my fingers. ". . . Yes."

We stood very still: she in candlelight on her side of the door, I in darkness on mine. I placed my hand on the doorknob and wondered what would happen, to my resolve, to my anger, to my perception of the world, if I threw it open and fell into her arms. It was so strange to think of that alternative future existing a mere twist of the fingers away, that I almost did it, just to prove I could.

Her dress rustled as she moved away, and the golden light faded from under the door.

Now I'm in bed again. I shan't sleep tonight, my last night at Orchard House, which is why I'm writing my diary instead. I am using a pen, since I can't find a pencil, and I've gone and dripped ink on the sheets. I wonder whether Miss Greenaway will be cross when she finds out? Not that it matters to me.

Friday, 18 August, 1876
Mid-morning
London train

~~Dear God, I~~

The Plan did not flow seamlessly into effect, that much is true. On the other hand, here I am on the London train, with my brother and without Miss Greenaway, so it is possible to argue (in fact, I absolutely shall argue!) that it has worked. Sawyer's Fen is miles away. Frank has been made unhappy by the forged note, but he seems perfectly persuaded by it. He sits pouting, with his arms folded and his boots up on the seat.

It's just as well we have the compartment to ourselves: shortly after I'd boarded, as the train was pulling away from the halt, I was sick down my coat. I can't think why it happened. There wasn't much substance to it, as I'd only had half a cup of tea for breakfast, but I still had to mop myself up with a handkerchief and lower the windows to get rid of the smell. I feel better now. The day is warm and sunny, the breeze is fresh, and there cannot—there simply cannot—be any reason for gloom or fear.

I've tried making conversation with Frank, but he says, "What on earth's got into you? You sound like a maniac, talking for the sake of talking." Of course I don't sound maniacal—it's he who is so dull and slow—but there's no point my arguing. I'm better off turning to you, dear diary, until my brother recovers from his disappointment.

I suppose you will wish to hear about the events of the morning, but I'm not sure I can remember them in order. Perhaps I'll have a sandwich first, since I missed my breakfast. I only had a mouthful of tea . . . but I've written about that already.

Miss Greenaway and I made cheese and pickle sandwiches yesterday evening, and wrapped them in waxed paper, and I've got them here in my bag.

I had a bite, but the cheese is perhaps a little sour, because although I chewed it well, I couldn't swallow. I tried and tried, but in the end I spat the soggy lump into my handkerchief. Frank didn't see because he was staring out of the window. It's a broad, empty landscape . . . but you know all that. You know about the flat meadows and vast skies. Never mind talking for the sake of talking, I think I'm writing for the sake of writing!

We will leave Cambridgeshire behind very soon, and I suppose I shall never see it again.

Do you remember The Plan? How I was meant to rush up to Miss Greenaway, at the last minute, with an urgent summons from Robert Stirling? Well, when the time came I slunk out of the kitchen door and jumped up and down on the spot with as much energy as I could muster. I knew exactly what I was going to say, because I'd rehearsed it a million times in my head. As soon as I was sufficiently flushed and out of breath, I dashed to the front of the house, where I expected to find Miss Greenaway.

I did find Miss Greenaway. I found her in conversation with Robert Stirling.

Neither of them noticed me. I slid to a halt (and, well, I suppose I gaped) while the Urgent Message from Mr. Stirling dissolved on the tip of my tongue. I stared and raked my hands through my hair, and eventually had the presence of mind to step back round the corner of the house, so that they wouldn't see me and ask what on earth was the matter.

"The little rosewood desk!" Miss Greenaway was saying. "Oh goodness, she's absolutely right, I did promise it to her, ever so long ago. How stupid I am!"

Mr. Stirling was equally apologetic. "Kitty, really, it doesn't matter a jot. I told Emily she should remind you in class, but you know what she's like: she goes all shy and begs me to have a word . . . I'd quite forgotten you were leaving first thing. It will wait."

"Are you sure?"

"Perfectly sure! Don't give it another thought."

He came into view again, striding down the path with Scout at his heels, smiling back at Miss Greenaway, waving his hat in the air. "Enjoy your holiday!"

As he stopped to unfasten the gate, she called out, "Robert? If I have a moment, I'll fetch it from the cellar and leave it under the porch."

Another cheery wave. "Very well, thank you, but truly it's no matter. For goodness' sake, don't miss your train!"

He saw me, as he clapped his hat back on, and acknowledged my presence with a nod before closing the gate behind him and disappearing back down the lane with Scout.

I could have sworn I heard our train whistle down the line. In retrospect, I wonder whether I imagined it? Miss Greenaway didn't seem flustered in the least as she patted her pockets, saying to herself, "Keys, yes. Bags packed. Plants watered. Windows locked . . . Emily's desk. Oh, hello Maude!"

What could I do? I hadn't enough presence of mind to wipe the cold sweat from my palms, let alone to speak. Dumbly, I followed her round the house to the cellar. It was the oddest feeling, like being a body without a soul. (Is that what I was? What I am?) I could see the normal world in acute detail—the spongy moss between the paving flags, the scuffing on her boots, the untidy stitches in the hem of her dress—but I couldn't understand it. Up until now, it had possessed substance and meaning, and now, all of a sudden, it didn't.

Miss Greenaway made some remark about the desk, and laughed, and I managed a "Hmm," by way of reply. I followed her to the trapdoor and watched her heave it open with both hands. She said, "I'll have to feel my way; there isn't time to fetch a light," as she started down the steps, and when I remained silent she glanced at me.

I'm afraid of what she saw in my face. What was there to see? I don't know. What if—

I can't think about that.

The train sounded again—not so much a whistle as a scream—drawing nearer and nearer to the halt. (Did I imagine it? It can't have been as close as all that.) The voice inside my head said: "You must be on that train, Maude, and Miss Greenaway must not be on it," and I answered, "What am I to do?"

So I

~~And so~~

And so, as she was inching her way down the steps into the darkness, I hauled the trapdoor off the ground, swung it on its hinges, and dropped it.

I dropped it, and the air convulsed as it crashed shut. Then I slammed the bolt across, picked up my bag (which was by the front door), and ran. Not a single thought entered my head all the time

I was running, and getting on the train, and handing Frank the note, and vomiting down my coat.

I only began to think again when the windows were wide open, and I noticed with relief what a rational sort of day it is. You know what I mean by a "rational" day, don't you? I mean that there are cotton-wool clouds in a blue sky, and the wheels of the train are making a genial clickety-clack, and we've just passed a woman driving a donkey cart, and a boy sailing a toy boat in a stream. Everything will be all right because the alternative is unthinkable, on a day like today.

~~Doubtless I imagined it (yet again!), but when the trapdoor~~

~~There was a noise, after I dropped the~~

~~Did I~~

~~Did the trapdoor knock her off the steps? Before it thumped shut I think there was a scream, and a tumbling flurry, and a horrible crack like~~

~~But the stairs aren't so very high~~

~~And even if she did~~

~~And even if she did, she won't be badly hurt~~

~~I can't~~

I feel sick again.

My farewell letter to Miss Greenaway is still in my coat pocket. I meant to leave it on the kitchen table.

Two o'clock (approx.)
London to Brighton train

A List of Comforting Thoughts

- *Mr. Stirling will return to Orchard House this afternoon, to see if the foldaway desk is waiting for him under the porch. When Miss Greenaway hears him open the gate, she will hammer on the trapdoor and call out for help. She <u>must</u> hear the gate, because the hinge has been squeaky for ages, and she never gets round to oiling it.*
- *If not Mr. Stirling, then the postman. She will certainly hear him because he whistles music hall tunes and his hobnailed boots ring on the path.*
- *There is a sink in the cellar—I remember the drip of the tap—so she need not suffer from thirst.*
- *Although it will be cool in the cellar, it will not be dangerously cold—not on a day like today. Besides, there are dust sheets; she can wrap herself up in them.*
- *Miss Greenaway is not afraid of the dark.*
- ~~*She might be able to burst the trapdoor open, if she beats it hard enough with a brick or some such?*~~
- *What if I were to send Mr. Stirling an anonymous telegram?? (But no matter how I phrased it, he'd know it was from me.)*
- *I should not have bolted the trapdoor. <u>Why did I do that</u>?*
- *Have I committed a crime? I mean incarceration. What's the penalty for incarcerating someone in a cellar?*
- *This is supposed to be a list of <u>comforting</u> thoughts. Remember: Mamma shut me in a cellar against my will, and nobody called her a criminal.*
- *Oh God, please do something. Send Mr. Stirling or the postman to release her. (But how will I know?)*
- ~~*Miss Greenaway is The Feline/The Siren, and these are her just deserts.*~~

- ~~*Even if I did accidentally knock Miss Greenaway off the steps when I let go of the trapdoor, which I'm sure I didn't, but even if I did*~~
- *It's better not to think anything—comforting or otherwise. All will be well, because it must be.*
- *Oh God, oh God, oh God, please*

5:30 p.m.
No. 8 Wimborne Street, Brighton

We are in Brighton. Frank has gone to his room and I to mine. Mrs. Simpson, who runs the boarding house, is a pleasant woman. When I took my bonnet off in the hallway, she patted my head and called me a pretty child, which was reassuring, because if that's all I am (and who am I to question Mrs. Simpson's judgement?), then I can't be guilty of anything terribly serious. I can't, can I? Everything will be all right.

I would like to describe Brighton for you, but I barely took it in en route from the railway station. Frank and I are going to walk the promenade after supper (at his suggestion; perhaps he is improving already?), so I will take the opportunity to observe my surroundings properly, and report back.

In the meantime I'll unpack my bag and wash my face and hands. My room has two beds with lacy covers, and is overflowing with doilies and china ornaments. Mamma would have liked it, which is—

As I was unpacking, some papers fell out of my bag and scattered across the floor: they were the ones I'd taken from Miss Greenaway's desk, when I needed samples of her handwriting. I thought that they consisted merely of household lists, but I was wrong.

She must have found this letter difficult to write, because it's full of crossings out. It wasn't dated, so I don't know when she wrote it, or whether she ever copied it out and sent it.

Dear Frank,

You are wrong to think I despise you. I am old enough to have fancied myself in love one or twice before; I know the pain of it, and am sorry for your sufferings. Nevertheless, you must understand that I do not reciprocate your feelings, nor ever will, and that this is my final word on the subject.

I am sorry to come across as brutal, but if I shilly-shally for the sake of politeness, you will think me persuadable, which I am not. My reasons for refusing you are sound and deep—it is not merely a question of disparity in age, as you seem to think—however, you must forgive me if I decline to enumerate them.

If you will promise not to embarrass me—or your sister—any further, by word or deed, then I shall accede to your Brighton scheme, after all. I was reluctant when you broached the idea because I feared (and still fear, to some degree) that you regarded it as an opportunity to win me over. You and I must go to Brighton as friends, and as Maude's joint guardians, or not at all, and if you will agree to that, then I'm sure we shall have a pleasant time. Indeed, a holiday with her beloved brother may be just what Maude needs. I could scarcely believe it when you told me she had never been near the coast! We must put that right. I shall enjoy watching her face when she first sets eyes on the sea.

Both of you are dear to me—for your father's sake, if nothing else—but Maude is a child, who has been entrusted to my special care, and I shall always put her first. I'm afraid you have a tendency to undervalue your sister, Frank, although she thinks the world of you. Try observing her more carefully, and you will see that she is not "just a girl" or "just a child"—as you would say—but a perceptive and sensitive soul. Over the last few months, I have come to love her dearly.

Strictly between ourselves, I am planning to take her to America in the autumn; there are friends in Boston and Philadelphia whom I've been longing to visit for years, and it will be a pleasant excitement to leave England for a while, once the final edits on my Homer book are done and dusted. (Please do not mention this to Maude, as I look forward to doing so myself, once our plans are finalised.) I am confiding in you because, in all truth, I believe it will do you good to be rid of us both for a while: in our absence you may come to appreciate Maude a little more, and me a little less. You might also get some work done.

Poor Frank: I know it has been a difficult year for you, as well as for your sister. Although your first instinct will be to dismiss this letter as heartless, I hope you will come to understand my point of view, in time. Everything I have said, I have said in a spirit of comradely affection and sympathy.

Yours,
K. Greenaway

Late evening
No. 8 Wimborne Street, Brighton

I sat on the floor for a long time with my head in my hands, and then Frank knocked on my door and said we should go and see Brighton, so we did. Do you want to hear what I thought of it? I'll tell you, if you like. I'd rather be writing than thinking, and I can't stomach the thought of supper.

When Frank and I walked onto the beach, the shingle clattered under our feet like broken bones. I looked across at the famous Royal Pavilion, but its domes and minarets struck me as no weirder than the scenery inside my head. Even the sea—the much-vaunted sea—was nothing but a sad silver wasteland.

We made our way to the water's edge and got our feet wet. There were other holidaymakers getting their feet wet too, but they squealed with laughter and ran and caught at one another, while we simply stood and let the waves break over our boots. I tried to push my thoughts away—thoughts of the cellar—but they kept rushing back, like the sea.

"You should leave Miss Greenaway alone," I said. "She doesn't want you to love her."

Frank snorted. "Do you think I'm going to give up, just because a woman tells me I must?"

"Well . . . I think you ought."

He didn't respond.

We strolled with the crowds along the West Pier and sat on a bench to watch the gas lamps being lit. Frank sighed and said, "What dreary company you are tonight," and I felt no urge to defend myself. I even opened my mouth to say, "Yes, I know, I'm sorry," but no sound came out because I felt that if I moved, or uttered a sound, I would shatter into a million pieces. Other than that, we didn't exchange a word.

Miss Wilson strolled past us in the blue twilight. I suppose this was startling, given what a busy town Brighton is, but it felt inevitable to me, like something that the gods had preordained. She had a tiny dog on a lead, and was arm in arm with a portly old gentleman who might have been her father. I heard something about "a small party for Granny's birthday," and "Timmy is threatening to mix his famous punch," and laughter.

Frank did not notice Miss Wilson, and she did not notice us. As she sauntered by, I realised several things, all in the same rushing moment, which I may as well record:

1. *Miss Wilson is an ordinary human being—no better, no worse, than most. (Can the same be said of me? Or of my brother? I think I am a great deal worse than most.)*
2. *Ebenezer disappeared all by himself, because such things happen, and sometimes there is no one to blame.*
3. *Frank did not choose Brighton because Miss Wilson lives here. He chose it because Henry Simpson's aunt was generous, and offered her nephew's impecunious friend a reduced rent for his holiday.*
4. *When Mrs. Potter said, "Don't trust her one inch, she'll do for you," she was confused, and dying, and thought she was speaking to Miss Greenaway about me.*
5. *Frank is not the be-all and end-all. He is not even a man; he is as much a child as I am.*
6. *Miss Greenaway will forgive me—even me—because, whereas*

I am made up of vanity, ignorance, and spite, she is made up of love.

Saturday, 19 August, 1876
4:00 a.m.
No. 8 Wimborne Street, Brighton

Of course I could not undress and go to bed. I had to go home to Orchard House, and thank God I had no difficulty in persuading Frank to come too. He was still fully dressed when I rapped on his door at midnight, and his bedclothes—like mine—were unruffled.

"I have to go back to Sawyer's Fen, at once," I said, from the landing. "If you won't come with me, I shall go on my own, but you've got all the money and I need some for a ticket."

One of the guests knocked angrily on a wall and someone else—Mrs. Simpson, I think—emerged from a downstairs room calling, "Shush! Please!" Frank hauled me inside and shut the door. I repeated what I'd said, word for word.

"All right! I heard you the first time!" My brother heaved his packed valise off the bed and placed it by the door. "I've every intention of returning to Orchard House, but then I've got particular reasons. What can yours possibly be?"

The room that Mrs. Simpson had designated for my brother was as ladylike as mine, full to bursting with pretty, fragile objects. I'd have liked to pick them up, one by one, and fling them against the fireplace with a roar: the china handbells, the ornate mirror, the picture frames full of pressed, brownish flowers. When I'd finished doing that, I'd smash myself against it too, and shatter my body to dust.

"Well?" said Frank.

How many times have I longed for my brother's full attention? Well, now I had it. I took a porcelain dog off the mantelpiece, weighed it in my hand, and took a deep breath.

"Yesterday morning, just as we—I mean, Miss Greenaway and I—were leaving the house to meet your train . . ."

"Yes? She handed you that note?"

"No . . . that is, forget about the note, for a moment. You see, just as we were leaving, Mr. Stirling appeared—"

Frank clapped his hands. "I <u>knew</u> it!" he cried. "I knew Stirling was involved!"

"No, wait . . ."

But my brother was pacing the floor, listening, with the deepest attention, to the whirl of ideas inside his head. I could have said anything—could have said, "Frank, I locked Miss Greenaway in the cellar"—and he wouldn't have noticed. I placed the dog back on the mantelpiece, as Frank wheeled to face me.

"Did he hurt her? Forbid her to leave? Force her to write the note? That's it, isn't it! The monster! I <u>knew</u> he was at the bottom of all this. Oh, you foolish child, how has it taken you so long to speak up?"

"But I've hardly—"

"We must go at once."

"Yes, but Frank—"

"I told you that Stirling was a villain."

"Oh, but you see—"

"I do see!"

And so we might have continued, if Mrs. Simpson hadn't burst in, all of a flurry in nightcap and gown, begging us, please, to be quiet. I explained our urgent need to leave, but she pointed out that there weren't any passenger trains to London at this time of night, adding that we were welcome to stay till morning, if we could manage to do so in a civilised and peaceable fashion.

I thought she might be piqued by the brevity of our stay, but she seems happy enough to see us go.

Early morning
Brighton to London train

At last, at last it's light, and we're in the train, rushing back to Sawyer's Fen. Yesterday I thought I'd never see it again, but yesterday I was living in a dark dream; today I am awake.

That phrase about one's heart being in one's mouth feels revoltingly literal: if I open my lips to speak, or sigh, or—God forbid—eat, I fear a red, slippery lump coming loose from my throat and dropping onto my lap.

Frank keeps telling me off for fidgeting, so I'm keeping myself busy by writing.

I spent the first half hour of the journey leaning out of the window, shredding my letters—the one I forgot to leave on the kitchen table for Miss Greenaway, and the forged one I never did give to Frank—and releasing the pieces into the pearly morning air.

They whirled away as if they'd never been—just as my errors will whirl away, once I'm home again, putting everything to rights.

What if she won't forgive me, though? Would I, if I were her? Probably not.

~~What if~~

Sawyer's Fen
Night-time

"What if?" There are no "what ifs" anymore, but I still end up writing. Even tonight, when nothing can possibly be worth saying, I open my notebook and scribble the nothingness down. Maybe I'm writing a noose around my own neck, weaving a rope of words; maybe that's my intent? It's a good intent; my best yet. When they find this diary, discover what I've done, and sentence me to death by hanging, I shall be glad. Frightened, but glad.

It's dark in my bedroom, even with the candle. I can see the gold lettering on the spines of the Dickens books, and the spatters on the bedsheet where I spilled ink, the night before last. (The night before last!) Everything else is swallowed up in shadow.

Frank kept asking, "Why are we running?" as we hurried up the lane to Orchard House, and "Where are you going?" as I dashed through the garden gate and round the side of the house.

I knelt on the trapdoor and wrestled with the bolt—I don't remember it being so stiff before—cutting my hand in the process. I hope my blood is poisoned with rust; I hope I die. I kept crying, "I'm here!" over and over again. "I'm coming! I'm coming!"

I forgot that Frank was there, until he seized me by the shoulders and hauled me to my feet.

"What is it?" he demanded. "What in God's name are you doing?"

All the different shades of green in the garden wobbled about, as he shook me. I tried hard to answer—I really did—but I couldn't. Frank struck my cheek very hard and shouted, "Maude! You're hysterical! Stop it now!"

Was I hysterical? I only know that it was difficult to hear myself think over the noisy memories of yesterday morning, when the trapdoor boomed shut and the air contracted and there was a broken cry that might have existed solely in my head but might, equally, have come from Miss Greenaway's mouth, and please God it was only in my head.

Frank slapped my other cheek.

I pointed at the trapdoor. "She's in there."

Frank stared, but didn't comprehend, so I tugged, and strained, and lifted it open by myself.

"But it's dark," said Frank.

So it was. Dark, cold, and lonely as a tomb.

"Maude? What do you mean, she's in there?"

"Go and get a lamp," I said. "The house is unlocked. You'll find one in the kitchen, on the shelf above the range, and the matches are there too."

"Maude?"

"Please."

Slowly my brother backed away, wiping his palms against his coat as if he regretted their contact with my face. I waited until he'd gone before feeling my way onto the steps, shuffling into the dank blackness of all my nightmares, groping for the rope that hung in loops along the wall.

"Miss Greenaway?"

I wasn't afraid to whisper her name. With anyone else, I'd have been flinching in anticipation of icy fingers round my neck, or vengeful nails in my eyes, but I could never flinch from her. Indeed, I longed for nothing more than to feel her arms reaching through the darkness—but nothing stirred in the cellar, and there was no answer to my call.

At the bottom of the steps I dropped to my hands and knees and began crawling, searching the floor by touch. I could have stayed upright and shuffled about on my feet, but I wanted to find her with my hands, not my boots.

There were metallic slivers lying about, which clinked under my hands and spiked my knees, so I paused to explore their shapes with my fingertips. Blunted needles? Twisted wires? Some sort of fastenings . . .

Hairpins. They were hairpins.

I crawled a little farther, and discovered an edge of fabric, whose splayed folds I followed until I was touching a solid body, which I patted gently—legs, stomach, breast, shoulders, face—whilst begging it to move. I ran my hands over her loosened hair. Most of it was springy to the touch, as it had always been, but some was clumped and sticky, as if she'd doused one half of her head with jam and left it to dry. My searching fingers travelled over her nose and lips, and I told myself I was mistaken; that this wasn't a person at all. The skin didn't feel a bit like skin. It was waxy and solid, like a brand-new candle waiting to be lit.

I tried to think what else it could be, this humanlike thing, but nothing came to mind.

Frank started down the steps. He trod with caution, one step at a time, the light swaying wildly round the walls, and stopped only when he reached the bottom.

"Maude?" My brother's voice was small and imploring, but I hadn't any words with which to meet it. I buried my face in Miss Greenaway's side and squeezed my eyes shut, but it was only a matter of time before the lamplight found us out.

We stayed in the cellar for a long time, because we weren't sure what to do. Frank crouched nearby but wouldn't touch her—wouldn't even look at her—so it was left to me to lift her head onto my lap and stroke her lovely hair (I didn't touch the places where it was clogged and matted). On one occasion I tried to lift her hand to my lips, but her arm was unyielding, and I felt faint when I tried to bend it.

"We should carry her up the steps," I said, but Frank shook his head and breathed, "I can't." His voice sounded too slight for his body, and his eyes looked too big for his face.

We were both shivering and the brick floor was imprinting ridges on my knees and turning them numb. I had no idea that a head could be so heavy.

"Stirling will hang for this," Frank declared.

I glanced up.

"Robert Stirling?"

"Mark my words, Maude, this was no accident. It was foul play. The trapdoor had been bolted."

I looked down again. Miss Greenaway's eyes were open, staring at Frank, and yet not at Frank. I wanted to close them, but if I did that—or tried to—I would never see them again.

"It wasn't Mr. Stirling's fault," I said.

"Believe me, it was. Remember, you told me he called round, just as you were leaving . . ."

"Frank, it wasn't his fault." I followed the curl of her ear with my thumb, first one way, then the other. "How do you suppose I knew where to find her?"

My brother had been staring at his knees, but he looked up at this.

"What . . . ? You mean . . ."

I considered a spluttered denial (it wasn't too late), but I took a deep breath instead, and nodded, and then it was too late.

Does either of us know what he understood by my nod? Or what degree of guilt I'd confessed to? Not that it matters. Who cares? Miss Greenaway is dead.

I thought we'd be in that cellar for the rest of our lives, growing colder and hungrier and unhappier until we died, because what reason was there to move? Yet we did move in the end, and Frank must have summoned people, because there they were: the doctor, the vicar, the policeman, and Mr. Stirling, among others. Miss Greenaway's body was taken away, when I wasn't looking. Somebody (I think it was Mrs. Banks, the vicar's wife) fetched a basin of warm, soapy water with which she bathed the gore from my face and hands, before helping me into a clean dress.

Everybody's kindness was terrible, but Mr. Stirling's was the worst of all. He sat with Frank and me at the kitchen table, grey-skinned and drawn, and placed his hand on mine. He said, "I don't expect you ever to forgive me, Maude. I know I'll never forgive myself."

I didn't understand what he meant, to begin with; I entertained a fleeting hope that he had killed her, after all, and that the guilt was his. Of course, he was only alluding to his request for the fold-away desk, and I wanted to say, "Oh, that's got nothing to do with it," but instead I shivered, and chattered my teeth, and folded myself tight inside my arms.

Mr. Stirling patted my hand, then he got up and pottered about the kitchen—big, coarse, "unfeeling" Mr. Stirling—fetching biscuits from the tin and heating a pan of milk for me and my brother to drink. Frank wouldn't touch his, but I was determined to drink mine, to show Mr. S. that I didn't hate him. As soon as I'd gulped it all down, I rushed outside and spewed it into the gutter.

I intended to hide inside the green skirts of the willow tree, where it was quiet and there were no people, but Frank had followed me into the garden. I was still bent double, spitting out strands of milk, when he called, "Maude? It's the police! They want to talk to you."

I won't deny that my insides twisted into a knot. I saw it all so clearly as I leaned over the gutter: the handcuffs locking around my wrists, the prison gates opening wide like jaws, the judge reaching for his black cap, the cell, the rope, the unthinkable drop.

"I'm coming," I murmured, but Frank had already come to me. His grip bruised my arm, but he spoke softly with his lips touching my ear.

"If you disgrace the family, I'll kill you myself," he whispered. "Do you understand?"

"No," I whimpered, trying to twist round so that I could read his face, but he held me fast.

"Here's the story. She sent you off on the train, and told you to give me that note. Nobody knows why she did, she just did: that much is true at any rate." He gave my arm a rough shake. "Yes?"

"Yes."

"You and I set off to Brighton, as instructed, but we were worried about her, so we decided to come back. We found the trapdoor lying open—OPEN, Maude—and that's how we knew to search the cellar. Yes?"

"Yes."

"The whole thing must have been an accident."

"Yes."

"There was no blood on the trapdoor. I checked. It must have been when her head hit the floor that her skull . . . that all the blood . . ."

I stared stupidly at my feet. His grip tightened, as if he contemplated ripping my arm out of its socket, but suddenly he let go, with a shove, and turned on his heel.

The police were represented by a tall, moustachioed constable, whom I'd seen about the village once or twice. I did not like his moustache, it was excessively large, as if its main purpose was to conceal his face. When we entered the parlour, he unfolded himself from the chair, and I glimpsed teeth among the hairs as he smiled.

"A sorry business," he said, shaking our hands. "Won't you sit?"

"Thank you," said Frank, "but we'd rather stand."

Frank proceeded to tell the story in his own words, and I followed with an identical version. Every now and then I looked at my brother, but he wouldn't spare me a glance, let alone any sign of approval.

My face burned when we came to the forged note, and I would have sat down if I could. The constable read it out in full, though I could have recited it by heart:

"Frank—I insist you travel to Brighton now, with your sister, and I promise to join you at the very earliest opportunity. Make no mistake: if you disobey me in this I shall not come at all. Your affectionate Kitty."

He paused at the end, and I tensed in anticipation of the inevitable . . . but the inevitable did not come. Rather than declare the note a blatant forgery, he mused, "Curious, isn't it? How anxious she was to be left alone."

"We thought so too," Frank agreed, smoothly. "It wasn't like her to be so vehement. The more we pondered it, the more worried we grew, and that's why we came back."

The constable stroked his moustache.

"You think . . ." He glanced apologetically in my direction before mouthing, at Frank, "Self-destruction?" and miming the action of someone slitting their own throat.

I expected Frank to protest, but he tightened his grip on my arm and said, "It has to be a possibility."

The policeman sighed and nodded. "The mysteries of the human psychology, eh, Mr. Gower?"

"Indeed."

No response was required of me, since the conversation had taken place entirely over my head. Nevertheless, as we were leaving, I shook myself free of my brother's grasp and said, "Sir? Miss Greenaway did not kill herself."

The constable's eyes were sharp, sharper than I'd taken them to be.

"How do you say she died, miss?"

Frank was powerless to rant, or glare, or dig me with his elbow. The best he could do was press his finger into my back, as if he should like to drive a nail through my spine. My mouth went dry, and I saw it all again: the cell, the rope, the drop.

". . . I say it was an accident."

"An accident, miss?"

"Those cellar steps are horribly dark and steep."

He seemed to ponder my words, and eventually he nodded, as much as to say, "Fair enough, and so they are."

Monday, 21 August, 1876

- Frank has gone away without saying goodbye.
- Pa's tobacco pouch has lost its scent entirely, and I can't even picture his face anymore.
- Mamma's ghost came to me last night, but I ordered her away in such a tone that she took fright and obeyed. That's to say, when I rolled over in bed, to look her in the eye, she wasn't there.

So the world turns. This time last week my home was Orchard House, and Miss Greenaway was alive, and I thought I hated her.

Now my home is to be with Aunt Judith and Uncle Talbot at the Firs in St. Albans, and Miss Greenaway is dead, and I know that I do not hate her.

Frank (or someone) must have telegraphed The Relatives, and they have lost no time in replying. The boy who delivers the telegrams has visited Orchard House no fewer than three times today.

Cousins John and Amelia were typically brief and disobliging: their telegram read simply, "God's will be done."

Aunt Janet wrote in a similar vein, albeit more expansively (and expensively): "For there shall be no reward to the evil man; the candle of the wicked shall be put out. Proverbs 24:20."

Aunt Judith and Uncle Talbot wrote, "Maude must come to us at once," which is at least pragmatic, although I doubt they'll desist altogether from crowing. They're probably saving their barbs for my arrival at the Firs, where they can address me face to face, day in, day out, free of charge.

Emily came upstairs this afternoon, while I was packing, and tapped on my open door. What could I do but invite her in?

I don't know how to judge prettiness anymore, and I don't know why I used to set such store by it. Emily and I are the same in all outward essentials: a red nose, a pair of leaking eyes, a layer of pasty skin, a head of unkempt hair, a body that's forgotten how to sleep.

"Emily," I said.

"Hello, Maude."

I was kneeling by my trunk, squeezing the backgammon set down one side and piling books on top of my clothes (only the books I brought with me in March; I won't take anything that belongs to Miss Greenaway and Orchard House), so she came and helped me. We worked in silence for a while, but her sobbing became ever more difficult to ignore, and eventually she burst out:

"That wretched, wretched desk."

"It's not your fault," I said.

"It is! If I hadn't pestered—"

"Emily, it is <u>not</u> your fault."

I sounded angry. Partly to show that I wasn't (not with her, anyway), and partly because I had nothing useful to add, I shuffled on my knees to her side of the trunk and held her tight while she cried on my shoulder. How I envied the honesty of her tears.

"I'll look after the cats until you send for them," she said, as soon as she could speak. "Or if you're not allowed to have them in St. Albans, don't worry, they'll be all right at the farm. If you'll give me your address, I'll write from time to time and let you know how they're keeping."

I nodded. I ought to have thanked her, and wished her well, and made reference to her university plans, but somehow I didn't think of it till later, when I was fastening the straps on my trunk and writing my new address onto luggage labels.

Miss Maude Louise Gower
The Firs
Broad Street
St. Albans
Hertfordshire

All the things I ought to do, I don't; and all the things I ought not to do, I do. Perhaps I can't help it.

I've lost my taste for diarising. Opening this notebook at random, a moment ago, I read: "He and I"—meaning Frank and I—"are not living through the best of times." When I wrote that, I was not a murderer, and my brother still liked me, and my future lay with Miss Greenaway, who was alive, and who loved me enough to take me with her to America.

So I'm going to stop. The world is unalterably bleak, and what is the point of recording this observation, day after day? Who wants to read it? You don't. I don't.

To paraphrase Aunt Janet and the book of Proverbs: the candle of the wicked is put out, and about time too.

Goodbye, diary.

PEGGY

September 1945

Peggy switches the lamp off, to ease her aching eyes. She rests one hand on the final page of the diary and smoothes her son's hair with the other. The shapes of things are newly visible in the gloom, as night fades into dawn, but she is not sufficiently familiar with the house to know what they are. There's a blotch in the corner that looks like a crouching woman, but is probably a chair. The oval to the left of the door is the right height and size to be the face of a child, but must be a picture or a mirror.

"Poor Maude," she whispers. "Poor little girl. You weren't really wicked."

No, says a voice inside her head. *Not then*.

Peggy pictures Maude the grown woman, lying every night in this bed, trying to sleep, dwelling on her secret.

What becomes of a person who kills the thing she loves?

What would become of me, if I . . . ?

Peggy's fingers tighten around Laurie's scalp until he whimpers in his sleep and she notices what she's doing, and stops.

Laurie rolls onto his side, and as the blanket lifts, the diary slips from Peggy's bent knees, and two folded papers fall out.

Letters?

Warily, Peggy opens the pages and checks the names and dates. There's a letter from Frank to Maude, written on 20 March, 1880, and another from Maude to Frank, on 22 March, 1880.

Peggy rubs her eyes, digging in hard with the heels of her hands, and flicks the light back on.

115b Weston Street
London
20 March, 1880

Dear Maude,

I gather that congratulations are in order? I was dining out with a few chums last night when I happened to run into our old friend Robert Stirling. We talked for a while on neutral topics—his work on the farm, my work at Guy's Hospital, his daughter's forthcoming trip to Italy (apparently she's going on a "dig" in the summer, with a gaggle of like-minded ladies from Newnham College, but doubtless you know about that already). As the conversation was winding down, Stirling suddenly said, "What about the 'heiress'? I hope she is well and happy?"

An awkward passage ensued, during which I was obliged to make it clear, as politely as I could, that I hadn't the foggiest notion what he was talking about. I was most embarrassed, but you would <u>not</u> have been. You would have had no difficulty understanding what he meant, because you are well aware—I'm sure—that Robert Stirling was appointed as a trustee in Kitty Greenaway's will, and that upon attaining the grand old age of eighteen, in a few weeks' time, you will inherit Orchard House and a "modest" income!!! Stirling professed himself "awfully sorry" if *he'd spoken out of turn, but he'd assumed (reasonably enough) that I'd known about it "for years."*

Well, I hadn't known "for years," had I? I'd no idea. I wonder when—or whether—you were going to break the news to your closest living relation? But never mind, never mind—reproaches are no use to either of us. I sat down to write this letter with the sincere purpose of congratulating you—and I do. It is a fine thing—a very fine thing indeed—to come into money. How do you intend to use it? I hope you shan't let Aunt Janet persuade you to donate the lot to one of her worthy causes! It's just the sort of romantic gesture a girl like you might make—that's to say, a little girl with a nasty secret and a heavy conscience.

No, no, I am not mocking you. Truly, I am not. Whatever dark deed you committed in the summer of 1876, I for one am willing to forgive and forget. It goes without saying that this inheritance will not fill you—as it would any normal person—with unalloyed pleasure. How could it? You know that Kitty Greenaway would not have singled you out for such a prize had she seen the darkness in your heart; had she anticipated, poor woman, the manner of her death, and your role in it. You know to what a tragic degree her affection was misplaced, and therefore you feel (that is, I do you the justice of believing you feel) burdened, rather than freed, by your good fortune.

How strange! I began this letter in a spirit of weariness (I have been working without rest, yet that chance meeting with Stirling yesterday evening deprived me of a well-earned night's sleep), and angry (with you, for what you did, and for the injustice of your sudden prosperity), but the more I write, the more vividly I recall the little Miss Mouse I used to love, and my mood softens. Perhaps I am unduly influenced by the restful quiet of my lamplit room, or the bottle of brandy by my chair, but I begin to wonder . . .

I wonder whether my poor, lost sister might be restored to me, after all? Is it possible? We used to share a dream of the future (you won't have forgotten) in which I was a doctor with a thriving practice of my own, and you kept house, and nothing troubled us—neither demanding lodgers, nor bossy governesses, nor inept servants, nor tiresome relatives, nor damp coal, nor a paucity of cats.

Of course you remember. It brings a tear to your eye, as it does to mine.

I am ignorant as to the extent of Kitty's generosity, but the sale of Orchard House alone—never mind the rest—would enable me to set up in my own practice far, far sooner than I could otherwise hope. Think of it, Maude! What a flawless end to all your troubles: in one stroke you would atone for your sins, make peace with your only brother, and create a home for us both!

What say you? Don't be afraid to accede to my plan; don't be hobbled by self-doubt. Despite all that has happened, I will welcome you with open arms, and call you sister, and take every care not to mention the past. What is done, is done.

Think how happy Pa and Mamma would be to know that we loved one another again!

Write back with all haste.

Your brother,
Frank

LETTER TO FRANK, IN REPLY TO HIS OF THE TWENTIETH

(A copy for my diary, by way of a postscript.)

The Firs
St. Albans
Hertfordshire
22 March, 1880

My dear Frank,

When I came down to breakfast this morning and found an envelope addressed to me, in your handwriting, I was too happy and nervous to eat. I had to endure an interminable lecture from Aunt Judith on Proper Gratitude for the Fruits of the Earth, and the Horrible Sin of Wastefulness, before I was able to escape to my room. How strange to hear from you again, after so long!

Once I'd opened it and read to the end, however, all my happiness evaporated, along with all my nerves. How transparent you are, when you are excited! The tone of your letter seems to waver between distaste and tolerance, depending on whether my past sins or my future wealth is uppermost in your mind—and the more you think about the money, the more you persuade yourself that you could learn to like me again. Really, Frank!

Apparently you are offended by my silence on the subject of the inheritance? I find this odd, and more than a little grating, given the number of times I have written to you since 1876—albeit on matters that did not relate to money—without receiving a word in reply. You expect me to exhibit an unusual degree of persistence!

Nevertheless, you are mistaken in supposing that I have kept the news a secret for years—I was apprised of it myself only last month. When the will was read, four years ago, The Relatives agreed amongst themselves that I should not be made aware of my good fortune whilst I was still a child, lest my moral character suffer as a result (i.e., if I were to know that one day, in the not too distant future, I would be free of them, it might have inspired me with impudence or complacency or—God forbid—hopefulness). It's bad enough, in their eyes, that I'm to inherit at eighteen. "Twenty-one would have been a more proper age," as Aunt Janet never tires of observing—the implication being, as always, that Miss Greenaway was improper in everything she did, thought, or said. (I have not told them that I mean to be improper in much the same way—only imagine the lectures and gruel suppers that would ensue—but I mean to mention it when my birthday comes round.)

The flippant tone of this letter is disgusting to you, I know. In your own letter you make much of my guilt—of my "nasty secret" and "heavy conscience"—and no doubt you anticipated several bolts of sackcloth and a mountain of ashes by way of reply. Oh Frank, how can I explain myself? Try to understand: the remorse I suffer is not something I care to describe—either to you or to anyone. Many people did Miss Greenaway wrong, but I was the worst of them, and I have borne that knowledge for years. I bear it still; I always will. It won't change because I spend my life weeping, or beating myself with a scourge, or abasing myself in front of you. It is a part of me—a leaden bullet, embedded in my heart's core—because I did what I did, and cannot undo it.

And yet you *are not entitled to the self-righteous tone that you affect in your letter! Most emphatically you are not, no matter how you have reordered the past to suit your memory. Have you forgotten all your talk of "felines" and "sirens" and "Pre-Raphaelite stunners"? I may have failed to perceive Miss Greenaway for what she was, but you were the one who taught me to see. You, among others.*

In answer to the request, which is the basis of your letter: I shall gladly use a part of my inheritance to help set you up in your own practice; however, nothing shall induce me to sell Orchard House. Nor (although I suspect, with this letter, the offer is revoked) shall I ever live with you, or be your housekeeper. Certainly I have not forgotten our dream, nor can I think of it without a sentimental regret, but it has become impossible. I—we—have altered beyond recognition since those days.

You may wonder at my firm attachment to the house. The fact is, I visited Orchard House last week, for the first time since that summer. I wouldn't have had the courage to do it of my own accord, but the two aunts and Uncle Talbot were desperately curious to see it, so they persuaded themselves, and me, that it was The Right Thing to Do in advance of my important birthday.

I needn't have been afraid. Not really. The worst part was the journey to Sawyer's Fen, and the walk from the halt, but my fears were calmed the moment I entered the garden. It was always a lovely wilderness, but after four years of minimal tending (which Mr. Stirling kindly arranged), it is lovelier and wilder than ever.

As for the interior of the house: no one appears to have touched it since the funeral. Miss Greenaway's desk was just as it was on the day of our journey to Brighton, with its ink-stained pens, and its piles of letters and books, and the spectacles wrapped loosely in a silk cloth. There was a colourless bunch of violets in a jam jar, which turned to dust when I touched them.

Do you remember Satis House, in <u>Great Expectations</u>*, where Miss Havisham withers from year to year in her wedding dress? When I saw those violets disintegrate, I thought: "I am free to be anyone now, why* *not be Miss Havisham?" Orchard House could provide the setting for my living death, and there would be a decided satisfaction to be had from such a theatrical semi-existence. Wallowing is always pleasant—even if the substance you wallow in is nothing more luscious than Self-Loathing.*

Meanwhile, the aunts' eager footsteps thumped about the whole house, and Uncle Talbot stayed downstairs to explore the bookshelves. There was an (unacknowledged) mood of deepening disappointment amongst the three of them, as they failed to make any scandalous discoveries. The pencil portrait of Pa, which Miss Greenaway kept on her dressing table, gave rise to a short-lived "frisson," but there was nothing else. Uncle Talbot declared the books "thoroughly tedious, bluestocking nonsense," and the aunts had to fall back on criticism of the accumulated dust and cobwebs. They trooped outside after a while, to my immense relief (later on I spotted them through the window, congregating around the infamous trapdoor).

After they'd gone, a cat sauntered in through the open window: a sleek grey cat, who may have been—who surely was—my own Nancy. She wove herself round my ankles, as if we were old friends, and blinked luxuriously when I rubbed her under the chin. I couldn't ask Emily to vouch for her identity, as she was away at college, but I decided to believe it was she.

Miss Havisham would have got along much better, I think, with a cat. (Or two, or three.)

It was unsettling to walk about the house again—I won't deny it. All those memories—all that guilt—which had grown amorphous over the years, gained a sudden solidity and shape. One moment I felt, "I cannot bear to be here a moment longer," the next, "I cannot bear to leave"—and so I continued to vacillate as I made my way from room to room.

I found the bracelet that I took from the cellar, the one that Pa gave Miss Greenaway—but I never told you about that, did I? It is a simple silver band with a hinge and a clasp, and Pa (presumably) had it inscribed with a Latin phrase: "Caritas Omnia Ignoscit." I believe this translates (though you will know better than I) as: "Love Forgives Everything."

When I first saw the bracelet four years ago, and looked up the words in Miss Greenaway's Latin dictionary, I thought it rather tawdry. When I retrieved it from the floor of my old bedroom, last week—having accidentally caught it with my foot and sent it rolling and skittering across the boards—it struck me to the bone. I fitted it round my wrist there and then, and have worn it ever since.

I know you will think it self-deceiving, to find comfort in something so small—but I do. I must. Comfort has been in short supply these last few years; I won't turn up my nose when it lands at my feet.

I don't yet know what I shall do with my house, and my new-found independence, but I'm determined to use them to <u>live</u>. Perhaps I shall turn the house into a school, or an orphanage, or a hospital; perhaps I'll live quietly and write novels at Miss Greenaway's desk; perhaps I'll shut the place up and go travelling, and make myself known to her American friends. Perhaps I'll do all of these things! Oh Frank, believe me: if I could bring her back by dying, I would die this minute. I've wished for nothing else since August 1876. It's no use, though, is it? I can't bring her back by dying, I can only honour her by living—so that is what I shall do. I shall make something good—something very good—of my life.

The other day I overheard Aunt Judith tell Aunt Janet: "Talbot thinks Maude has been more subdued than ever since we told her about her inheritance, but I'm not so sure. There's a fire smouldering away behind those cold blue eyes, which wasn't there before, and I don't like it." Aunt

Janet agreed. Far be it from me to look to The Relatives for wisdom and insight, but there is something in what she says that rings true.

I hope you have read this letter to the end, and that you will forgive its occasional harshness of tone. I think if you listen—really listen to my words—you will understand.

Let us meet soon, and try to be friends again. You will always be my dear Frank, for the sake of those who have loved us both, and—even more—for the true affection we bore one another as children.

Your sister,
Maude

PEGGY

September 1945

The room smells of coal, but there's no accompanying warmth. Draughty daylight flows over her sleeping face. She rolls onto her stomach and reaches across the bed for Laurie, but the covers have been thrown back, and the mattress is cold.

There is someone else in the room: someone still and watchful. Not Laurie. Not the cat. Peggy opens her eyes and there is her father-in-law, sitting beside the bed in a straight-backed chair.

"Frank . . ." Her voice is too groggy with sleep to express the unease she feels. She gropes at the buttons on her pyjama jacket to check they haven't come undone and discovers, with relief, that she's wearing her husband's blue sweater.

At least Frank Gower is old again, the white hair and the liver spot are present and correct, but, even so, it's like seeing him for the first time. She notes that he's holding Maude's diary on his lap.

"Where's Laurie?" she murmurs.

"In the bathroom."

Peggy raises her head from the pillow. Sure enough, a lavatory flushes across the landing, and the taps over the basin creak and gush.

She lies down again, and is about to remark on the diary when Frank says, "It was Laurence who let me in, at first light. He was filthy—covered from head to foot in cobwebs and coal dust and I don't know what—his pyjamas will need a good scrub. I asked if he'd been sweeping the chimneys."

"What did he say?"

"He said . . ." Frank glances down at the diary, and up again at Peggy.

"What?"

"He said he'd been playing in the cellar."

Their eyes meet and Peggy hauls herself into a sitting position. Even with Jonathan's sweater, she's freezing.

"I told you we should never have set foot in this place." Frank leans forwards in his chair. "Now will you believe me?"

Peggy answers with a sceptical look as the bathroom door creaks opens and small footsteps pad across the landing. Laurie's hair is dripping, and his skin is rosy, and he's carrying his filthy pyjamas in a bundle under his arm.

Peggy pulls him in for a kiss and fusses mildly about the fact that his hair is wet.

"Come on, let's get you dressed," she says, helping him on with the clothes he was wearing yesterday: green jersey, grey shorts and socks, scuffed shoes. As she sits him on edge of the bed and kneels to do his socks she wonders, airily: "How did you discover the cellar, you clever old thing? Grandad thought it was bricked up."

Laurie has covered his head with the towel and is rubbing his hair vigorously. By the time he emerges, Peggy has to ask again, and the question loses its casual air with repetition. He stares at her with anxious eyes and says, "I didn't!"

His grandad makes an impatient movement, but his mother kisses him. *Not now*, she mouths wearily, over his head, at Frank.

"I'm hungry," says Laurie.

"So am I," Peggy agrees. "Let's go down to the kitchen and see what we can find."

Not enough, she suspects. There's the heel of the loaf they bought yesterday, and the rest of the week's ration of butter and tea, which won't amount to much. There's the billycan of milk they bought, yesterday, from Willowbrook Farm.

"Was it you who opened the window, Frank?" She crosses the room to shut it. The landscape is misty, as it was yesterday, and grainy with bonfire smoke. She wonders whether the fields across the way belong to Willowbrook Farm, and whether Willowbrook Farm still belongs to the Stirling family.

"I did." He is unapologetic. "The air in this house is fetid."

He's still sitting in the chair with his hands neatly folded over the leather-bound diary and his face as stiff as a mask. How long Peggy has known him—years and years—and yet not known him at all. His sister ought to be the greater mystery, and yet Peggy seems to have known Maude forever.

"Perhaps it would be better for all of us if it burned to the ground," he adds, but when she looks at him sharply he raises a placatory hand. "I don't mean that. We should sell the place for all it's worth and put the money to good use. Buy you and Laurence a little house in—"

"In Hendon. Near you."

Frank shrugs modestly. Jonathan's voice flashes across her mind: *My father has a knack of getting people just where he wants them*. She's forgotten precisely why he said it, but it struck her, at the time, as enlightening. Perhaps it's unkind to remember it now.

Peggy prises the diary from her father-in-law's fingers. Momentarily he resists, but he knows she's stronger, and lets go.

"Perhaps Laurie and I want to live *here*?" she says, as lightly as the mood will allow. "Poor Aunt Maude; I'm not convinced she is, was, as hateful as you make out. Laurie? What do you think? Would you like to live in this house?"

Laurie is on his knees, retrieving his colouring things from under the bed, too busy to answer questions. The towel is draped over his head, concealing his face, and he's singing a song under his breath. Peggy doesn't recognise the tune. When she turns back to Frank, she's conscious of feeling less bullish than she sounds.

"It's all nonsense," she says, "all this talk of ghosts. The past can't linger in that way, except in people's minds. It's just a house."

"You didn't hear anything last night? See anything?"

Peggy swats the air. "Nothing that can't be put down to tiredness, or suggestibility. Or having to field a telephone call at some unearthly hour of the morning." It crosses her mind—though she daren't accuse him—that Frank is toying with her. Until yesterday, she wouldn't have had him down as a trickster—but until yesterday, he was an unknown quantity.

"You've read this?" he asks, indicating the diary.

"All of it. Have you?"

"I skimmed it this morning, while you were asleep. It's quite the work of art, isn't it?"

Peggy folds her arms across her chest and makes sure Laurie is occupied before responding. It is strange, unheard of, to face her father-in-law in pyjamas and a much-darned sweater, with her hair awry and no make-up. He's as dapper as ever, of course, in his dark woollen coat and homburg hat. She ought to mind the contrast, but doesn't. It makes her feel free and unguarded.

"Maude was so young," she says. "You both were. What happened was terrible, but you were children—or practically children—and it was all so long ago. I don't see the point of going on and on feeling angry . . . or guilty . . . especially now Maude is dead."

Silence, except for the *rasp, rasp* of Laurie's pencil sharpener.

Outside the front door, the mist is thickening to fog, and she can't see beyond the lane. It isn't raining, but the grass is wet. Peggy puts her hands in her pockets and wanders barefoot among the apple trees, before turning to look at the house.

How does one read the face of a house? she wonders. Then again, how does one read the face of a human being? She could kill for a cigarette, but she smoked her whole week's ration last night, while she was finishing the diary—and for a while afterwards.

There's the tortoiseshell cat, stalking along the hedge. When she crouches and twiddles her fingers, whispering, "Cat! Hey, cat!" it glances her way, but doesn't come.

Peggy wants to love Orchard House. She pictures Laurie with a clutch of new-found friends, running about the garden and climbing trees, while she sits in the sun, drinking a cup of coffee—strong, black, fragrant, pre-war coffee—and reading a book from Miss Greenaway's library.

She reaches on tiptoe to pick an apple, and as soon as she bites she's comforted by the piercing sweetness of its taste.

"Margaret?"

Frank is standing in the doorway with the diary under his arm.

"Margaret, Laurence needs his breakfast."

She twists another couple of apples off the tree and follows him inside, trailing wet footprints along the hall floor.

*

Peggy butters bread while the tea brews, and Frank sits in silence at the head of the kitchen table. Laurie is at the other end, engrossed in his drawing.

"Why did you say Maude's diary was 'quite the work of art'?" Peggy speaks quietly, so that Laurie won't hear.

"Because that's what it is. It's a fiction."

"It doesn't read like fiction. She was a child, writing from the heart—anyone can tell."

Frank struggles to match her softness of tone. There's a part of him—Peggy can hear it—that wants to shout.

"My sister was a skilled storyteller," he replies. "You know that's how she made her living, don't you? Writing novels under a variety of pen names? She knew how to spin a yarn, and I know she didn't write that diary when she was thirteen. I remember what her handwriting was like, and how it changed over the years. Besides, I never set eyes on that notebook till today."

"Well, why would you? It was private."

"No. She constructed the whole damn thing, years later, in adulthood. Can you not tell? The story has shape, for heaven's sake; real diaries don't have shape! As for that letter at the end, supposedly from me, wheedling for money—that's a forgery. I never wrote anything of the sort."

Peggy is silent, stroking her knife over and over the same corner of bread, though it's already well buttered.

"But Frank, why would she do that? For what possible purpose?"

Frank shrugs. "To win an audience. To have the last word. To bend the ear of someone like you."

Peggy frowns as she places a mug of tea and a slice of buttered bread next to Laurie, along with one of the apples. She does the same for Frank, and for herself, before sitting down.

"I've got a different story to tell," says Frank, "but you won't want to hear it, because Maude has slithered her way into your confidence and turned you against me. You've not been here twenty-four hours, and already you feel privy to the deepest secrets of her heart, don't you? She has flattered you with a pretence of confidentiality, and you have fallen for it . . . fallen for her."

Frank's palms hover over the tabletop as if he longs to slam them down. He goes on:

"Well, I confess, I'm not talented in that way. Intimacy does not come easily to me. And because I never weep when I'm sad—because I never say the right things—you conclude that I'm cold and unfeeling . . . but I am not."

If there is a slight tremor in his voice, there is none in his upright frame, and his face is as secretive as ever. In all the years of their acquaintance, Frank has never spoken so much, or with such feeling—at least, not in Peggy's hearing. She remembers how he was when the telegram came about Jonathan. *Now then, my dear, Jonathan wouldn't have wanted a fuss.*

"You're not an easy person to talk to," she admits.

He hasn't touched his breakfast. Peggy sips her tea, by way of encouragement, and burns her tongue.

"Well?" she says. "Why not tell me your version of events? Here I am. I'm listening."

He scowls at the tabletop. "I don't know how . . ."

Then: "I loved her, Kitty Greenaway, and she loved me in return. As unlikely as it was—as improper as it was, in every way—we got engaged to be married, that summer of '76. And Maude couldn't bear it, she simply couldn't bear it. She had to have me all to herself—said I was breaking my solemn oath, and that she'd never forgive me. That's why she murdered Kitty. There was no element of accident, or panic, or naivete in what occurred. She knew precisely what she was doing. It was murder. Murder in cold blood."

Peggy pushes her chair back and goes to put the kettle on again, although there's no need for more hot water. *I don't believe you*, she thinks, as Frank gets up and joins her. There is a rail at the front of the stove, where the tea towels hang to be aired, and she holds on to it with both hands. Frank touches her arm—Frank never, ever touches her—and says, "Margaret? Peggy? My dear?"

She turns to him and says, flatly, "I'm sorry, Frank, but I don't believe you."

"You don't?"

His grey eyes are watching her; that's all she can say for sure about those so-called windows to the soul.

"But, Margaret . . . at least ask yourself . . . why not?"

Why not?

Peggy ignores the way his words echo in the depths of her mind. *Why not?* She swings away from the stove, resolved to change the subject, one way or another.

Laurie is watching them, and Frank lowers his voice to a whisper.

"Whatever else you may think of me, you know I'm not a liar."

When Frank leaves the kitchen and pounds up the stairs, Laurie questions her with a look, but Peggy doesn't know how to answer. She stares back at her son, and several seconds pass before she remembers to fix a smile on her lips and in her eyes.

"Drink that tea while it's hot," she says. "Everything's fine."

Out in the hall, Peggy peers at the staircase, listening to her father-in-law's urgent tread and feeling his agitation in the floorboards and joists. She is as frightened as she was last night, when she seemed to hear ghosts.

When he returns, he's carrying a silver picture frame. Peggy follows him into the study, where he wheels round and places it in her hands.

"Recognise that?"

Peggy takes the picture to the window, squinting as she angles it towards the milky daylight. It's a pencil drawing of a debonair young man in a tall collar and a cravat. *George*, she reads, in the bottom right-hand corner. *K. G. June 1849.*

"It's the portrait of your father that Miss Greenaway made when they were young. Maude describes it in the diary."

Frank nods significantly.

"What of it?"

He takes it from her hands, lays it face down on the desk, and unclasps his pocketknife. Before Peggy can protest, he's slid the blade along the four edges of the backing board and lifted it off.

"Maude never knew—at least, I hope she never found out—that Kitty concealed another portrait behind the one of my father. She wanted to put it on display, but I made her hide it. I knew it would rile my sister, and I was afraid of what might happen."

The object lies in pieces on the desk: silver frame, protective glass, portrait of George, backing board, and, sure enough, a second drawing. Frank picks it up and looks at it for a few seconds, before handing it to his daughter-in-law. His eyes and lips are as rigid as ever.

It says *Frank, July 1876.* Underneath the date there's a dashing signature: *Kitty Greenaway.*

Peggy opens her mouth to speak and closes it again.

"You were very good-looking," she says. Seconds pass before she dares to add, "It's obvious from the drawing that you loved her."

That much is true. The boy leans forwards with his yearning smile, as if he wants to detach himself from the page and topple into her world. He is so eager and young, and Peggy's own lips twitch in a slight, answering smile. No flesh-and-blood man has ever gazed at her with such intensity. Jonathan certainly didn't; if he had, Peggy would have teased him.

Frank paces the study with his hands clasped behind his back.

"Describe that portrait in one adjective," he commands. "Go on, quickly, the first word that comes into your head."

Peggy hates it when Frank flusters her. He does this to Laurie, when he's testing him on his alphabet.

"Tender?" she offers.

"Tender!" Frank pounces triumphantly, and Peggy feels committed to something she doesn't necessarily mean.

She studies the picture again. The soft gradation of light on the lips; the shadowed sliver of skin where the collar opens onto the neck; the tiny hairs that curl at the temples: yes, "tender" is a good word for these things.

Peggy clears her throat. "But surely an artist can draw tenderly without being in love with her subject? Perhaps she felt tender towards the process itself: the subtlety of the light and shade, and the beauty of your face?" She shakes her head, embarrassed. "I don't know, Frank. I'm no expert."

Frank's pale eyes are filmy. Oh God, not tears; he never sheds tears. Peggy touches his arm in a sketchy gesture of pity, unsure whether she really feels it.

"Kitty Greenaway loved me," he says, his voice so small that it evokes the boy he once was. "Look at it, Peggy. Look at it properly! The way her pencil moved across the page . . . How can you not see?"

Peggy is afraid of him: afraid that he is playing games with her; afraid that he is not.

"What can you say?" he insists.

She hesitates. "That perhaps there's no such thing as proof, either way, in this case?"

Poor Frank. He is the very picture of hopelessness, with his old head bowed, and his arms hanging at his sides. When she says his name, a note of apology creeps in despite herself, but he leaves the room without a backward glance. She listens to the front door open and close, and goes to the window. The fog has crept closer to the house. Frank walks among the fruit trees, looking most unlike himself, with his coat falling open and his head bare.

Her breath forms a circle of mist on the glass, obscuring the view. Peggy wipes it with her sleeve and searches for his silhouette again. Sometimes Frank stands out clearly among the trees. Occasionally he wanders too far away and disappears. Most of the time he is the merest suggestion of a figure, drifting amidst the half-formed shapes and moving shadows of the garden.